THE KALAMA DAGGER

AN ALYSIA ROSE NOVEL – VOLUME 1

A. SCOTT WEST

[signature]

8/24/2021

ISBN:978-1-7371143-1-4 (eBook)

ISBN: 978-1-7371143-0-7 (Paperback)

ISBN: 978-1-7371143-2-1 (Audiobook)

Library of Congress Control Number: 2021911145

This book is a work of fiction. While the described artwork, historical references and science are factual, the characters, incidents and dialogue are drawn from the authors imagination and are not to be construed as real. Any resemblance to actual events or persons, living or dead, is entirely coincidental.

First printing edition 2021

Formatting by Ross Jeffery

Circlefox LLC

4730 University Way NE

Ste-104 #

Seattle, WA 98105

www.ascottwest.com

The gift of a book, Christine by Stephen King, to a thirteen-year-old boy sparked a yearning to read and create. This book is dedicated to Toot Reid, who opened the door to new worlds and new adventures.

CONTENTS

Kalama Dagger

Eboli Cross

Eye of the Mathed

Ehecatl's Breath

Maphe's Tear

Anshul's Glow

CHAPTER 1

Alysia Rose opened her eyes as a rough breeze peppered her face with sand. Ocean waves crashed to her left. Generally, this was a sound that calmed her, but these waves smashed the beach with brute force, each one a booming concussion, cannon fire in her ears. The smell of sea salt was thick, stirred by the pounding waves. Under her back, the feel of gnarled timbers, the pithy odor of tar and petroleum mixed with the tangy smell of salt assaulted her nose. Above her was a night sky. Not one star shone, no moonlight, only a cold, empty blackboard staring back at her. Alysia let her arms fall to her side and rest against the splintery wood. With the cool roughness of the timbers under her palms, she adjusted to her surroundings. She turned her head to the left, where the waves hammered the shore, but the night was too dark to see them frothing against the sand. She turned her head to the right. Her gaze captured an amusement park ride, a ride that scratched the back of her memory from a long time ago. Was it Bulgy, the Whale Carousel? Her eyes took in the ride and traveled up.

Barely visible in the darkness, a sign hung above what appeared to be a roller coaster, Logger's Revenge. A feeling of unease enfolded her, forcing a shiver to run through her body, goose-bumps growing along each arm. The scratching within her memory turned to talons, digging deep. She was on the Santa Cruz Boardwalk, a place she had not visited and refused to visit, in the last twenty years.

Pressing her palms into the splinter-ridden timbers, she pushed herself into an upright position. Her head swam, and her stomach lurched, forcing her to tuck her head between her knees to counteract nausea.

Accessing another's mind during REM through the act of transporting was a technique she did frequently, but the dizziness, headache, and need to vomit never improved. As she battled wave after wave of queasiness, she wondered for the hundredth time what transporting was doing to her physical body lying on a hospital bed in her home. At some point, the mental stresses would begin to affect the corporeal. At what cost to her future self? If the mind began to accept transport as reality, would it alter her ability to recognize truth from deception? In her current state, this world felt authentic, the taste of sea salt, the feel of a breeze, she could not distinguish a difference. It seemed impossible, but she knew her mind was a powerful machine, concocting realities from whatever it could wrangle together, real, or not.

After a moment, her lightheadedness dissipated, and she lifted her head from her knees. Stable, she used her hands and legs to stand. A brief flash of dizziness swept over her but swiftly fled as she stood her ground.

Orienting herself, she glanced down and watched as rough timber changed to flat concrete. The smell of ozone and lime-stone replaced the rich scent of tar. This was a new experience.

One she could only fathom was her memories meshing and clashing with the ones of the child whose mind she was currently occupying. Typically, the child's memory controlled the scenario, Alysia had never experienced a blending of memories in the past. Testing her balance, she took three steps forward, and as her right foot came down for the third time, the dark was pierced with the harsh glow of boardwalk lights. Her dizziness came back with a fury as her eyes tried to adjust to the sudden brightness. The strobe effects from a ride called Wipeout forced her to turn her head out towards the unseeable ocean. As her eyes adjusted to the change, her ears captured the sound of a child, only a whisper over the cutting breeze, a voice in terror. This was the young girl she had come to find, nine-year-old Bethany Wild. Bethany was lying in a bed not ten feet from her own. Should Bethany be thrust out of REM, Alysia would be thrown back into her own consciousness, time was critical.

The boardwalk environment continued to cycle around her, timber to concrete, rides interchanging, the smell of cotton candy replaced with the scent of rotting popcorn. Alysia shook her head, trying to acclimate to the disorienting experience, forcing herself to stabilize the memories, but her intense focus just intensified the disruption.

Only Bethany's cries and the sounds of waves reached Alysia's ears. A boardwalk should be a place of laughter and excitement, no trace of joy resided here, its emptiness foreboding. Alysia continued forward. To her left, she passed more rides. The Cliff Hanger and Riptide, then the Giant Dipper Rollercoaster towered over her, a wooden monstrosity with old-fashioned white lights twinkling amongst its massive girders. Alysia's momentum slowed as she approached the entrance to the rollercoaster. The increasing dread reached full boil as she realized the next attraction would be the Haunted Castle - if she were to continue forward. Alysia tried to comprehend the intensifying feelings of anxiety. This was a new sensation to her, normally her confidence would be high, she was in control here. The uncomfortableness made her doubt herself, and self-doubt was dangerous. Any signs of weakness could be used to harm her or the one she was here to protect.

"What the hell, Alysia," she said out loud, her voice sounding flat. In response, a soft ghostly sound of laughter, not pleasant but grotesque, scraped across her skull. The sound was intensifying her need to leave this place, to abandon the child. Abruptly, boardwalk lights began to pop, thousands of miniature explosions, until only the lights from one ride glowed, the Haunted Castle. "Shit, shit, shit!" she murmured. This was all wrong. Why was she terrified of a goddamn amusement park ride? She could feel her memory monster fighting to the surface, a prehistoric beast beating against her brain, a memory so powerful but held back by rattling chains.

Forcing her feet forward, she found herself standing in front of the Castle. Gargoyles stared down from turrets on both sides of the ride entrance created from what looked like old sandstone but was only painted concrete. Laughing skeletons over the door dared her to enter their domain.

"Bethany, are you in there," Alysia called out with a slight tremble in her voice.

A graveled voice responded, "Bethany is in here. She is all alone. You know the feeling, don't you, Rose?"

Her ears never acclimated to the voice of a demon. The best she could relate it to was if someone gargled glass, swallowed one hundred razor blades, and then drank an entire cup of saltwater. Copper nails on a chalkboard.

"Hello, demon," she replied with as much confidence as she

could muster. "I have little expectation we can settle this with words, but hell, I am willing to try. Can we skip the Rules of the Dead, the ritual, and you simply move on so I can get back in time to catch the next episode of the Mandalorian?"

"Come now, Rose, how much fun would that be, especially since the Rules of the Dead no longer apply? Didn't Father Teabag deliver the memo?" it laughed.

"You think you're a funny fucker, don't you," she mumbled. "No. Father Tealander never said shit about rules changing, demon. Between you and me, you might be the one who does not understand the outcome. You should talk to a few of your brethren. Ask them about me."

Its reply was but a whisper, "Speaking of my brethren, Crimson sends his regards, Rose."

Crimson. The name sent a shock wave of deep shivers along her spine. Nerves already on edge ticked up a notch, forcing her to redouble her focus. This place, this name, why was it forging such a reaction? The memory beast pounded harder, rattling its chains wanting to be free. Something was faulty. Alysia did not feel in control. She needed a moment to gather herself, and so she pressed back. "Tell me, demon, why should I know that name? Why should I believe anything a vile creature such as yourself pours from its wretched mouth? Your kind is the speaker of lies and untruths."

"Seriously, Rose, you throw shade? Bitch, you have some balls, well, figuratively. By the way, I taste your fear from here. It is delectable. Sweet as sugar, mix it with Bethany's, and you have one hearty meal," the demon chortled.

The demon's taunts did not trouble Alysia. She had faced off against many like it in the past. Demons were full of bravado, salty words, and theatrics. Broadway could make a mint off them, except they were ugly as hell and smelled of rotting meat and sulfur, not the kind of thing the public was willing to pay to see.

"Again, why should I know Crimson?" Alysia responded.

"I think the real question you should be asking yourself, why would one as regaled as the lord demon ask me to speak to you on its behalf personally?" it growled.

As a professional poker player, she could play with the best of them, but her current hand was not strong. Her opponent appeared to hold the better, she decided to do what she did best, bluff. Engage the demon on her terms, regain the upper hand. From rote memory, she spoke into the darkness. "As set forth by the Rules of the Dead, I request you name yourself, and therefore, you must name yourself. We shall address each other by the names presented to us by the dead. I speak to you as Alysia Rose. I address you as...?"

The demon chuckled. "Ah, I see. The rules, well, did you not hear me say the rules no longer apply? Rose, if you must know me, I am Infantmeal. Shall you demand further conversation, you will need to enter this wonderful attraction. I have been advised not to harm you or harm the child if you repay in kind. One more thing. Although I was told to cause no harm, should you try to damage me, I have been instructed to hurt you and the girl, badly, very badly should you not comply."

Infantmeal, holy hell. Demons tended to take the names of commercial products, but only phonetically and or misspelled, many times inspired by something in their past. Lower-level demons were denied titles, and so you get an Infantmeal. Demons were not creatures of high intelligence, at least not the demons Alysia had faced off with in the past. Their strengths were intimidation, torture, torment, mayhem, manipulation, and lies. Skills they practiced well.

"Okay, I am entering. Although you claim the rules no longer apply, I am holding you to your promise."

"Whatever, Rose. I grow weary of our banter and am hungry. Bethany would make a wonderful meal, so enter, or go away and let me feast on her fears alone and without interruption from your incessant babble."

Bethany's screams increased. Alysia was out of options, so she stepped into the Haunted Castle.

CHAPTER 2

Her first step into the attraction caused the chained beast in the back of her mind to shrink back in fear, a warning to go no further. She ignored it. The only lights within the attraction were the lights along the pathway providing just enough illumination to walk without stumbling. As she stepped around the first bend, a werewolf jumped from behind a large monument within a graveyard. Alysia's heart rate increased. She found it difficult to breathe. The demon had turned on the animatronics. She would need to be prepared so she did not launch out of her skin. Alysia's body was already tense and amped.

Entering the next room, a mad scientist performed a grizzly operation on a screaming patient. Blood and gore soaked the floor as the patients' eyes rolled in their head. A coil of intestines sat upon the floor, slithering as if alive. The scientist turned and smiled. His yellowed, rotted teeth presenting an ominous smile. In its hand, a beating heart which he offered to her. She stepped back, her feet propelling her from the room.

Each turn revealed a different room with life-like settings, enhanced nightmares, as no amusement ride on a boardwalk would suffer such atrocities. Alysia felt like she was turning the handle of a Jack-in-the-Box, not knowing when the top was going to pop, and a clown demon would jump out on a long spring. Speak of the devil, and he may rise! The next room was a demented circus.

Demonic clowns wandered the space. Red makeup on their lips was replaced with the blood of the dying, which they trampled under their large shoed feet, squeaking with every step. The clowns held bouquets of severed floating heads, each attached to a red ribbon. The heads howled in misery, their eyes protruding from their sockets. As she passed, a clown offered her an offal offering of what appeared to be lungs and kidneys. She could assemble a whole body by the time this ride was complete.

"Alysia, are you enjoying the memories? Don't they just make you feel warm and gooey inside?" the demon taunted from deep within the ride.

"I am going to kick your demon ass back to Jarapenth when I reach you," Alysia responded with more bravado than she felt.

She entered a room where a dragon guarded a giant mountain of gold. At the foot of the treasure was a cage of silver. Within the enclosure was a young girl with dirty blonde hair, blue eyes, and blood smeared on her cheeks.

Alysia hurried over to the cage. Taking the child's hands in hers, she tried to provide her reassurance, something she lacked in herself now. As she spoke to the child, she observed the cage. There were no doors and no locks. It was one solid piece of silver. Once again, this was new, and she was unsure how to react. The cage was supposed to be a representation of the demon's possession, symbolic. This felt permanent, solid.

She pulled her hands free from Bethany's and ran them across the smooth, almost translucent bars. She felt them humming under her palms, the silver neither hot nor cold. She felt no spurs, no imperfections. It was as if someone had taken a single piece of metal rod and bent it into this form. Alysia shook the cage, banging her hands on the tops and sides while listening intently for weaknesses. Bethany whimpered within. Alysia's fingers wrapped around the silver rods and worked to pull the bars apart. She felt no give.

"Pointless Rose, pointless," Infantmeal shook its head as it rounded the head of the dragon.

As with all demons, most human traits were gone, except for the ability to walk upright, well, for most of them. It was impossible to know who or what they were before becoming this. It stood at least six feet tall, with crisped blackened flesh, which released a crinkling sound every time it moved. Burnt beyond recognition, its entire form was covered with a map of red lines just under the charred remains of its skin, a network of magma streams, like the Hawaii lava flows. The angrier a demon became, the more defined those lines would be. It was a great emotional read. Parts of its malformed body were covered in weeping pustules which oozed a black substance. The substance never reached the floor. It always absorbed back into the demon's burnt flesh. Spikes and ridges ran along its shoulders and knees, adding to a demon's bizarre appearance. Infantmeal had horns upon its head, wrapped with tattered straps of tanned human skin. The reek was formidable. A blend of death, sulfur, rot, decay, and bad earth. Demons were just unpleasant. They held no redeeming qualities.

For all its ugliness, the scariest aspect of a demon is its eyes. Every demon has crystal blue eyes—Sapphire bright. The remains of a demon's soul shine through those glowing orbs. One look and a human could read every ounce of pain and suffering, hit with not only the insane and crazy, but what is left of the demon's humanity. If one stared too long into those glowing blue flames, one could find themselves slipping into the demon's madness.

"Let her go, then we can talk," Alysia countered.

"Right, yeah, I mean, sure, let her go. You wouldn't think of sticking me with the knife you have hidden in your left pants leg, would you?" Infantmeal chortled. "Hang on a minute." It patted itself down as if it were looking for something, "appears I misplaced the key." It smiled and spread its hands. "Besides, not sure you noticed in your shaking and rattling of the bars, Rose, there are no locks or chains or doors."

"How the fuck am I supposed to take her with me when we are done? You said we would not be harmed."

"Oh, I never said she was free to leave. I simply said I would not harm her." It walked over to the cage and stroked the bars, touching Bethany's hair, watching her flinch each time it did. "Besides, I kind of like her, it's like having a pet," it said distractedly. "Wait, where were we? Right, letting her go, not going to happen. This cage was built by Crimson and can only be opened by Crimson. Crimson will only let her go if Crimson gets what Crimson wants."

"What's its name again," she asked sarcastically.

"Ha Ha," the demon responded with its sense of what sarcasm would be. It sounded wooden.

"Take a joke, you burnt rump roast. What does Crimson want, or Crimson want what Crimson wants? However, you wish to Yoda speak it. I still have no idea who or what this creature is, so let's stop playing games and get to what it is I was brought here for, or, I can begin the rites of banishment."

The demon took a step back from Alysia's rising anger and wheezed, "Crimson wants the Kalama Dagger."

"What is the Kalama Dagger?"

"You don't know? It is one of the six artifacts of Carpathica."

This only led to further confusion on Alysia's part. What was this demon blathering on about? "Carpathica? What is Carpathica, I don't understand your demon speak."

"You are versed in the Rules of the Dead, but you do not know the six ancient artifacts or Carpathica?" The demon was perplexed, its body shifting left and right in a nervous dance.

Infantmeal was speaking to the most potent Demonspeaker his kind had ever encountered. Even Ka's Council of 120 feared her. Yet, she seemed to have no knowledge of what it was speaking. The demon could not imagine her power should she even hold *one* of the six artifacts. His kind cower before her now. With an artifact, she would become a legend.

Just being in her presence was terrifying. Even with fear coursing through its malformations, the monster admitted it was enthralled by her. She was striking in many ways. Beautiful and dangerous, her auburn hair like the embers of hell, she radiated power. It crashed into the demon, soundwaves ebbing and flowing. The sudden surge of admiration was quickly swept away as Alysia advanced towards it.

"Again, what is Carpathica, and what the hell are the six artifacts?"

Cowering and in fear for its existence, the demon whimpered, "I can't tell you. Crimson said you would know. Crimson wants it in six days, or Bethany will die, oh and you and anyone who assists you." Infantmeal prepared to be stricken down, but Alysia was simply watching it when it looked back up.

"I am to bring Crimson the Kalama Dagger in six days, or we all die? Tell Crimson to go fuck himself. I am not his gopher."

Infantmeal panicked as Alysia turned and walked away.

Bethany's cries for help became louder, resonating through the room. She indeed had no heart. There would be a place of high regard for her among the 120 when she passed. "Wait," it bellowed, "Crimson said it would kill one child per day after the six days until you bring the Dagger."

Alysia stopped and turned. Her face unable to hide her concern, "It told you this?"

"Crimson did, yes, Crimson was very clear, Crimson would capture, torture and kill one child per day until Crimson owned the Dagger."

The threat of one life lost per day was outside the Rules of the Dead, strict rules on the number of souls and such. Most people believed demons were free to do as they pleased, it was an inaccurate belief. Rules applied to the living. Regulations applied to the dead. Crimson would know those laws and would not make a threat lightly.

Could Crimson break the rules? If it was able to do so, then all bets were off. "Alright. I do not even know what this Crimson wants or even who Crimson is. I have never heard of artifacts or Carpathica? Help me understand."

"Ask the Father, Father will know. I can tell you no more. Alysia, once you step out of the Castle, your time starts, the days begin, you have six and no more. Once you have the Dagger, return here, give it to me, and the children will be freed. Crimson gives Crimson's word."

"Crimson's word is the children will truly be freed, mind, body, and spirit. No games here, demon."

It stared at her as if she had gone mad. "Crimson would not go back on Crimson's word."

"Tell me, Infantmeal, if I was to just ignore all this bullshit, start the ritual to excise you from this child's mind, what exactly could you or Crimson do about it?"

"Nothing. I would be excised. The child would be free. For a moment, you would have your victory. Ask yourself, Alysia, do you believe my master cannot inflict the pain it promises? Can you, alone, save hundreds of children when Crimson begins to demonstrate its wrath. Do you wish to find out?"

Alysia returned to the cage, once more giving it a good shake, even kicking it in frustration as the demon watched. Bethany grabbed her fingers through the bars, pleading to not be left alone. "Bethany, honey, I have to go, but I will be back. I promise."

Bethany screamed and pounded on the bars. "Please don't leave me here, it smells like feet, it touches my hair, it leaves its glop in it. I just want my mom!" Bethany could barely choke out her words as tears rolled down her cheeks and tremors racked her petite form.

Alysia felt hopeless. A part of her desperately wanted to harm this demon, thrash it. Send it sniveling back to its home within Jarapenth. But if the demon spoke the truth, if its master was willing to torture hundreds of thousands to get its way, was she willing to risk many for one?

Before Infantmeal could react, it found Alysia's hands twisting around its neck, pushing it against the head of the dragon. Her gaze one of pure rage, raw and unforgiving. It awaited her to strip it from the child's mind and throw its tortured shell into the ever-burning fires of Jarapenth. Her hands further tightened. Then the fire left her eyes, and her hands released it.

"If over the next six days, you touch her, breathe on her,. do anything else which makes her uncomfortable, I will not only expel you, but I will also perform the Rights of Treason. I hear demons cast into the Plain of Teeth within Jarapenth truly suffer."

"I won't, I won't," it screamed. "I swear, please!"

Alysia turned her back on the demon and the child. Bethany's screams ripped at her heart. She felt her own tears fighting to escape, but she would not give the demon more pain to feed upon. Alysia would not allow it to further feast on her. Out of sight, she wiped her hands on her pants, removing the sliminess of the demon, its sluffing burnt skin staining her jeans. The smell was vile. It was a damn good thing this was not reality, or her clothes would be ruined. The smell would never come off.

Retracing her steps through the castle, she pondered the confrontation. She was left with more questions than answers. Who was Crimson, and why did the name frighten her? What was the significance of the six artifacts, and why did Crimson want the one called the Kalama Dagger? Why did she not know about them? The chained creature within her mind was now quiet, huddled in a corner, fearful it almost escaped. It had answers she desperately desired, but it refused to share them with her.

She felt betrayed. Why would Father Matthew Tealander hide something of this importance? Or was it a clever ruse by the demon to shake her, forcing her to doubt herself? If so, the demon was the smartest she had yet met, and she would need to reconsider the whole demon intelligence stereotype. Or it was the dumbest of demons and she would stomp the shit out of it in the end. The sadness she felt for abandoning the child was all-encompassing. The thought Matthew might have been keeping secrets from her made the pressure in her chest worse.

Alysia exited the Haunted Castle into a foggy landscape. The boardwalk was gone, the ocean silent, no night sky covered her. Only a cold gray blanket surrounded her, the fog of Bethany's terrified mind. She could feel the girl's terror clinging to her skin. It tasted of acid in her mouth. She glanced over her shoulder and watched as the Haunted Castle turned to vapor and was absorbed into the gray.

The demon said her time started once she left the castle, so she set her watch to one hundred-forty-four hours. Alysia lay flat upon the fog and pressed the tiny button on her watch's left side. It sent an electrical current through her body, transporting her away from this place.

CHAPTER 3

Alysia Rose awoke to the sound of Debussy's Claire De Lune. It was one of her favorite piano pieces and reminded her of her mother, a talented pianist. Her mom had played it almost every night to help her daughter fall asleep. Although her mother tried playing other artists, Alysia would have none of it, forcing her mom to play only Debussy. This argument always made her mother laugh. Alysia's heart rate slowed, matching the flowing rhythms of the piano keys. She tried to sit up, but a gentle force against her chest pushed her back down.

"Nope, take it easy. I need you to take a moment," a soft voice spoke to her reassuringly.

Alysia's vision was blurry upon return, but she recognized the voice and was comforted by it. As her sight cleared, her gaze met a set of brown, caring eyes behind a stylish pair of round glasses. Her complexion was perfect with a round face, well-pronounced smile lines and small lips. A look without blemishes, something Alysia would occasionally feel jealousy of its perfections. Alysia reached up and brushed a strand of long black hair from the woman's worried face. "Martha, we need to stop meeting like this?"

Martha Ortega removed her hand and smiled. "I see your sense of humor was once again undamaged." Her tone grew dark, "What happened in there? You and the child's vitals were all over the place. I had to sedate Bethany, or she was going to come out of REM too soon." Martha's gaze drifted over to the young girl in the bed nearby, her eyes a pool of worry and concern.

Alysia rolled her head to the left and saw Bethany sleeping. She appeared at peace until you witnessed her hands dancing next to her side, the effects of fear. Alysia felt a single tear fall down her cheek. She abandoned a nine-year-old to face her terrors alone. Locked in a cage with a demon standing watch. Laying here would not help the child. She once more lifted her body, but Martha's hand on her arm tightened.

"Martha, let me up." Alysia's tone made it clear, the moment was over. Martha knew she needed to stay relaxed a little longer, but Alysia would not be contained.

Martha raised her hands in surrender, allowing her to rise. "What the hell happened in there?"

Alysia's head began to pound the minute she raised up. It was the reason Martha tried to keep her horizontal. Martha deserved answers, but she was uncertain she understood herself. "I am going to go grab a hot shower. Would you reach out to Matthew and let him know I need to see him immediately. Not a phone call, but in person. I will fill you in once he arrives."

"Okay, I will contact him while you are cleaning up. What else do you need?"

"Could you ask Roland to prepare my usual? I feel like my stomach might crawl out my throat and start hunting its own prey."

She flipped her legs over the side of the bed and stood up. Martha caught her as she wobbled. Alysia gently pushed her away and left the room, leaving Martha worried and perplexed.

Coming out of transport left her feeling soiled. It was a unique sensation because her physical body was clean and untouched. But her memory remained smudged, and all the soap and hot water in the world could not clean the beast hidden within. Alysia's steps were cautious as she worked to regain her equilibrium. The room exited into an open concept area with a large kitchen and living area which overlooked the ocean. She stopped for a moment and stared out the floor-to-ceiling windows, which not only took in the ocean but the infinity pool on the vast terrace. She truly hated this place, but it was the dream her parents left her, half-built before their tragic death. She and Roland, at the time her co-guardian, had it completed and lived within its walls. It was not her, and she was not it, but she knew this was what her mother and father would have wanted, and she acquiesced to its refinements.

Gaining confidence in her balance, she continued towards the wrap-around staircase which led to the top level of the three-level home. She looked down as she moved up the stairs and could see the first floor, a vacant space below. The plans had been laid out to be a bar, movie theater and a safe room with vault. Two years later, it still laid empty, except for the safe room, which Matthew, her other co-guardian, had insisted be completed. Not for the first time, she imagined herself falling from the stairs and ending her life on the floor below. Still, she knew what was waiting for her after this world ended and she had no desire to arrive early. These feelings of self-harm were expected after a transporting session, her work over-whelming at times and sometimes unsuccessful. Today was a day she felt strongly about letting go. What was the point of her existence if she could not save every child? Alysia hurried the rest of the way up the stairs not allowing these feelings to shroud her in misery and doubt. There were questions needing answers. She exited onto a balcony area that led to a hall which led to her master bedroom, which led to a master bath. Her glass shower overlooked the ocean. The windows facing the ocean had a smoked glass feature, but she was too damn drained to turn them on. If someone wanted to watch her, then so be it.

She placed her watch on the counter and let her nightdress fall to the floor (it was always strange to her to be dressed in only a gown upon waking, her clothing within transport seemed real). Refusing to look at the time, she set the water temperature as hot as she could handle and stepped into the steam. Her body reflexively tried to pull back, but she forced herself to stand under the scalding water. Her pale skin turned a bright red. After a moment, she became used to the heat. She washed not once, not twice, but three times, scrubbing herself raw. Just like her clothing in the transport state, the ability to touch, feel, see, and smell all resided within her mind. Which meant, when she grabbed the demon, it did not actually occur. It certainly felt real. The memory was accurate.

Rinsing from her third intense scrubbing, she stepped out and grabbed a towel. As she dried herself, she gazed at her reflection. Her daily workout routine was brutal, so she was lithe and fit. Not an ounce of fat resided on her toned body. It was necessary to keep her body strong, her agility and strength mirrored in the transported state. She turned to the side and admired her curves. She tried to remember the pop artist who said, "*all the right curves in all the right places,*" and smiled. But it was not her body tone, long auburn hair, or all those curves which caught her breath every time she saw herself. It was the scar that started above her left eye and went down her entire body, just below her navel. The tear was deep, and due to the shower, inflamed as if someone had taken a hot poker and slashed her open.

Unconsciously, she traced the mark with her finger, feeling its roughness, the depth, and was shocked she was still alive. The event that took her parents left its permanent mark upon her body—a constant reminder of her loss. The scar was why she had so far not been able to find a solid, lasting relationship. People spoke of not caring about looks until you were on a dance floor and the entire room was staring at your date's face. Alysia was used to the long stares in the grocery stores, or the scrutiny others gave her at restaurants. The women she dated could only handle the attention for so long before it ate at them. She had been fortunate to find someone special three years ago, someone who understood her, but the relationship ended in tragic form. Nancy would not even speak to her anymore, blocking her from all contact. She shook her head. This was not something she needed to rehash right now.

She pulled another towel from the warming rack and dried her hair. The towel was wonderfully warm and fluffy. She would let the cool ocean sun finish drying her lengthy hair. She was not much of a blow-dry person. Body dry, she entered the master closet. It was large enough to park a small car in but held ten shirts, one formal dress, six pairs of pants, and an assortment of socks, undergarments, and shoes. She was not one to gather garments. They were meaningless. She slipped into a favorite AC/DC t-shirt, a pair of ripped jeans, and sat on the edge of her king-sized bed to put on a pair of socks with Master Chief on them and a couple of old tennis shoes, well-worn and loved.

CHAPTER 4

Descending the stairs, she observed a helicopter landing in the dunes. The blades created sand devils which danced around the dunes, whirling madly in the wind. Matthew exited and navigated the well-worn path up to the terrace. Winds must have been on their side today, she thought as she continued her descent. The flight usually took forty-two minutes from Seattle.

For Moclips, it was relatively warm, a balmy sixty-five, a temperature she observed on her little home weather station which sat on a small table, before stepping through the large accordion doors leading out to the terrace. Her parents had chosen Moclips to build their forever home, as they both loved the ocean. The coastal town was a small community along the Pacific coast where everyone kept to themselves and out of their neighbor's business. They relied on tourism to survive but were just as glad to see them leave come summers end preferring their peaceful ocean views. Alysia loved the peace and quiet, the mansion she resided within was several miles from any other home, as her parents purchased the land around them.

She had no interest in creating neighborly relationships, as she did not want anyone asking questions about her line of work. The people she worked with were her family, and for now, that was good enough.

Roland Mears, her once co-guardian and now steward and mentor prepared the terrace table with pastries, an assortment of teas and a steaming pot of coffee. She considered herself blessed to have Roland as part of her life. It was the only part of her parent's past she embraced fully. Her mouth watered just seeing the glazed delicacies. Her stomach came alive and rumbled with excitement, screaming to be fed. She craved sugar after transport. Instead of candy, carb-filled bites such as the apple turnovers and mini cinnamon rolls filled a two-tiered stand. Martha already sat at the table drinking her chamomile tea and eating a croissant with fresh raspberry jam. Martha was watching Matthew stumble through the sand on the way up to the terrace. Alysia could hear Martha's quiet laughter as Matthew swore loud enough for them to hear. Someday finishing the helipad and paving a way through the dunes would become a priority.

Roland followed Alysia onto the terrace with fresh-squeezed orange and pink grapefruit juices. She thanked him with a smile while letting the sharp tartness of the juice pucker her mouth. The tarter, the better. It was the main reason Roland squeezed it fresh. She took her seat, reached over, grabbed an apple tart, and shoved the entire morsel into her mouth.

"Surprised you have not choked to death," Martha exclaimed, watching her boss and friend doing a decent imitation of a chipmunk.

Alysia smiled through a pastry-filled mouth and tried to make a comment but realized all she was doing was spitting crumbs all over the table.

Martha cringed, her full eyebrows coming together over her petite nose, "Gross. Alysia, seriously?"

Alysia finished chewing, swallowed the massive amount of sticky sweet dough, and drank a full glass of grapefruit juice before trying to speak again. "Is Bethany stable?"

"As stable as I can make her. We need to talk about what happened there. I was not prepared. I am not a doctor, Alysia. I am research and technical, not medically trained. If we end up in a serious situation, I am unsure what I can do. Roland is better suited for this, Dr. Black even more so."

"I know Martha, and I am sorry, it was scary for both of us. Losing Dr. Black was unfortunate and could not have occurred at a worse time, but we must work with the team we have until we find a replacement. I agree we need to rethink what we are doing after this morning. All that aside for a moment, I discovered some information only Matthew can answer. For now, the focus needs to turn to him."

Alysia was nervous about confronting Matthew regarding what she gleaned from the demon. If the demon were correct, and Matthew was holding back information, would she ever be able to trust him again? Alysia placed her shaking hands in her lap as Matthew arrived at the table and sat in one of the seats where he could see the ocean. She knew he loved the ocean. It was soothing to him. Sometimes he would sit on the terrace for hours, staring out into the dunes, allowing the ocean air to blow what little gray hair he had left. Just watching, waiting.

Roland presented Father Tealander with a cup of Earl Grey, two sugars, and one teaspoon of cream. He thanked him and started to take a sip when Alysia addressed him. "What can you tell me about a demon named Crimson and an artifact called the Kalama Dagger?"

Matthew's body tensed, causing the tea to slosh over the top of his cup, spilling onto his jeans. He picked up the cloth napkin and blotted the tea, the liquid hot, but her question was more burning and frankly unfortunate. He finished blotting the tea with a cloth napkin and returned his attention to the table only to find Alysia staring directly at him. Her scar burned red, a dangerous sign. He would need to tread carefully. He had been her co-guardian with Roland for many years. He understood her moods and would not be intimidated by her. However, she could be very intimidating and highly persuasive. He sat back as casually as possible and drank his tea. Only after regaining his composure did he speak.

"Where did you hear about Crimson and the dagger?" he asked in a calm, articulate voice.

Alysia's gaze probed him. Her left eye a dull milky blue, damaged in the accident, while her right was as blue as an Arizona spring sky. Her gaze would leave most unsettled, but he kept eye contact with her never permitting his eyes to waver from hers. Alysia could be predatorial when she wanted to be. It was part of what made her a great Demonspeaker. Matthew refused to show weakness. He knew of Crimson and the dagger but was unfamiliar with their importance. What she shared next made him realize he would need to reach out to the Sect of Light and inform them of her discoveries.

"I transported this morning to extract a demon from Bethany Wild, and although it is never normal, what happened this morning was highly abnormal. I was out of my element the minute I awoke in the child's mind. Things were displaced, out of order. Matthew, I was in Santa Cruz. The child's and my memories were fighting for dominance. It was as if this demon knew the location would throw me off balance, and it did. I could not pin why I was suddenly afraid. The closer I came to Bethany, the more afraid I became. Walking along the boardwalk, I felt as if I was meant to be there. When I arrived at the building Bethany was being held, The Haunted Castle, I was certain I was there for more than her. I felt something banging against my memory. It wanted to be freed but reaching for it only made it disappear."

Matthew's eyes left Alysia's and wandered out into the dunes and towards the ocean beyond. He made the right choice sitting here. The soothing sounds of water swishing across sand traveled across the barren dunes on an ocean breeze. His thoughts swirled around Bethany. Was the girl a snare? Had the demons taken her for a specific purpose? What if the child were simply a way to shake Alysia's confidence, to disorient her so her work would stall? If all Alysia shared was true, and he had no reason to doubt her, then specific prophecies were unraveling faster than he, or the Sect of Light had estimated.

"Alysia, why do you think you were there for more than Bethany? What made you feel this way?" Matthew calmly asked as he let his gaze return to hers and drank a sip of his cooling tea.

She sat back, crossing her legs, placing her hands on her knees, "I don't know. I feel I should know. I entered the Castle, but it just felt wrong and at the same time it felt right. It left me feeling confused, shaken to my core. I found Bethany in a cage with no locks and no doors, kept there by a demon calling itself Infantmeal."

Martha, who sat quietly next to her, snickered, "Infantmeal, seriously?"

Alysia smiled, "What can I say? They are not the brightest creatures."

Matthew did not want Alysia to lose focus, he pressed her to explain the cage. "You say the cage had no access points, one solid piece of silver. I thought these were just mental constructs and therefore breakable?"

"You are right Matthew, and this is another reason why I am further confused by the confrontation this morning. The whole point of what I do is to free a child from possession by forcing the demon out, and in return, the demon frees the child's mind. Most times, the cage is symbolic of the mind's imprisonment. The structure can change based on the child or memory I have seen netting, sometimes locked rooms, but there have always been ways to free them and force the demon out. This time, I could do nothing. I was as ensnared as Bethany. Infantmeal said to free Bethany, I would need to locate an object, the Kalama Dagger created in some place called Carpathica, and return it within six days. Here is the thing, the creature was visibly taken aback by the knowledge that I had no idea what it was asking. It told me to speak to the Father. Matthew, what the hell am I looking for and why?"

Matthew's shoulders slumped as he placed his empty cup on the table. At seventy-five years of age, he was tired, not just physically but emotionally. He reached up and ran his fingers through his hair. Well, the little hair left, which at one point in his life had been a stunning black, was now nothing more than wisps of gray stuck to a balding pate. His entire life had been spent in the work of the Sect, fighting a battle with no clear beginning or end. Well, until today. The Dagger and Carpathica, fairytales regarding final days, so much bullshit, yet here they were. He would need to contact the Sect and let them know what he learned. In doing so, the door would open, dragging Alysia deeper into the Sect of Light, placing her in further peril. It was something he hoped would not occur this soon in her life.

"I have to make a phone call," he informed the table as he stood. Alysia started to rise, but he put a cautionary hand up. "No, there is no discussion to be had here," Matthew said and walked away to the other side of the terrace, withdrawing his phone from his pocket and making a call. He watched as Roland placed a steady hand on Alysia's shoulder. He knew she did not like being told what to do and being pushed away only further pissed her off. Luckily, Roland was as sensitive to her moods as Matthew and worked to calm her before it spiraled out of control. Matthew saw Roland lean down and whisper something to her and then moved away. He turned as a voice answered his call.

Alysia heard the words Roland spoke to her, but her emotions were high. Yes, she was tense, yes, she was angry, she had her reasons, and Roland was not privy to them. Alysia stood from the table, excused herself, and left Martha to sit alone.

"She's too damn young. It's the wrong time." Father Tealander said into the phone.

"I agree, but it was not us who made a move. If we had more time, we would take it." A female voice answered from the other end.

"Her parents were killed, seeking the same answers. Are we really going to place the target on her now? There must be another way. Someone other than her. This is too damn dangerous." Tealander begged over the phone.

"I am sorry, I know how you feel for her. She has become like a daughter. I warned you to avoid becoming overly attached, but now your feelings will need to be packed away. It appears our journey is about to begin in earnest." The woman on the other end of the phone disconnected.

Matthew stared out at the ocean, allowing himself to be hypnotized by the rhythmic sound of waves on sand. God help her, and God help him. He prayed this day would not come, but now that it was here, his heart was heavy with fear and dread for the safety of his ward Alysia.

As ALYSIA ENTERED THE HOUSE, she felt an atmospheric shift. The smell of sulfur assaulted her nose. Fight or flight mode kicked in as she cautiously moved towards where the odor was most pungent. The stench was emanating from the operations/conference room. The door was slightly ajar, she nudged it open with her foot. Standing in the room, fifteen feet away from her, was the demon Alysia confronted this morning. Due to the confrontation outside with Matthew, she was emotionally keyed up. She needed a punching bag. This demon would work fine as a replacement. She darted into the room, fists and teeth clenched, itching to pummel the living shit out of this creature.

"Wait," Infantmeal shouted, waving its taloned hands. It held no desire to instigate a confrontation on Rose's territory.

The demons' motions made Alysia slow her progress, but it did not prevent the clenching of her fists or the tightness in her chest. "What are you doing in my home. You are not allowed here. How are you standing in my fucking home!"

"Wait, wait. I have information. Please, Alysia, listen to me." The demon placed hands out, trying to be submissive. It knew the risks coming here, but it must speak.

Infantmeal did not appear to be a threat for the moment, so Alysia took a deep breath, working to remove the lump in her chest and throat. She clenched and unclenched her fists to release the tightness but would be ready in an instant should the demon move towards her. Seeing the demon standing in her home, in daylight, on her turf verified what it had told her this morning. The rules were no longer being observed. The demon was obviously as uncomfortable as she, for it was shaking, its fear spilling from it like a waterfall. "How are you here, Infantmeal?"

Its voice trembled. "I am sorry for what happened. I really am. I was only doing what Crimson wanted me to do. I need to speak with you. I bring you information, information which can save this girl, all the children. It could free you as well. I felt your pain and fear this morning. I know something is hidden from you. I could maybe help?"

Alysia could not feel herself blink, her full attention on this creature. What could it possibly share? "Speak, demon."

"You are in danger, Rose. You are a pawn in a game, one you and I have played for years, but others have played for millennia. The Council of 120 discovered things which they were not supposed to acquire. Now a battle rages within the realm of Jarapenth, one unlike any has seen."

"I heard you speak of the Council earlier. Who or what are they?"

"They are hand chosen by Ka itself. They are truly unclean, the very definition of evil. Until six months ago, Ka was able to control them, but something changed, and Ka lost dominance. Crimson now manipulates the council. Crimson exiled Ka to the deepest level of Jarapenth and has instructed the 120 to tear Jarapenth apart. No one knows why Crimson is destroying its home. Without Ka's reign, it is only a matter of time before hell is unleashed upon Earth and your universe. You cannot fathom what it means Rose, no one can." The demon's head hung low, a human trait of despair.

"Why share this with me? Why are you not overjoyed with the idea of your kind ruling over us?"

The creature released a hot breath, the stench overpowering. "See, you do not understand. I am no more than a low-level demon. If Jarapenth is torn asunder, I am no different than a human soul. I will be thrown at the mercy of the darkest of demons, spinning in chaos, torture beyond human thought. Your horror movies cannot express the true hell we will live within. It will be never-ending pain, grief, and loss. It would make the Plain of Teeth feel like a kiddie ride."

Alysia's confusion grew with every sentence the demon spoke, and her frustration was showing. She could feel her face flushing. Her scar must be glowing bright. "Demon, I cannot keep up with all these names you speak, I have no idea who Crimson is, and now there is Ka. Is Ka good or bad? Is it Satan?"

"Ka has many names and many stories. It is timeless. You might know it as Lucifer or Satan, but it is neither and both. Ka represents evil, anger, hatred, war, corruption, but it is not this simple. Ka is balanced by another entity known as Akh, Akh represented love, compassion, and understanding. They equalize each other, but the scale is tipping, which cannot be allowed to happen. "

Demons could not help but speak in half-truths, it was their way. Alysia was not getting that half-truth vibe from Infant-meal, so everyone could be getting a first-class ticket to hell in a handbasket, literally. Alysia threw her arms up in frustration, overwhelmed with all she was learning in such a short amount of time. "What am I supposed to do? I have nothing to go on here. It is all one big riddle."

"Rose, you are part of a much bigger plan than you can fathom, the x in a larger equation. Your parents acquired significant knowledge, what they learned I do not know, but it led them to search for enlightenment. Instead, the path turned darker. To prove I am speaking the truth, Tealander is about to call out to you. He is going to bring you to meet the Sect of Light, one called Madame. They believe their cause to be true, but like any cause, there are two sides. Your parents were close to uncovering truths and were eliminated, an accident that nearly killed you as well."

"Wait. What do you know about my parents ..."?

The demon waved its taloned hands in front of it, interrupting her. "It is all I can tell you because I know no more, but they are key. You cannot let the Sect know what I have told you. The Sect will distract you. They will try and get you to see things their way, but Rose, you must remember, balance is needed. You will hear things that will make you want to turn against the demon world, and after all you have seen, I would not lay blame at your feet. I must go. If Crimson finds I was here, I cringe imagining it. I will help where I can. All our futures lie within the balance, you are the only one who can restore it."

With an audible pop, Infantmeal disappeared, leaving only the smell of sulfur and charred flesh to remind her it even existed. Alysia stepped into where it had stood. She could still feel the heat it left behind. Things were unraveling fast. This must be what a prized fighter feels like getting knocked to the mat multiple times in the first round. She heard Matthew calling out to her from outside, his voice carried by the breeze carried in from the ocean. She walked over to Bethany and touched her forehead before once again stepping out of the room. Alysia would need to rethink her feelings about demon intelligence. She just witnessed one who communicated only too well.

CHAPTER 5

As Alysia stepped out onto the terrace, Matthew beckoned her over. "It's time for us to go."

Matthew avoided eye contact with her as she spoke to him. Something he only did when he felt guilt or fear. "Where exactly are we going, Matthew?"

"It's time you are introduced personally to who you really work for, The Sect of Light. I do not have time to explain. If what you say is true, and I do not doubt it, we have limited time. I only have a rudimentary knowledge of the questions you seek answers to. Considering what occurred this morning, the Sect believes it is time to enlighten you to the cause which has been hidden from you, hidden for your protection."

Alysia knew the Sect was her employer, but she had never met anyone from the order. All assignments were brought to her by Matthew. Roland submitted financials, and money was transferred to a linked account which, due to her parent's legacy, she promptly donated. The Sect was a profound mystery to Alysia, but if they continued to support her efforts to free as many children as she could, she rarely questioned their motives. She felt that was about to change.

Turning to Martha, she made a request, "Watch Bethany while I am gone. And, if a moment presents itself, can you dig into the dagger and Carpathica legend? Even on one of those crazy conspiracy sites?" Martha agreed and gave her a hug. Although Alysia was no hugger, she reciprocated the hug absorbing the warmth of human connection.

Matthew and Alysia walked through the sand and stepped up into the waiting helicopter. As it ascended, she stared out over the ocean, where it appeared the water dropped off the horizon in a beautiful straight line. The sun kissing the wave crests, reflecting the white caps and oceans spray. The aircraft turned and headed east, over the Olympics.

FIFTY MINUTES LATER, the helicopter landed on the helipad at the top of the Columbia Tower in downtown Seattle. She learned little on her flight, other than the Sect of Light dedicated itself to preserving innocence and the understanding and containment of evil. Regarding funding, Matthew explained it was complicated. Unbeknownst to others, the top three floors of the Columbia Tower were the headquarters for the Sect of Light. Most people believed it was the offices of Malcolm, Quidfield, and Row, Attorneys at Law with a focus on Intellectual Property Rights, and Lightflay Technologies, a publicly traded company employing over one hundred thousand people worldwide. A company with its focus on data collection and artificial intelligence, data used to inform the Sect of changes in politics, social trends and religious fervor. Both organizations funneled millions to the Sect of Light through creative accounting.

Stepping out of the helicopter, she was struck by the beauty surrounding her. The Puget Sound and the Olympic Mountains popped against the vibrant blue Washington summer sky. Not one cloud marred the blue canvas. The light winds and heavy rain earlier in the week had washed away the smoke from fires burning to the north and south of the city, clearing the ugly brown haze which had clung to the Sound like old cellophane. She could have stood on the top of this building for hours looking out over the Sound, but she did not have hours to spare. She turned quickly and followed Matthew to the steel door leading down to the main offices for the Sect of Light.

CHAPTER 6

Madame loomed in front of the floor-to-ceiling windows on the seventy-sixth floor of the Columbia Tower. She deserved this view. She led this organization through hard times and harder yet to come. She forced them to adapt to changing situations and to not linger in the past. Many within the organization called her ruthless, but she saw herself as a warrior, preparing her tribe for battle against an unknown force. If anyone else in this organization knew what she knew, it would undoubtedly drive them mad.

Father Tealander shared what Alysia had been told by the demon. Were they on the brink of Armageddon? She found herself dreading, and at the same time, relishing the coming meeting with Alysia. She was tired of the worry and the fear. It was time for the dam to break so she could just be done with it.

She turned her gaze down to the stack of journals she would hand over to Alysia. They sat on her mahogany desk, mocking her. She had read through them multiple times and could only decipher half of the data within. What she could figure out made her blood run cold. Many called it the End

Times. It was not. It was the beginning of something even worse.

The journals were mysteries defying the laws of physics. Some were light, like a feather. You might think it would float from your hands down to the table. Instead, once it was out of the readers' hands, it dropped like a boulder. Sometimes leaving pits on the top of her hardwood desk. The best scientific minds in the organization continued to be perplexed. Her sharpest employees were flabbergasted as the journals properties changed based on who handled them, the time of day or even objects the journals might interact with surrounding them. With so many competing factors the team was hard pressed to decipher the physical changes.

She reached down and picked one up from the stack. It weighed as much as a Webster's Dictionary an hour ago. Now the weight was surprisingly normal, not unlike picking up a favorite story from a library shelf. Frustrated, she let the journal drop from her hands back to the stack. She expected it to settle with a resounding thud. Instead, it drifted as soft as snow to quietly land on the top of the stack. Finding reason was, at times, a futile effort. Realities within her world were often rigidly-flexible.

Her gaze returned to the window as the helicopter carrying Alysia and Matthew flew past the neighboring buildings for a landing. On cue, her assistant, Christopher, spoke through the conference speaker, informing Madame her guests would be arriving in the conference room shortly.

How much should she share? How much to let Alysia to figure out for herself? There was not enough time. Opening certain doors only led to more questions, which required opening more doors. If what she had become privy to six months ago turned out to be accurate, the time for opening steel barred and locked doors was quickly coming to an end.

Heavy battering rams would be necessary if not acted upon soon.

Mysterious informants shared what Ka's Council of 120 discovered, which led to the banishment of Ka. With Ka's banishment, the universe began its slow unraveling. Nothing could return to the way it had been. Balance was tipping. If the Sect were fortunate enough, Alysia might be the hand that would restore the unraveling balance of good and evil. At the same time, she could accelerate the destruction of all life.

It was not Madame's place to say, for others had seen the future before Madame rose to lead the organization. She was simply a messenger, a mouthpiece for a master, a puppet on strings. She hated to think she was someone else's to maneuver, but Madame was chosen from an early age to lead the Sect of Light, and so she did with little questioning.

Casting her eyes downward, she saw people scurrying about, doing their menial work, never knowing what awaited them once they passed from this reality. The Tesla's, the million-dollar condos with water views, none of it mattered. Looking out on the snow-capped mountains from her palatial office, she did not lose sight of the irony in her thoughts.

Turning from the floor-to-ceiling windows, she walked to the two huge double doors which led from her office to the conference room and pulled them open.

ALYSIA CAUGHT her breath as the older lady dressed in an expensive Alexander McQueen all-black business suit with Christian Louboutin shoes opened the large garish doors, revealing a massive antique desk and sweeping views beyond her. The woman who approached walked with the ease of someone who had been in charge for a long time. She was decadent in her movements, as if she came from royalty. She stood about five feet eight, an inch or two taller than Alysia. Her brown hair was going gray, amplifying her power. Hazel intelligent eyes glanced across the table. Alysia found her features to be sharp but not harsh.

Madame glanced over the table, observing Alysia as well. She was more beautiful than any picture she had seen. Her lines were perfect. The makings of a model if another calling had not been answered or forced upon her. This young lady was a force to be reckoned with, her body built upon well-defined muscle. Her beauty was only marred by the scar which started above her eye and traveled down past the t-shirt she wore. It would never heal properly, even after several surgeries. Doctors were baffled as to why the grafts did not take, the scar returning to its exact shape, length and depth. Madame knew why and in time, she would share with Alysia the reasons, but it would not be today.

Madame moved to the opposite side of the large conference table and bade them sit. Father Tealander and Alysia did so and were offered something to drink. Alysia preferred grapefruit juice if they could acquire it, and of course, Tealander had his Earl Gray. As her assistant Christopher served beverages, Madame watched in silence. Much could be learned from silence, and she was glad to see Alysia felt the same. Their eyes locked, seeking an understanding or perhaps the upper hand, neither pulling nor pushing the rope, but ready should one try. After a few moments, she spoke.

"Thank you for coming on such short notice, Alysia." Her voice soft but powerful, a hint of refinement.

"Did I have any choice in the matter?" Alysia countered.

"One always has a choice Alysia, but sometimes our choices lead to the same place and to the same answer. Neither is where you wanted to go or be, but there it sits. What you do with it is up to you." She crossed her left leg over her right knee and waited for Alysia to respond.

Alysia wasted no time. "Madame, I need explanations regarding information which has been shared with me over the past ten hours.

"First, who or what is the demon called Crimson? What role does the creature play within the Council of 120?

"Second, what are the six artifacts of Carpathica? More importantly, what is the relevance of the Kalama Dagger, and why would the demon Crimson want it so badly?

The demon set a trap for me this morning. One I believe to be personal. The reasoning for my involvement I do not yet understand. Should I fail in finding this dagger, it has promised to not only kill Bethany but an additional innocent child per day until I acquire and return it. If I am successful, Crimson has provided its word the children shall not be harmed."

"Do you believe it will let them go should you recover this artifact?"

"If shit were not as fucked up as it appears, I would have told you yes, because I have never seen the Rules of the Dead be broken. I have witnessed things today which test my beliefs in all I have learned and been taught about the Rules. The demon I confronted this morning, calling itself Infantmeal, told me the Rules no longer apply. You see, I would say that is bull-shit, but then again, why would a demon tell me this?"

Madame locked eyes with Alysia. It was critical Alysia heard and understood what came next. "Once I share this infor-mation with you, there is no turning back, there will be nowhere for you to run or hide. You are neck deep in the future and our cause. Those opposing us will become aware of your knowledge and hunt you down. You think you are in the thick of it now, but you are not even up to your knees. I want you to understand, the Sect of Light is grateful to you for the services you have rendered in the name of hundreds of children, I want to provide you this chance to walk away. If you stay, you will need to be open to all things."

"I confront demons almost every day. What more can you share with me which will cause me to walk away?"

Madame took a deep breath, releasing it before speaking. "Things that could drive you mad, question your reality, force you to make decisions you should not have to make, and perhaps watch as friends die around you. If you are ready to make this commitment, I believe the best way to educate you is to start at the beginning of time."

"Frankly, Madame, I do not believe I have a choice in this matter. If I walk away, children die. If I stay, friends die. If I do nothing and a darker world is on the horizon, I allowed millions to die. I cannot think of a better example of damned if you do or damned if you don't."

Madame nodded her head in understanding. This young woman was precisely what they needed right now. She only hoped even with her young age, her wisdom was refined enough to understand what she was about to hear.

Madame began the story of time.

CHAPTER 7

"The history of our becoming is too expansive to share with you this evening. A condensed version will be provided due to our lack of time. Much of what I will share with you will require setting aside disbelief, religious teachings, and many of our scientific theories of evolution. Try to understand as best you can. Can you do so?"

Alysia found the statement to be somewhat condescending, but due to the pressures of time, she let this slide and simply nodded her agreement.

"Our species continues to search for meaning, purpose, reason. Why are we here? Are we a cosmic mistake? Created by a higher power or evolved from the muck at the bottom of a river? These same questions were asked by the first sentient being, Ka, who originated from light and carried the same fears we feel. It was all. All-encompassing. Ka had no gender, no religion, no culture, it just was. Ka did not know its origin, it sought its creator but found itself alone. It called out but was met with silence.

"A sentient being alone can become quite mad, fearful,

paranoid. Ka suffered. The being began to speak to itself, and the answers it received scared it more than it wished to acknowledge, it could feel its mind slipping away. So, Ka decided to create another like itself, so it would no longer suffer alone. Since it did not know how it became, it began to experiment. Each of its attempts failed, until Ka packed all its fears and delusions into a single creation. Ka found itself rewarded with a creation of darkness, one it called Akh.

"Ka could not understand Akh's being. It was not like itself, Akh was darkness, built of shadow. But what would one expect when born of fears and doubts? To Ka, Akh was subservient but appeared to carry many of Ka's powers.

"Since Akh knew its creator, its focus turned to pleasing Ka. Akh was like a child, it built things and brought them to its creator, desperately seeking Ka's approval. Akh had a creator to love, so it began to form new emotions, such as compassion, belonging and empathy. Ka could not understand Akh's changing emotions.

"In a fit of rage and lack of ability to connect with its creation, Ka tried to destroy Akh. But Akh being an equal could not be destroyed. Failing, Ka abandoned Akh and traveled through time searching for one that would genuinely be equal or its better so it may learn."

Madame readjusted in her chair. Sitting for long periods at her age created fiery shoulder pains which radiated across her back. She rotated her arms hearing them crack and pop, instantly reliving some of the pain, even if for a short while. She could see Alysia's impatience showing, so continued.

"Akh, left alone now began to suffer as its creator had with loneliness. But Akh understood connection and creation and therefore filled empty spaces with stars and moons, galaxies, and by accident, Akh molded life. Akh was astounded by life, fascinated with the ways it evolved and learned. It enjoyed watching its creations like one of us sitting back at our desk and watching our characters in SimLife evolve and interact. Akh choose to not interfere, it did not manipulate, it simply derived pleasure from watching its creations evolve and adapt.

Life became intelligent. Beings began to communicate through drawings and words, stories were born, and from stories, religions were created to explain the unexplainable. Examine any civilizations and you will find this to be a common factor. We are frightened by what we do not understand. Therefore, we created stories to ease our fears or prevent our young from approaching the Sabretooth Cat. As we evolved, we created new gods and monsters to bring our stories to life. The expressive gods of the Romans and Greeks, worship through pagan rituals, rites of the seasons to explain an eclipse It was easier to blame our failures on an angry god.

At some point, Akh did begin to interact with its creations. Ancient civilizations have recorded interactions with higher powers and the lessons learned. We need to look no further than the Nazca Lines, Crystal Skulls, the Great Pyramids, or the heads of Easter Island to bare witness to these advancements. Science continues to try and find answers to each of these but is unwilling to accept the unacceptable."

"You mean aliens?" Alysia crossed her arms over her chest, her voice sarcastic in its response.

Madame smiled, "Well, not the aliens you are thinking of, Alysia, the greys from *Close Encounters* we have all come to love or fear. And by the way, yes, there are other lifeforms out there, we are not destined to be alone here, but that must wait.

In time Ka returned and discovered Akh's constructs. Jealous of its creation's accomplishments, it destroyed all but a few of Akh's creations. Only sparing what was left because Akh begged its creator for mercy. Ka agreed to allow the remaining of Akh's beings to survive if it could rule in tandem with Aka but rule with fear, for Ka believed it was the only way to receive love. Akh loved its creator and so therefore agreed, believing Ka to be a great ruler even after Ka tried to destroy Akh.

After much deliberation, the two entities negotiated a truce. Ka would rule with fear, Akh with compassion, a balance born of need. In return, Ka would harvest half the souls that passed and place them in his newly created world of Jarapenth, our hell. Akh would take the other half and allow their energy to remain here, on this planet, heaven."

"Hold up a moment," Alysia held up a hand and leaned forward. "Am I hearing you correctly? Ka, which is light, became the ruler of hell, and Akh, who was darkness, became the ruler of heaven? And we are not judged, just half of us go here, the other half there? And when did we get souls?"

Madame held out her own hand to pause Alysia. "There are many questions I cannot answer now Alysia, we do not have adequate time. They will need to wait, and I promise to answer them when time permits. But, let me address the easier of the three you asked.

"We tend to associate darkness with fear. But when we sleep, we are in darkness. When we die, we are in darkness. Many of our most peaceful moments are shrouded in darkness. When you are stressed, you close your eyes, embracing the darkness. You look up to the heavens, and the stars shine down upon you, but the night is dark, and you find peace. Our universe is wrapped in a blanket of darkness. The light reveals our blemishes, our discomforts. We see color in light, but in darkness, we are all the same. We are afraid to reveal ourselves, our true selves to each other. But in darkness, we can be who we want to be without fear of repercussions."

"This is difficult to conceptualize if I am honest. It goes against everything we have been taught or understand." Alysia said as she pondered the information Madame shared.

"Yes, that is why you must let go of your beliefs and prepare yourself for new truths.

"Now where was I? Yes, Ka and Akh created balance but needed to set rules so neither entity could easily dethrone the other. They set aside their differences and squabbles to write the Rules of the Dead, with which you are familiar, to govern both sides and not give one or the other advantage. A moral code if you will. With this work accomplished, they needed to spread these new Rules to Akh's creations." Madame's hands parted, spreading wide over the table before bringing them back and interlacing her fingers.

"I do not understand how any of this relates to our current situation," Alysia said as she stood to refill her glass at the buffet. She did not realize how thirsty she was until finishing her first.

Madame waited for Alysia to return, taking a moment to lightly stretch. Her body did not enjoy sitting for long periods, her standing desk was where she spent most of her time.

"It will come together in a moment. Please allow a bit more patience," A diamond bracelet on Madame's right wrist caught the ceiling lights and flashed across Alysia's face.

"With the Rules in place, Akh worked to convince Ka that their influence on creation created too much chaos. Would it not make more sense to have a being that resembled our kind, humans, deliver the entities Rules, the morale code?

Ka acquiesced to Akh's idea if each entity would have its own messenger. Ka's representative came to be known as Crimson, and Akh's was Kalama, or as you know him, Christ. Each entity gifted their creations with unique powers to help convince their followers."

"Lucifer had a prophet?" Father Tealander sat forward in anticipation of an answer. He had been a quiet spectator during the conversation up to this point, but the idea Lucifer had a prophet was one too many new revelations for Tealander to take.

"Let's not call them prophets, Father." Madame said with a quick wave of her hand as if she batted away a buzzing fly. "They were much more, think of them as the old-world Twitter influencers. They were the creations and loved children of the creators. Ka adored Crimson, finding his creation to be its greatest accomplishments. It believed Crimson would deliver the Rules and grow a large following of worshippers. We know however, this did not occur. It is why we are in our current predicament, but I am getting ahead of myself." Madame found herself slouching in her chair so straightened to relieve tension in once more in her shoulders.

"Crimson and Kalama traveled their creators lands separately at first. But at some point, we do not know when, the two became friends. They discovered their messages were generally the same and therefore decided to travel together. Neither was aware of the other's origins. Ka and Akh had not anticipated them coming together.

"Kalama grew to become a true leader, and Crimson was eager to follow, for it loved Kalama. Watching Crimson fall in line with Kalama angered Ka. It felt betrayed, manipulated by Akh. Ka sent a secret message to Crimson. It was to tempt Kalama to turn from Akh and follow Ka instead."

"The temptation of Christ in the desert," Matthew nodded in excitement. Finally, something relatable to his education and teachings. He felt a knowing smile cross his face.

"Exactly Matthew," Madame acknowledged, "but neither Ka nor Akh could predict how strong Crimson and Kalama's bond of friendship had become. When they met in the desert, Crimson spoke truthfully to Kalama about what Ka had wickedly asked it to do. Both realized their creators were too powerful and held too much jealousy. They would need to balance out their creators to prevent chaos from reigning. Crimson shared with Kalama a secret place Ka had created, a world called Carpathica. This world was kept secret from Akh, it was a place Ka could plot and scheme, a place of its own. Crimson was sure Ka would not be aware of their presence as its focus was on this place, Earth. In agreement, they created spectral images of themselves here and traveled to Carpathica."

Madame stopped suddenly. "Are either of you hungry? I am famished with all this talking, and I see the hour is growing late. I can have my assistant, Christopher, order some food, and we can eat while I continue? Besides, a quick rest and stretch would do all of us good."

Both Alysia and Father Tealander agreed reluctantly, shook from their trance realizing they were stiff from listening intently to Madame's story. They, too, were hungry but were eager to learn more. They gave Christopher their sandwich order and stood to stretch out tired limbs. Madame excused herself to her office after showing the two where the restrooms were located. When Alysia and Matthew returned, they discovered Madame had not yet returned.

"Well, at least I know who Crimson is now," Alysia said with a sigh.

Matthew took her hand and hung his head low. "This is shaking the very core of my faith. I feel my entire life has been one large deception. I do not even know what truth is anymore. Why would the Madame allow me to follow my religious teachings when she knew they were all for naught?"

Alysia squeezed his hand lightly. Matthew's seventy-five years were clearly showing today. He looked tired, no, exhausted. The bags under his eyes the color of dark soot. His posture ravaged slouching as he walked. She could smell the cologne he was wearing but also the nervous sweat underneath. She realized he was scared, and she did not blame him, herself terrified. Absolutely none of this could be good. The story was leading to an answer she did not want to hear.

Food arrived shortly and Madame returned from her private office. She was carrying a stack of books, and some rolled parchments held together with rubber bands. She placed them on the conference table while Christopher passed out the sandwiches.

Alysia did not realize how famished she was until she sat down and took her first bite. The mini pastries from the morning seemed a long time ago. Half her sandwich was gone before she even looked up to see if a bag or chips or a maybe a cookie awaited nearby. When she did, Madame was smiling at her as if she had been reading her thoughts.

"What," Alysia said through a mouth full of turkey on rye.

"You have a little mustard right here," she pointed to her own mouth.

"Oh," Alysia wiped the corner of her mouth, then realized it was the other corner. Swiping off the yellow liquid, she popped her finger in her mouth, the tangy mustard tantalizing her to finish the other half.

"Shall we continue?" Madame asked as she forked a bite of salad into her mouth.

Since no one objected over mouths full of food, she finished chewing, took a drink of water, and continued with the story of creation.

CHAPTER 8

"Crimson and Kalama traveled to Carpathica where the two of them worked for forty days to design and forge six unique artifacts, three of light, three of dark. They then combined their powers together and divided them into six portions, placing a portion into each of the artifacts. With the dregs of their remaining powers, they had distributed the six artifacts across the unknown regions of Earth. Neither knowing where the artifacts were distributed and hidden to ensure their creators could not locate them." Madame's arms once more stretching to either side to show the enormity of her statement She removed a rubber band from one of the parchments and unrolled it onto the table. She shifted some of the journals she had brought to hold it in place.

On the parchment, a circle was drawn with a line separating it horizontally. In the middle of the larger circle was a smaller circle, with one half representing the moon and the other half the sun. Around the larger circle spaced apart and across from each other were six symbols. Madame pointed to each as she spoke.

"The center circle represents light and dark, Akh, the moon, and Ka the sun. Around the circle are the six artifacts. At the top sits the Kalama Dagger, the others are as follows, moving clockwise. Elohi Cross, Eye of the Marked, Ehecatl Breath, Mahpe Tear, and Anshul Glow. Each artifact is across from its compliment, the Kalama Dagger, an artifact of light, sits opposite Ehecatl's Breath, an artifact of darkness. Balance."

Alysia observed the parchment then asked, "Why is Crimson keen to have the Kalama Dagger when there are five other artifacts it could obtain?"

Madame was impressed with Alysia's willingness to accept the bigger picture and turn the conversation back to the critical discussion. She allowed the question to hang in the room for a moment, rolled her shoulders, and proceeded. "Good question. When Crimson and Kalama returned from Carpathica, they parted ways. Both agreed it would be best. In retrospect, it was not a wise decision.

Kalama's following grew as Crimson disappeared beneath Kalama's shadow. Ka tortured Crimson, forcing the child to do horrible things. Ka tasked Crimson to turn Kalama's followers against it, but to no avail as Crimson loved his friend and would not turn on Kalama, until Crimson met Judas." Madame watched Father Tealander jump slightly at the name.

Tealander was a mystery to her. He had been a servant of the Sect for years, and yet, he still believed in his higher power and was fervent in seeking signs of proof. Her eyes held Matthews as she spoke the next part. "Judas was a weak-minded greedy man. The promise of riches, fame, and fortune placed before him was all it took for him to deny and forsake Kalama, and Kalama was subsequently tortured and killed by his followers. The stories of nailing Kalama to a cross a gentler recollection of what really happened to Crimson's friend.

Crimson's shame and loathing for its treacheries was

intense. Not able to resolve its conflicting emotions it turned its anger towards hating his once friend, Kalama. But most of all, Crimson feared a life without its friend and resented Kalama for not taking Crimson when his friend ascended."

"It wants to find the dagger out of anger because of its namesake?" Alysia pondered aloud, lightly tapping her fingers on the table. Envy and rage were powerful emotions, she could only imagine the intensity with which they would affect a being such as Crimson. "How did the Sect of Light discover all of this?"

Madame stood from her chair and slowly paced the room, knowing that what she was going to share could set off a tornado of pent-up emotions. "The Sect has known of Ka and Akh since the organization began. We were unaware of these six artifacts until your parents became employed by us."

Due to her morning confrontation with Infantmeal, she was aware her parents were connected to the Sect but to what extent?

Alysia's body language changed. She tensed. Her hands balled into fists on the conference table. She felt her eyes close to slits, sharp and aware. She turned towards her friend Matthew and let her words fly from her lips, sharp as razor-blades, her tone meant to cut deep. "How were my parents involved? Matthew, did you know my parents were involved? Why did you not tell me?"

Matthew's face turned red, and he was forced to turn away from Alysia's glare.

Madame raised a hand. "He was forbidden to speak to you for your own protection. You have always believed your parents were killed in an accident. We believe they were murdered because of what they knew. You were lucky to have survived. It was determined to not involve you at a higher level until the moment presented itself." Madame spread her hands, "the moment has presented itself."

Madame watched emotions play across Alysia's face. Sadness, anger, and resentment. The scar, always her emotional giveaway as it changed from fiery red to pale pink in a matter of seconds. Much information could be gleaned in how the scar changed and with the scrunching of Alysia's face or the squinting of her eyes. These tells were the map of Alysia's emotions.

"In time, you will better understand why we kept your parents' involvement from you." She had to ignore Alysia's emotions, brushing them aside, not allowing her to become confrontational. "When the stories of Kalama were documented by its followers, Crimson tried to rectify its betrayal by submitting its own Book. It shared the stories of Kalama and Crimson's friendship and their work to balance good and evil. Prophets and ancient scholars considered its accounts to be lies, and Crimson's Book was denied as part of the narrative, its tale was never allowed to be part of the holy scriptures. Crimson hid its narrative after being denied, and its name was forgotten.

Centuries later, your parents were exploring the Chal-e-Nahijr Cave in Iran on one of their many visits to the region. The floor in a fragile part of the cave collapsed, dropping your mother over fifty feet. Miraculously she survived with not even a scratch. In this undiscovered portion of the cave, she discovered an ancient scroll written in a language she did not know. She should have returned the find to the Government of Iran, but she was enticed to keep the scroll. Within the scroll was the document before you, and your parent's obsession was born."

"Wait, who or what enticed my mom to keep the scrolls?"

"That, Alysia, is one of many unanswered questions."

Alysia felt such a deep well of sadness for her parents, so many things she did not know or understand. She had been so young when her parents were torn from her. These emotions still so difficult to understand. So, why did she expect her parents to share this information with her? Could her ten-year-old self have even comprehended what she was hearing? No, she would not have. And learning the world was facing unexplainable evil would have only given her untold nightmares.

Her annoyance blossomed at knowing Matthew had been aware. She felt he should have informed her as she grew older and began working for the Sect. She was strong, she could have handled it. Her thoughts were interrupted by the sound of tapping on the table. Her eyes followed the sound finding Madame lightly tapping the stack of journals.

Madame took back the conversation from Alysia, returning the focus to the tasks at hand. "These journals represent over fifteen years of research into the artifacts shown on the diagram before you. Your parents realized the importance of what they had discovred, and the dire consequences humanity would face should the artifacts fall into the wrong hands. The Sect has tried to decipher as much as possible, but we have not had much luck. Now, with Crimson seeking the dagger, it is necessary to accelerate our understanding of the journals and find these hidden relics before it does."

Madame slid the stack of books to Alysia and watched as Alysia picked the top one up and opened it. Alysia glanced up from the journal and saw the inquisitive look on Madame's face.

"What?" she asked.

"The book does not seem strange to you?" Madame asked as she leaned slightly across the table.

Alysia flipped the book from hand to hand, opening and closing the book to different pages. "It's a journal. Why, is it bound in human skin?" she mused. She then handed the journal to Matthew, and his reaction was immediate.

"It is so light!" he exclaimed. "It feels like it has no weight at all. It should be floating," He tossed it from hand to hand, laughing at the weirdness of it.

Matthew and Madame exchanged glances before returning to it Alysia.

"Wait," Matthew asked. "You don't feel it, do you?"

He handed back the journal, and Alysia held it in her hand. "What the hell are you two talking about? It's a damn book." Alysia grabbed another. It, too, felt like a book should feel. The bindings were well worn, creased from consistent opening and closing. At the bottom of each binding, a symbol was written in gold.

Madame moved around the table to Alysia, placing a hand on her shoulder. "No matter. I have more to share, much more, but it will need to wait. Lives are at stake Alysia. Other questions and answers will need to be put on hold. The hour grows late. The answer to finding the Kalama Dagger is within these pages. At least we hope it is. You have extraordinarily little time and a lot to do," Madame sighed, "besides, I grow tired and need rest. Christopher will show you the way out and back to the helicopter."

She turned abruptly and walked back to the open double doors leading to her office. Before she could close the doors, Alysia asked the question Madame had hoped she would ask.

"Madame, I do not see Crimson's Book here. Where is the rest of what my mother found it that cave?"

Madame turned to her, "We do not know. We have been unable to locate it. Hopefully, you can discover its location within those journals."

The doors closed, and Alysia was left staring at the intricate artwork carved into them. For a moment, the carving seemed to come alive, the script rearranging itself. She closed her eyes briefly, then opened them. The illusion disappeared, the door returned to normal. Alysia stood and went to the doors, letting her fingers trail across the carvings. She felt a slight tingling, electricity flowing up her arm. It was like ants marching along her skin. Unpleasant. She wiped her arm with her hand to remove the sensation. A cold shiver ran through her. There was more here than she was being told, ancient information to disclose.

Alysia picked up the books and parchments from the table, placing them all into a canvas bag that Christopher provided. She and Matthew followed him out of the conference room and back to the awaiting helicopter.

CHAPTER 9

M adame was truthful with Alysia. She was exhausted. The weight of what was to come pushed her down into the chair. She stared out the window and waited for the helicopter to leave. Only after, as she watched the helicopter lights disappear, did she acknowledge the other in the room.

"It is done," she said with as little emotion as possible, not even turning to acknowledge its presence.

"You have done well" the shadow figure replied, its form shifting between fully formed and translucence.

Madame turned and witnessed the shifting entity, its orange eyes casting a glow within the shadows. Its form released a dark energy which seemed to supp on her own energy, turning good thoughts bad, and bad thoughts into squirming nightmarish hallucinations.

Madame tried to turn the shadows focus to something other than herself, "Do you think it strange Alysia did not have the same experiences with the books as everyone else?"

"I find much about Alysia Rose strange. It is why her

involvement was necessary," was its only reply. It then disappeared and the room returned to normal.

Madame called her assistant on the speakerphone. "Prepare the Sovereign Guard. Tell them it is time. They need to be ready to escort Miss Rose to wherever she needs to go. Oh, and bring me a bourbon on the rocks, for Christ's sake, better yet make it a double. I need a goddamn drink."

CRIMSON WAS PLEASED as it sat upon the throne of Ka, gloating over its recent victories. Once it discovered the ruse, the taking of Jarapenth had been swift. Those who opposed Crimson joined Ka in the deepest pits of Jarapenth. Once a few thousand had been cast down, the others had come around quickly to its grim way of leading. Over time, all would see Crimson's way was the only way, and if they did not, the Kalama Dagger would obliterate them.

One of Crimson's guards had just informed it of Alysia's meeting with the Sect of Light and the handing over of the journals. After Alysia's parents' death, Crimson was sure it could acquire the diaries and its own Book before the Sect discovered them. Still, fate was fickle, and the Sect of Light was quicker to acquire them.

Now those journals were in Alysia's hands. The question to be answered, did it steal the journals from her and locate the objects on its own? Or should it strike enough fear in her to continue her quest? Crimson was confident that if it stood back and allowed her to continue, she would have greater success than its army of fools.

Crimson would wait, play the game for the short term, bring terror to her and her friends to inspire them to continue the search. If necessary, the demon could always change the rules to ensure a successful win for itself. Besides, Crimson's informant would keep it apprised of Alysia's progress.

"Ispep," the demon lord bellowed into Jarapenth, "Come forward, I have work for you.

CHAPTER 10

I t was a good day. It had been a fantastic two weeks with her
parents. Alysia could not remember a happier time in her
ten years of existence. She was usually lucky to see her parents
once a week for dinner. But she had seen them every day and
night for seventeen straight days. The trip had been centered
around her. Her parents asked what she wanted to do, denying
her nothing. The fun started in San Diego with trips to the Zoo,
Safari Park, Sea World, and Legoland. Then the Rose's went
north and stayed at the Disneyland Resort, in a suite. It was
magical, overlooking the park, waking up to breakfast with her
favorite princesses, dinner at fancy restaurants.

To top it off, on their way home, her dad suggested the
Santa Cruz Boardwalk, a place he used to go with his family as
a child. Knowing nothing about the boardwalk she looked it up
on her phone and saw it had a big wooden rollercoaster. She
loved the way thrill rides made her feel, frantic and exhilarated
at the same time. That feeling of her tummy flipping, and head
spinning was the bomb.

Unfortunately, it was the last day of their trip. They would return home soon, and she knew things would return to her parents leaving for days, or weeks and sometimes for months at a time. They told her the trips were vital for her, but they would never say why, even when she begged to understand. Instead, she was left feeling unwanted or that they were ashamed of her. Sometimes, on nights when she awoke with screams in her head, bed soaked with sweat, her body feeling as if the sun were laying directly on top of it, she could hear her mother crying softly in the room next door to hers. In the morning she would ask her mother what was wrong, but her mother simply kissed the top of her head and told her not to fret.

But right now, she would take all this special time granted her. And she did, loving every ride, the caramel apples, cotton candy and the sand beneath her feet, even though her parents kept warning her to watch for broken glass buried in the sand. The cold Pacific Ocean waters lapped her toes like her puppy would do at home when she awoke in the morning.

As night arrived and the boardwalk lights switched on, it took on a different appearance, a darker, more muted sinister tone. She noticed that families were replaced with teenagers hanging out in groups, leering at tourists as they passed. Her parents noticed the shift too and told her it was time for one last ride, and then they would head back to their hotel. Alysia had ridden every ride at least twice, some three times, except for one, The Haunted Castle. She had been purposefully avoiding this ride all day, she loved thrill rides, but was not a fan of scary dark rides. Her father continued to rib her throughout the day, and so, finally she agreed to go in with him.

They arrived at the castle with darkness pushing against their backs and the wind of the ocean blowing her mother's and Alysia's hair into their faces. Her mom said she was tired and would sit this one out. She sat on a bench under the light by the entrance to the ride. Her dad took her hand in his and handed the ticket taker the correct number of tickets. Alysia's hand felt small in her father's, but it also felt safe and warm.

The first room was pirates. Her dad called them animatronics, she called them bad robots. Swords clashed, thunder and lightning struck, cannons fired. She could not help feeling a bit disappointed because the Pirates of the Caribbean ride had been ten times more awesome. The next corner brought them into a Haunted Graveyard, and she grabbed hold of her dad's hand a little tighter. Ghosts jumped at her from all sides, making her lean into her father's leg. Her grip tighter and tighter with each step. Leaving the graveyard, they entered the lair of a Giant Dragon, its eyes a beady red, its colossal head blocking the way forward. As they approached, the Dragon spoke, "Who dares to disturb my treasure?" Her father, never being the humorous one, always serious, replied with a rare moment of lightness, "Bitch, we are all up in your treasure." He turned and smiled at his daughter while the Dragon's head lifted and revealed a staircase. They walked cautiously to the base and began ascending the dark metal staircase. Each step released a loud clanging which jolted her eardrums.

At the top, they found themselves at the entrance of a house of mirrors. Her father stepped in but smacked straight into a mirror after the third step. Startled, he laughed, then stepped forward, hitting another mirror immediately. This time his laugh sounded the same as when Alysia had done something wrong. It was the kind of laugh letting her know he was at his wits end with her goofiness.

They made their way through the maze until a clown appeared. It was the scariest clown she had ever seen, with a giant red nose and red weeping eyes. Its makeup was running down its gaunt face, leaving rivulets of black, red, and white. When it smiled, its sharpened teeth gleamed from within a mouth which seemed too large. From where she stood, she could smell its reeking and fetid breath. Her first thought was it must have the worst cavities ever.

She jumped back, letting go of her father's hand, her feet taking control as she propelled herself towards the way they had entered. Smacking into mirrors, falling backward and immediately getting up and going again, not knowing front from back and left from right. If others had seen her, they might have found this comical, but Alysia was not laughing. She could hear her father calling her name, but the panic was too great. Her need to escape clawed its way up her spine compelling her to move faster. Blood ran down her face from what she thought was a broken nose as she continued to smash into mirrors. The sound of her father's voice became distant. She was collapsing into herself, drowning. Then a hand touched her shoulder.

A voice that was not her father's spoke her name. "Rose."

"I want my daddy!" Alysia screamed into the mirrors.

"Wake up, Rose!"

Alysia's eyes opened. Her mind focusing on multiple thoughts as she adjusted to the darkness. She smelled sulfur, which in turn caused her body to tense and immediately move into a sitting position. Her head turned left then right, trying to pierce the darkness around her. As her neck swiveled, her eyes focused on a blurry image at the base of her king size bed. The blue eyes of a demon peered back at her.

The dream forgotten, she turned her anger to the demon Infantmeal. How dare it enter her bedroom, her private space. "Get the fuck out of my room, Infantmeal, you worthless piece of shit!"

"Oh, you were expecting Infantmeal," the creature spoke as it leaned over, placing its taloned hands upon the bed. Alysia watched as the bedspread began to smoke. Its voice was like a thousand children screaming in pain all at once. "Yeah, sorry to disappoint, but your charred boyfriend is not available right now. Maybe I will suffice? You can call me Ispep," it bowed its grotesque form in a false sense of chivalry, "oh, Crimson once again sends his best wishes."

It leaped onto her bed, crawling quickly on all fours. The damned thing was fast. Alysia countered with a roll to the left, but the sheets wrapped around her legs and she found herself pinned on her stomach. She could feel the weight of the creature moving up her back, pressing her down. The heat of its body breaking her own into a pouring sweat. The stink of Ispep filled her nostrils. His odor was mixed with the scent of smoke. Her bed clothing was close to catching fire from the demon's hands. Panicked, she worked to free her legs from the bedsheets, but the sheets were tightly bound, her lower half wrapped like a mummy.

"Mmmmmm, Alysia, your fear is palatable, a fine red wine paired with sweet, sweet chocolate," Ispep laughed, close to her ear. The demons weight shifted just enough so she could move her hands to her sides, providing the leverage she needed to lift her body. She used all her fear and strength to lift herself up onto all fours in one quick motion. Her momentum thrust the demon away from her, but it corrected swiftly and prepared to attack.

"Ohhh, doggy style, my favorite," it laughed, an undulating pitch, which was even more horrifying than its voice.

Alysia gagged at the thought of this thing having its way with her. She shifted the sheets and could feel the mattress adjust to the weight of Ispep right behind her. She rolled across the bed and landed with a thud onto the floor. Alysia did not stop her momentum, belly crawling under the bed to the center where her parents had hidden a sawed-off shotgun. Knowing it was there had always provided her a sense of security. Now, she could only think of how stupid it was to have the thing in an utterly unreachable location. Ispep landed on the floor and fell to its stomach, peering under the bed. "Where are you going, Alysia? Crimson said I can play with you as long as I don't kill you, and it has been so long since I have gotten to play," it sneered.

Grabbing the stock of the gun, she twisted herself in the tight space and aimed at the demon. Her finger pulled the trigger before her arm stopped moving. The kickback jarred her arm and pushed it up towards the box spring, knocking the gun from her grasp. Small trickles of black ooze seeped from the demons' wounds. Unfortunately, the shot went wide, so damage was minimal.

"Bitch!" it screamed as the demon's form was peppered with shot. "I see we are going to play rough. I love rough play."

Alysia retrieved the weapon, but the demon did not give her time to aim again. It disappeared only to land on the top of the mattress and demolish the fabric with its talons. Alysia could not fire the shotgun again as there was no room to maneuver it into an upright position. Nails tore through the mattress, the metal springs slowing the demon's progress. She was thankful she had not switched out her current bed to a Sleep Number. This thing would have been on her already. She could hear the springs breaking, their sharp twangs in protest as the demon continued its frantic destruction. She thought about rolling either left or right, but she would be vulnerable if she moved and the creature broke through. Alysia had only one chance. Wait for Ispep to tear through the box spring and then use the gap to position the shotgun for what she hoped would be a head shot. She knew if she fucked this up, it was over. She had nowhere else to go or hide.

Tensing every muscle in her body, she held the shotgun to her chest, ready to push it through the hole the minute she saw the demon's shape. What felt like years were mere seconds as a talon tore through the cloth, nearly missing her body. She shifted slightly to the right, removing herself from the direct path of the creature's frenzied digging. The hole was now large enough for the demon to look through, and even in the dark, she could see its wicked smile, its blackened teeth shining like pools of oil. Alysia felt the weight of the creature shift on the bed above as it adjusted itself for the final attack. She used this moment to push the shotgun through the hole. The recoil had nowhere to go, but directly through her arm and into her chest, it felt like being whacked with an aluminum baseball bat. The shotgun fell to the side, and her arm and chest went numb, but not before her brain registered the impact. She cried out as the pain radiated through her body assailing every nerve.

The demon shrieked, throwing itself to the bottom of the bed, thrashing and screaming. The sound pierced Alysia's ears like an ice pick, adding to her current misery. She felt Ispep dismount from the ruined bed and run into the bathroom. She scurried on her belly to get out from under, what she now realized to be, an outrageously enormous bed, dragging the shotgun with her. She wondered if the gun held any more shells. She further wondered where the hell additional shells would be and why she had never considered this before.

As she exited from her near tomb, she sprang to her feet and pointed the shotgun forward. The gun waivered unsteadily as she had to use her right arm as her left was still numb and non-responsive. Her eyes moved to the now destroyed bed, smoldering and smoking in ruins. Maybe it was time for a downgrade, she thought as she tried to rationalize what was happening.

The demon was no longer in the room, but she could hear it yowling and destroying her bathroom. It screamed obscenities thrown together in confusion. If the situation were not dire, it would have been comical.

But the situation was dire, and it was far from comical as Alysia approached the bathroom. She had never been attacked on her turf. The Rules of the Dead forbade demons from entering the world of the living. Infantmeal had done so to warn her the previous day. Twice her territory was invaded. The idea she was now open to attack at any time filled her with dread.

Ispep continued its verbal outrage and onslaught as she entered the bathroom, sweeping the shotgun back and forth. The room was large. In this moment, she was grateful for its size because as she flipped on the lights, Ispep stood at the back of the room, a sizeable distance away from herself. It was ripping the toilet from the floor, water shooting up like a fountain, and flooding the bathroom. Her flicking on the lights caused it to flinch and cower but only for a moment. It regained its composure, standing to its seven-foot height, and turned towards her. She was mesmerized by the massive hole in the demon's chest from the shotgun blast. How the hell could it still be standing?

Ispep, feeding on her confusion, giggled as it ran its hands along and through the ragged hole. It felt no pain, no discomfort. I mere mosquito bite compared to its other sufferings. Toying with her, the creature began taking small steps towards the front of the bathroom. Water from the broken toilet fell like rain around the creature, water droplets hissing as it hit Ispep's hot charred flesh.

"Don't step any closer, demon," Alysia said, her voice shaking. She continued to stare at the hole in Ispep's chest, unable to glance away for the damage. The demon's laugh grew boisterous, feeding on her discomfort. Damn it, she wished it would stop laughing. The sound would haunt her for the rest of her life, or for the next few moments, whichever came first.

Ispep ignored her command as it continued pressing forward, the entire time running its hands around, in, and through the hole, a sickly seductive motion. Alysia just could not stop staring at the gapping, weeping wound. It was so disturbing, her brain unable to grasp what was happening. Her finger tightened and loosened on the trigger, but never with enough pressure to engage the deadly weapon. The creature appeared to float across the room, finding pleasure in her discomfort, until it suddenly reached within striking distance. Alysia pulled the trigger. No gunshot. She pulled again. This time harder, desperate for a reaction from the shotgun. The sound of an empty click echoed in the large bathroom, a lonely sound matching the low moan of desperation that escaped her throat. The demon grabbed the end of the barrel and plunged it through the hole in its chest imitating a perverse sexual act.

The demon's other taloned hand thrust outward and wrapped around her throat, lifting her, blocking her airway. She tried to lift the gun to use as a bat, but it was stuck inside the demon. She let go of the gun, her hands fluttered to the crisped arm and tried to pull free. She could feel the heat of the demon as she clawed off large chunks of its burnt flesh. Its skin sluffing off in putrid puddles of black goo and landing with a sickening plop in the water flooding the bathroom. Her hands burning, she smashed her fists into the creature's chest, arms, and face. Her throat grew hot but Alysia felt the rest of herself grow cold. "*I never had a chance,*" she thought as her brain numbed, turning memory gray.

Ispep giggled uncontrollably, finding her struggles humorous. It shook Alysia like an old rag doll, watching her legs jiggle and dance to its violent thrusts. Her blue eyes began to protrude from their sockets, her hands trembling at her side.

The demon drank her fear in gulps lapping up her despair. What was all the fuss about? These little toys were easy to kill. It felt Alysia's strengthen waning as it held her in the air. "Bitch, you are nothing. A weak, inferior creature unworthy of licking my feet. Oh, how the 120 trembles with the mention of your name, Demonspeaker, but I cannot fathom why, you are a powerless husk. You are not worthy of being feared." It shook her again, enjoying the rubbery movement of her body under Ispep's control, "You. Are. Nothing. When you are gone, I am going to kill everyone you ever cared about, and I am going to reap the children of this world like a farmer cuts wheat."

Alysia wheezed, just a whimpering cough, "Crimson is going to kill you. Your lord needs me to find the dagger."

"Crimson will reward me once it realizes you are no longer a threat. I can find the dagger," it growled and tightened its grip.

Alysia's vision blurred further, and in her last seconds of her life, she did not feel pity for herself but fear for those she cared about and all the others she could not save. Bright pinpricks of light flashed in the darkness of her mind.

In her final moments, she had a vision of Ispep's head exploding into millions of pieces. Its blackened brains splattering across her face.

Then she was gone.

CHAPTER 11

Alysia tried to open her eyes, but they were glued shut. Frightened, she reached up with shaking hands and felt a thick fluid covering her face. She was dead and in Jarapenth. Perturbation overtook her as she scooped the gore from her face. She opened her eyes, using her fingers to avoid getting the thick fluid into them. A demon was staring down at her. Terrified, she crab-crawled backwards, her movements causing small waves of water to wash across the bathroom floor. She was unable to swallow due to the painful swelling in her neck. This also stopped her from screaming aloud, although it did not stop the sound in her mind. Her back smacked against a wall. She was trapped with nowhere to go.

"Rose, it's okay, it's me."

"Itsa me, a Mario," she rasped out, giddily laughing at the craziness of it all. Phrases flooded her oxygen-deprived brain, movie quotes, video games, memes, great poker hands. Desperate to be away from wherever this place was, her mind rolled through things she loved. The end credits to her life.

"No, Rose, it's me, Infantmeal. You're okay. You're safe."

With each gasp of air, she moved from illusion to reality. Unless her hell was a destroyed bathroom, with a geyser of water turning the sheetrock into a paste, she was still in her home. She was not dead. Infantmeal stood over the one called Ispep, now a headless husk lying in a growing puddle on the floor. Alysia stumbled over her words as she continued to remove the sticky black mess from her face. "It would not die. I shot it straight through the chest. It acted like it was hit with a BB gun. It nearly killed me! I was defenseless. The goddamn thing was so strong. Demons are not this powerful in transport." She gagged as a part of Ispep's brain matter slipped into her mouth.

"You can't kill a demon with human weapons. The rules might have changed but killing a demon has not. The weapon must be holy or blessed. You can hurt us during transport because you have been trained to believe the weapons you use on our kind work. You fully believe, even though the weapons only exist within your mind. Your belief is so strong you can project the belief to us through the rites of the dead.

Or," it held out its hands, "a demon can kill another demon. Having done so, I am now a traitor. I will be hunted by my kind and sent to the Plain of Teeth or worse."

Alysia was trying to focus on what the demon was telling her, but she was still gasping for oxygen, her brain not fully functioning, "Did I just hear you correctly? You are trapped here?"

"Yes. Until I am sent back by demon hand or a blessed weapon. Ispep is already informing the others of my treachery."

"Wait," she gazed at the body before Infantmeal's feet, "it's not dead?"

"Technically, it was dead before it arrived here," it said as the demon gently nudged Ispep's husk with its own burnt foot. "Once it has been removed from this plane, it can never return here, but it does return back to Jarapenth. The only way a demon can be destroyed is if an angel is destroyed at the same time. The whole balance thing," it said with a shrug.

This was as complicated to understand and interpret as a 5000-piece puzzle of a blizzard in the artic, impossible to put together. Alysia stood up, shaken but thankful she was able to move at all. She trod past the burnt husks, the one standing and the one on the floor, and bent over to turn off the water valves where her toilet once stood. The water slowly became a trickle, adding only a few more drops to the flooded bathroom. How was she going to explain to a plumber how her toilet was literally ripped from the floor?

She turned and found Infantmeal watching her. She could not get over the revulsion of looking at it, and at the same time, it had saved her life at the risk of elevated torture and punishment. If she focused on its eyes, she could still see its dwindling human element. The sadness, pain, and the sympathy it held for her. She dared not hold its gaze too long or its madness could seep into her mind, warping her.

"If you are here, then what is with Bethany?"

"I was only a messenger. The demon within Bethany is Otrebo. It would not reveal itself to you as it fears your wrath. Bethany is still within her cage and safe for now, well, as safe as a child infected with a demon can be, I suppose."

"If you are stuck here, I am going to put you to use," she said as she walked over to Infantmeal and lightly patted its shoulder. It crackled like a pork rind and felt warm under her hand.

"Alysia, are you saying I can stay?"

"Yeah, but you are going to work, and that name has to change. I am not walking around calling you Infantmeal."

She stopped for a minute, inspecting the creature, "How about Char?"

The demon tipped its head to the left not unlike a puppy hearing a new noise. "Am I to assume that is a joke?"

Choked laughter burned her tortured throat. "Yep. Now I just need to figure out how to introduce you to the rest of the team. I do not think they will be as appreciative as I am, you know, under the circumstances and all."

Alysia's eyes turned hard. "Char, if this is a ruse, if this is all to get me in a vulnerable position, if you turn on me, I will fucking destroy you, and you will wish you had never met me."

She spun towards the door and left Char standing in the swamped bathroom.

CHAPTER 12

I spep hung upside down from a large hook, which was currently shoved in what was left of its spine. It never felt the gunshots or its head exploding when the traitorous Infantmeal used its hands to crush its skull. No, it was not bothered by any tortures, but what Crimson had done to it in the last hour, well, eternity was a long time. It could not imagine this pain for even another moment.

"Crimson, I did what you asked, I tried, and I would have succeeded if Infantmeal had not interfered," it pleaded.

"No. You were to toy with her, stoke her fear. I told you to ask about the journals to make her worry we wanted them. Instead, you allowed your ego and demon desires to sway you. You almost killed her, which I explicitly demanded you not do."

Crimson's voice never raised in tone or inflection. Ispep wished the demon lord would show some emotion, any emotion would be better than the slinging of his blade across its tortured form.

Crimson took the long blade in its hand and sliced through Ispep's lower body. The pain was excruciating. Although Ispep did not want to give Crimson the satisfaction of hearing its pain, it howled, its body thrashing on the hook, a fish awaiting the net.

"Ispep, to say I am disappointed, well," Crimson drug the blade farther down, listening to the demon's pain, feeding on it, growing stronger with each twist of the knife. "I am willing to give you another chance." It withdrew the blade and awaited a response.

Ispep was sure this was some form of trickery. It could not go back, it was banned from entering the human plane upon expulsion, but it could not take this pain. Its eyes flicked left then right. It saw others being tortured, heard their screams and pleas. The vastness of Jarapenth was immense beyond compare. The ritualistic torture that took place here, for all eternity, was beyond comprehension. Ispep was willing to take the bait, even if it distracted his tormentor Crimson for only a single breath "How? I would do anything to serve you lord."

Crimson smiled its sharpened teeth, stained red and yellow from the blood of centuries. "I am sending you back, but not as you, as it."

Crimson stepped back, allowing Ispep to see behind the demon lord, and what it saw destroyed all hope. Aloc Acoc was being held by another of the 120, Magenta. Aloc Acoc was beyond mad, tortured for longer than Ispep could remember, and it could recall a long time. This demon was no more than a shell, and Ispep knew what Crimson was going to do. It would be forced to ride along inside Aloc Acoc's warped brain as a passenger, sharing control over the mumbling husk. Ispep audibly moaned. Crimson and Magenta simply laughed, the sound rattling around in its hollow head like two metal balls clashing against each other.

"Please, Lord Crimson, anything but the ritual, I beg you!

Allow me to serve you in another way." Ispep whined and thrashed on the hook.

Ispep wished vehemently for Crimson's blade rather than the Ritual of Replacement. But it could see the decision was made and all its begging and pleading would only feed his lords hunger for suffering. Crimson and Magenta began the chant, and Ispep felt its form squeezed and compressed. Brittle bones shattered, tendons shredded, muscles torn asunder. Ispep wailed as its structure was reduced, crushed into a shapeless mass.

Crimson picked up what was left of Ispep, a simple blob of material small enough to fit within Crimson's palm. Returning to Magenta and Aloc Acoc, Crimson tore the top of Aloc's head open and pressed Ispep's matter into the cavity, then sealed the skull shut.

Crimson smashed Aloc Acoc's face with a tightened fist, awakening the passed-out Ispep. "Ah, there you are, Ispep," Crimson said, peering into the eyes of Aloc Acoc. "There is further work to be done, do not let me down again."

CHAPTER 13

T he morning could not arrive soon enough for Alysia. She embraced the dawn and the opportunity to see friends. Martha and Matthew sat at the large conference table in the operations room while Roland tended to Bethany, checking her vitals. Alysia noted she would need to inform the child's parents that treatments were taking longer than expected. She could not risk having them travel here to see her. Their lives might be sacrificed if they became involved. If things continued to worsen, they would need to move the child to a safer location if a safer place existed anymore.

Alysia's focus returned to her friends sitting around the table. She spoke loud enough so Roland could hear as she described all that had occurred since leaving on the helicopter the day before. She held nothing back, except for a few bits of information Char shared before she visited the Sect of Light. They handled it well until Alysia told them of the attack within her bedroom and that a demon had saved her life. Even though the master bedroom was the only room on the third floor, and her parents had heavily soundproofed the entire home, she was amazed no one had heard anything during the night. Her friends all appeared mortified and shocked as she shared the enormity of the attack.

"I would say it was impossible if I had not seen the state of the bed and bathroom," Roland commented from Bethany's bedside, continuing his morning check. "It is a disaster zone up there. I have no idea how I did not hear the ruckus. It is troubling, to say the least."

Martha shook her head in disbelief, "I was sleeping here, in this room, I heard not one thing, and I even had to get up twice to use the bathroom."

"Well, what I am about to share with you is not going to make your day much better. Char, come in here, please," Alysia called out to the demon.

Char entered the room to the sound of chairs scraping across tile and horrified gasps as Matthew and Martha pushed back from the table. The reactions were what Alysia expected. How could they not be terrified of this creature? She certainly was. Its looks were one thing, its smell another, as it sulfuric stench permeated the room. She watched as her friends placed hands over their mouths and noses. Roland had a hand behind his back, Alysia knew he carried a small weapon tucked under his shirt for emergencies.

"We are just supposed to trust that thing? After everything we have learned about their kind over the years?" Martha pointed to where Char stood. Her face contorted into a mask of fear and outrage.

"I am not saying we have to trust it. It saved me and I am still waiting for it to pounce on me like a cat playing with a mouse" Alysia glanced over at the demon and could see her words affected it, she did not feel much sympathy.

Char lowered its head. It did not blame them for their fear.

Roland sized up the demon, "creature, why wasn't Alysia

able to kill the demon Ispep? She has been trained to do this work, has done it many times, but why not here?"

The demon turned to the one Alysia introduced as Roland. This was a formidable opponent and one the demon would need to watch closely. A slight accent, maybe British, resided just under the surface. His black hair curled over his shoulders as hazel eyes held the demon's gaze. "As I told her, she is fearless when transported. Her training is in her mind. She can manipulate surroundings in the transported state, but more importantly, she believes she can excise a demon. She does not believe that here. You must use holy weapons to send a demon back, and even when you do, it is not dead, only unable to come back here."

Alysia knew her friends had many questions, but a clock was ticking. She needed their focus on helping to understand what the Kalama Dagger was and its current whereabouts. It was time to take control and turn her friends' thoughts to the dagger, and away from the demon.

"I understand everyone's fear and desire to have their questions answered. But we are pressed for time, those things will need to wait. Martha, were you able to locate any information on the Kalama Dagger or Crimson yesterday?"

Martha, unable to take her eyes off the demon, played with her shoulder-length brown hair nervously as she answered Alysia's question. "Two mentions of the word Kalama. One is a township in Washington State, it translates to *pretty maiden* from the Cowlitz Tribe dialect. The second mention is from Hawaii, where it means flaming torch. As far as Crimson, there is no mention of this demon, even in satanic sites or dark web ritual sites. Crimson is very biblical, symbolizing the blood of martyrs or even the presence of God itself. Another interesting tidbit, it is strongly paired with humility and atonement."

"I knew Kalama sounded familiar. The definition of

Crimson could be valuable in understanding the demon's motives. Still, I don't hear anything which gets us closer to understanding the dagger." Alysia quietly chastised herself for sounding disappointed when Martha had only done what was requested of her.

"Here is the situation," Alysia said. "We have to find the Kalama Dagger. We only have five days. Madame has promised to provide us any resources we need once we have discovered its general location, so I need your help." She started handing out journals to each of them. She unrolled the parchment with the six-artifact diagram in the middle of the table. "My parents spent fifteen years researching these artifacts, there has to be data in these journals about each. Your job is to locate all you can on the dagger and the dagger only at this point. We do not have much to go on other than this diagram with an icon representing each artifact. Maybe we look to see if we can locate this icon in any of my parent's notes."

Martha reached for her journal but found she could barely lift it from the table. "Holy shit, what is up with this book? It feels like a boulder."

"Another unexplained mystery to pile on to the growing list of other mysteries. For some reason, these journals do not obey the laws of physics, at least our knowledge of physics. Some are light, others are heavy, some are difficult to open and, once open, difficult to close. I appear to be unaffected by their changes. The Sect of Light offered no explanation. These strange characteristics might be important in time, but for now they contain information we need to locate the artifact Crimson seeks. I know you all have questions, and by all rights, I should have more answers, but I do not. So I am asking each of you to move forward on faith and a desire to save that child over there, and possibly many others."

Her friends agreed hesitantly as there was a demon in their

presence. They picked up their assignments, giving the demon a wide berth as they left the room in search of a quiet place to research.

"What do you wish me to do, Alysia?" asked Char from the corner.

"For now, nothing. We need to give everyone time to adjust. A lot is going on, take a walk around, get a lay of the house." Alysia tried to smile, but it came out as a half-grin, half frown. Char acknowledged her with a nod and left. Within seconds, the temperature dropped, and the air became fresher.

ALYSIA WAS STILL SEATED at the table, deep in thought, when Roland returned to the room. He was an intricate part of her life, just as much as Matthew. She could not remember a time when Roland had not been here. Her parent's professional assistant, and now hers. Jokingly she had called him Alfred once, but Roland found little humor in the reference, so those comparisons ended quickly. For a man in his late fifties, his spirit was youthful. She teased him about the daily application of anti-wrinkle cream, but it worked, as his face was still youthful and vibrant. Like her, he was vigorous in his exercise routine. He carried himself with pride, his walk that of a military general, which is why Alysia believed he was ex-military. But, Roland shared little of his past. After her parent's tragic passing, Matthew and Roland shared the duties of being her father figure. Matthew focused on her education while Roland focused on her physical strengthening and combat training. She loved them both dearly, and at the same time, resented them for having the opportunity to spend more time than she with her parents. Emotions were confusing.

"Finished your studies already?" Alysia teased.

Roland sat across from Alysia, folding his well-manicured hands on the table. "Are you all right, Alysia?"

"Yeah," she said with a tired voice. "Why do you ask?" Her voice was a little more acerbic than she meant it to sound.

Roland locked eyes with her, his tone one of concern. "The master bath has about three inches of standing water, the toilet lies shattered in a million pieces, the carcass of a headless demon sits on the floor, and I had to douse your smoldering bed to avoid it catching the house on fire. Your throat matches your hands, both blistered from confrontations with creatures who, in the past, were unable to physically harm you. Oh, and there appears to be a demon wandering the halls of your home."

Alysia rested her chin in her hands which rested upon the table, causing a mild ripple of pain to flow through her arms from the earlier burns. "I don't know, Roland. I have faced a lot of shit in the last twenty-four hours. A demon named Crimson is hunting me and its presence seems familiar in a strange way. Plus, I discover my parents were caught in the middle of something otherworldly before I was even born, and not one person thought I should know. I must ask. Did you know and willingly keep me in the dark? I trusted you. I trusted Matthew."

Roland's hazel eyes held hers. When she was determined, she was determined. All her emotions flowed across her face in tiny rivulets, like watching the wind move sand in the dunes. "Fifteen years ago, your parents took a trip to Iran for a college lecture tour," Roland started.

"Madame already told me this."

Roland lifted a hand and brushed it through his curly black hair, the gray flecks catching in the light. "Hold on a second. Sometimes you are so damn stubborn, Alysia." He took a breath, continuing. "Upon returning, they were disturbed, their attitudes changed. Their drive and focus went from their professions to darker more disturbing material. They began to research exorcisms, demonology, the occult, witchcraft, crypto-zoology, aliens, anything outside the realm of normal. Most troubling was their separation from each other. A deep distrust began to form between them. Before the trip, your parents were the happiest couple I have ever known. After it, they grew cold, many times not speaking to each other for what felt like days. I tried to ask questions, to help, but they collapsed into themselves. Your father refused to tour, and his work in Neuroscience began to slip." Roland stopped. His focus on a distant memory.

"You know, your father, Eric, was one of the most respected surgeons in the world?" His hazel eyes returning to meet her own. "He was flown around the globe, performing surgeries on world leaders, two of our nation's Presidents, actors, authors, you name it. He was brilliant and respected. His fortune grew. Eric and your mother Zooey created a non-profit focused on caring for children with brain abnormalities and those who could not afford the services he provided. His research changed the way we think of the brain.

"But lest we forget your mother." His gaze grew hazier once more, his pupils dilated with a memory from years ago. The memory of Zooey bothered him more than that of Eric. So, he stood and stretched, letting the tension of the conversation leave his body. It was too damn early, but Roland walked over to the mini fridge, grabbing a pink grapefruit cider. He pointed it at her, but she shook her head, declining. These were the only alcoholic beverages he would consume, and he was very careful with them. His family had a bit of an ism problem. This was one he did not want to inherit. Roland snapped the ring top and allowed the cold, fizzy liquid to moisten his throat.

"Zooey was a brilliant psychologist, and when you put the two of them together, well, their research changed brain science as we know it. They traveled together, sharing information, and in return, soaking up information from whomever they could gather it. After finding the scrolls, their research into the brain became darker. They started performing unauthorized brain scans on people who claimed to be possessed. Hospitals and research facilities that once welcomed them began to shun them and denied requests for use of their medical equipment. Murmurs within the scientific community erupted with some asking for your parents' removal from the charitable boards they sat on. At one point, your father claimed someone could enter the mind and excise an infection without an exorcism. A statement so outlandish he was removed from most speaking circuits. But he was not incorrect as you are currently aware." He tilted his cider can in her direction.

Alysia turned the conversation back to the scrolls. "Did you know The Book of Crimson was missing?" Alysia stated. "The Sect of Light does not have it, the only document from the Book is the parchment in front of you. Were you aware of my parent's journals?"

Roland drank the rest of the cider, calculating his answer. Anything to do with Alysia's parents could set off a hailstorm. He needed to avoid knotting her up, she needed to remain focused. He wanted another cider but instead reached into the refrigerator and snagged a Coke Zero. He offered one to Alysia. This time she accepted. Roland spoke as he returned to the table.

"Yes, I knew of their journals, but I was never allowed to touch them. Sometimes, when they were open, I could see writings and symbols. I thought I was witnessing a fall into madness. In the end, I think your parents hid the Book of Crimson, finding it too dangerous for humankind. Two weeks after your mother shared the news that she was pregnant, your father's work intensified. He acquired his own MRI to continue brain scans and increased travel to visit with those who claimed possession. He was obsessed with hauntings and locations of gruesome murders. Three months after this flurry of activity, Eric, and Zooey left. They would not disclose to me where they were going, but I am certain it had something to do with Crimson's book."

"What makes you think the trip had anything to do with the Book? Maybe they were just trying to get in one more vacation alone before I entered their lives?" Alysia asked as she popped the can of soda open.

"Well, because I saw the Book. It was in a carry-on bag. I assisted your parents with packing when I saw what looked like an old parchment in a Ziplock bag." Roland believed in calm and removing emotions from a situation, but the feelings he felt at this moment were a tidal wave of intensity. He was uncomfortable sharing them with Alysia, afraid they could be taken as weakness. "I cannot explain it, but the parchment spoke to me. It wanted me to open the bag. I could not stop myself, my fingers worked without my brains consent. I remember the feeling of the plastic zipper as I opened it. My fingers touched the Book. For a moment, I saw such horrible things, nightmares. Until today, I had forgotten about the experience. I believe my mind blocked it. The memories too frightening to recall. The second my fingers touched that cursed manuscript, I understood your parents slow slip into madness. What I saw were horrors unimaginable. Dark monstrosities wandered through cities. Their maws so large they could consume hundreds of people in a mouthful. Scooping the screaming up like a vacuum cleaner from hell. Demons butchered bodies in the streets, cutting off limbs, disemboweling them as they writhed on the concrete sidewalks. They threw the living into bonfires and danced around the flames as those within bellowed for forgiveness. Winged terrors swooped down from the heavens and feasted on the flesh of the mangled and dismembered. What was left was greedily devoured by hounds with human arms. Our blood flowed in the gutters, turning lakes and rivers a horrible shade of pink, from which the demons drank. I thought I was witnessing Revelations, only to realize it was far worse."

Alysia's body collapsed in her chair, shoulders slumping forward, face wrought with doubt and disbelief. Her auburn hair fell limply into her eye. She reached up and tiredly tucked it behind an ear. "Did Matthew know of any of this?"

"Little. Tealander is employed by the Sect of Light and assisted your parents when requested. He was a trusted ally and loved by both, enough so that he and I were placed as your co-guardians." Alysia noticed a touch of bitterness but let it slide. "Your parents trusted no one with their research, and so Tealander only knew what he was told, which was about the same as I knew."

Alysia played with the ring top on her soda can, lifting it under her thumbnail and listening to the snap. She glanced up and saw her actions were annoying Roland, so she moved her hand away from the can. "What happened after they returned from the caving expedition?"

Roland stood, picking up his assigned journals from the table. His eyes took in his hands. They betrayed his age, a few sunspots, a little more wrinkled than the year before, his wrinkle cream failing to stop time. He no longer held an interest in this topic. The memories were hard to assimilate, even after the passing years. "You were born. They became savagely protective of you while at the same time distancing themselves from each other. They obsessed over their journals. You were left alone with me so they could continue their research, and then they died horribly in the same crash that left the scar across your body."

"Roland, what happened in Santa Cruz? It is familiar and

yet, distant. It has significance. It feels like a chained monster in my head, desperately trying to escape."

"It was your last vacation with your parents before the tragedy, nothing more."

His eyes and the deepening of the lines in his face betrayed him. She recognized he was holding back. Alysia was about to push when Roland turned and walked away, leaving Alysia with nothing but her thoughts, two journals, and a diagram of six artifacts her parents were murdered for trying to discover.

CHAPTER 14

Alysia screamed as a hand fell upon her shoulder. The voice behind her was calming, telling her not to worry, but the pressure on her shoulder was heavy, threatening.

She launched herself into a standing position, once more screaming for her daddy, but only her reflection called back, mocking her. Her voice ricocheted off glass mirrors, her reflections mocking her. She stumbled through the maze, all the while a gentle voice followed her, assuring her it was okay, just take its hand.

"Daddy! Daddy!" she screamed. Her hands held out iron straight, desperately trying to avoid crashing into the mirrors.

The clown ambled around the corner, its face a twisted caricature of the ones she had seen at the circus with her parents a couple of years ago. It was making a balloon animal, but instead of a long balloon like the one at the circus, it used someone's intestines.

"Alysia, your father wanted you to have this giraffe. Slow down while I finish tying his insides together. It's slippery work." Its grin grew more prominent, its teeth gnawing on a bloody piece of meat.

Alysia froze, unable to move, not even a finger. The clown knotting together the bloody length. A squishy sound assaulted her ears with each twist and turn of the human cord. In her head, she was screaming for her daddy, but her mouth only opened and closed silently.

"You know," the clown said as blood drizzled down his lips, "you are a special young lady. It is not often my master sends me out to welcome new arrivals. I am usually locked away. It says I can be a little too frightening and a tad overdramatic." The clown performed two perfect summersaults, coming within inches of her.

"Here, it's finished. Just for you, dear."

The clown thrust the creation toward her. The offal animal was dripping foul-smelling fluids to the floor. It was not what it was made of or the smell that drove Alysia to her knees. It was her father's face staring out at her, moaning. His mouth twisted in a display of grotesque pain. Her father uttered a low mournful moan of such sadness and loss, she wished for it all to end. To just be taken away by whatever wanted her.

A heavy hand fell once more on her shoulder. "Rose, take my hand and I can protect you."

She awoke with a start, her body leaping upwards from the table and found Martha across the way, who had just dropped the journal she was reading on the table. She could feel the sweat dripping down her face, her body shaking with chills. "Alysia, are you okay? Jesus, you look like you just got out of a damn sauna. You're soaked."

Alysia was trying to come out of the nightmare, fighting her way back into reality. It felt like swimming through thick water. Martha came around the table and placed a hand on her shoulder, which Alysia angrily swatted away.

"Hey, okay, sorry, you just look like shit," Martha said as she backed away, her face a mixture of worry and hurt, her eyebrows knitting together with concern.

Alysia's vision cleared, her heartbeat slowed, and the shakes which racked her body subsided. Her voice tripped over words as she spoke. "Martha, I'm sorry, I am not thinking straight. I must have dozed off. That was one viscous nightmare."

"I'm not surprised you were sleeping," Martha said, "it's not as if you have had much sleep in the last twenty-four hours. What the hell were you dreaming about?"

Alysia stood and went over to the coffee pot. "I would rather not talk about it now. It was a little much." A part of her did want to talk about it, to force it forward and gain more clarity. But a more decisive element of her desired to keep it hidden for her own protection.

"Yesterday and then today, the same answer. Alysia, I understand. I cannot imagine what you're going through. I am not sure how I would have dealt with finding out my parents were at the center of potential world annihilation. But at some point, you need to talk to me because coffee can solve only so many problems." Martha said, trying to add a little levity to the discussion.

Alysia poured the rich black liquid into a large mug. The hot beverage burned her lips as she noisily slurped it down, forcing herself into the present. The dream was unraveling. Trying to grab onto strings of thought only made them disappear faster like a strand of spiderweb floating in the air. There one moment and then gone the next. As she turned, Roland and Matthew entered the room, Char following several steps behind, keeping a respectful distance from the rest of the team.

"Any luck?" she asked, blowing on her coffee.

"Nothing. Not a damn thing. Not an image, not a word, no dagger, no references," Martha said, rubbing her hands together in the way she always did when things were not going the way she expected. She battled anxiety like a dragon. Sometimes, it was vanquished, other times it required the wringing of hands.

Father Tealander sat in a chair and pulled it to the table. "I was unsuccessful as well. Although, I did find information on these artifacts representing darkness," he said as he pointed to the three artifacts on the diagram.

"Hey. Hey, yea," Martha exclaimed "I saw a reference to those three as well."

Alysia returned to the table. "Okay, wait, did you all see these other icons?" The three nodded in agreement. "How about any of these?" She pointed to the three artifacts of light. All shook their heads. "We must be missing something. Why would my parents only have information on these three but not the others? It does not make sense."

"Maybe your parents were focused only on the artifacts of darkness, thinking those were the most important?" Martha pointed out.

"I suppose," Alysia said, disappointed. They were forced back to zero with no further clues or information. She could see everyone was discouraged. She was about to provide a few words of encouragement when Matthew spoke.

"Did anybody else's ears just pop? It felt like I was coming down out of the mountains."

"I felt it as well," Roland said. "Also, is it just me, or did it get considerably warmer in here?"

Everyone turned to look for Char, but it was no longer in the room. Together they moved into the great room where Char was staring out the giant plate glass windows towards the ocean.

The demon was glowing hot as a forge, his body heating the room to a roasting temperature. Alysia was glad the floor was porcelain tile, or Char would have lit the house aflame. "They are here," its voice barely above a whisper as it continued to stare out the windows.

"Who is here, Char?" Alysia asked nervously.

Roland did not give Char a chance to respond as it pointed out the glass to a sandstorm moving toward the house. Swirling within were driftwood timbers and other items found within the dunes. The wall of debris moved silently towards the mansion, growing taller and more expansive the closer it came.

"Run!" Char yelled as the entire wall of windows imploded.

CHAPTER 15

Ispep stood with its back to the Pacific Ocean. A passenger within the shell of Aloc Acoc, whom it was now calling AA. AA's thoughts were not unlike a cheese grater. Adam Sandler doing one of his baby talk bits, Aba Dobi Babba Obi. The ritual placed Ispep here like two magnets, opposite poles, pushed together, straining for dominance, even though both resisted and pushed away.

Ispep watched as thirty-five demons paced frantically on the beach, awaiting their chance to tear the humans apart. It was open season on everyone but Alysia. Ispep tried to convince Crimson it was too soon after last night's attack. Alysia's team would be waiting, prepared. Crimson only laughed and replied they would not be able to defend themselves from the demon onslaught even with the traitor Infantmeal assisting them. Ispep was certainly glad not to be Infantmeal. The Council of 120 had created a whole new space of pain for it in Jarapenth. Ispep searched the surrounding area for any humans who could interfere with the upcoming assault. It saw none. The beach was clear as far as it could see.

Ispep began to recite the Rite of Ehecatl to summon the demon wind. Moving its burnt hands in time with the chant, it could feel the wind collect behind it. Ispep moved the wind forward, allowing it to capture the sand and driftwood within its force. Ispep glanced towards the demon commander and nodded to attack the home.

The demons sprinted across the dunes with an unnatural grace which boggled Ispep's mind if a demon mind could be boggled. The sand did not impede their progress in the least. As they drew closer, the line began to break apart, creatures moving left, right, and continuing down the center, following Ispep's plan perfectly. They would breach the home from multiple entrances, catching them off guard, giving them no escape. Ispep waited, watching, releasing the demon wind to destroy as it saw fit.

Char had sensed their arrival the second they appeared upon the beach. The tsunami of sand and debris was summoned by the demon wind, a powerful force as strong as a tornado. Should it hit the home, everyone inside would be obliterated. Char did not have time to gain access to the terrace before the storm struck. Char yelled to the others to run and began to chant a counter rite, the Shield of Gargolot. It watched as the wall of debris advanced. If Char had been an instant slower, the shield would have failed. It thrust the shield outwards as the entire front wall of glass imploded. The rite forced the wall out past the terrace. The water from Alysia's infinity pool was sucked out and added to the massive moving structure.

Char and Ispep fought for control, competing against the other for dominance. The demons on the outside of the storm tried to find a way around the swirling debris. They were hungry and anxious to destroy. Char could only hold them back for so long before the demon army's appetite for destruction drove them to break through the barrier even at the cost of their own existence.

CHAPTER 16

Raegan Marie sat in the back of the helicopter as it came over the top of the turbulent Olympic Mountains and flew over the Hoh Rainforest en route to Moclips. She was on the edge of her seat with excitement. This was the first mission of the newly formed Sovereign Guard, the special forces unit of the Sect if Light. Raegan assembled what she believed to be the best in class across multiple fields. They spent the last year in intensive weapons and hand-to-hand combat training. They were ready for action.

The Sect of Light already had highly trained security staff capable of handling most situations. Raegan had been hired to prepare for contingencies that were outside of the normal. She was hopeful they were going to finally see the full capabilities of their weaponry and protective gear in action.

Across from Raegan sat Mary Mueller, a sharpshooter unlike any she ever met. Accuracy was an understatement. Perfection was Mary's game. Her body was covered in tattoos, each telling the story of a moment in her life, each story fascinating. Her arms were a tapestry of color, which changed as her muscles tightened, the images appearing to move.

Next to Mary sat Christine Carlyle, a master in hand-to-hand combat and a whiz with close combat weaponry. Her hair as an ombre of color which went from a dark black to a beautiful smokey gray blue. It was flowing around her face as the wind came through the open doors. Martin nicknamed her BAB, Bad Ass Beyonce.

Martin Kyle sat next to her in the chopper. He was the only non-military trained personnel on the team. His skills were adventure-based. Martin had climbed Everest and traveled the Amazon. He knew cultures and regions. He was a walking wall of muscle. Christine called him Bane. She was a bit of a comic hound.

Martin won the coin toss for music selection so Disturbed was pumping through the helicopter's sound system. The song changed to the thumping drum opening of *Down with the Sickness*. The team joined together, yelling the opening line, "Do you feel that?" When the pilot joined in with "Oh shit," they realized he was not singing along.

"Holy shit, hold the fuck on!" The pilot yelled over everyone's earpiece. He had been flying low to land in the flattened area they called the helipad. A massive, fast-moving wall of debris forced him to adjust, pulling up quickly, but not before the wind whipped the chopper in the air like a kite. He struggled to hold the helicopter steady and prayed no one was falling out the sides. The aircraft came up over the top of the storm, a huge log, an entire fucking tree, just missed the helicopter. The pilot watched the tree sail past as the wall of sand rushed onward, then, just as suddenly, the wall was forced back out towards the ocean. "God damn it," he yelled as he worked to move the helicopter out of the way. Silently, he prayed the sand would not fuck up the engines.

Raegan Marie was thrown around with her team in the back of the copter. She held on for dear life as her curly reddish-brown hair thrashed her face. Raegan wanted to remove the hair from her eyes, but to let go of the handhold would be suicide. Now she understood the military haircut.

Mary Muller was having no better luck, her hand reaching out for anything to grasp as her body lunged for the open side door of the helicopter, her tattooed arms a colorful display of disoriented madness as they flailed around for purchase. She thought her life would end in glorious battle or mad sex. No, she was going to die launched from a helicopter in the middle of a sandstorm in Washington State, on a beach for that matter.

Martin Kyle grabbed Mary by her pants and yanked her back in before she was jettisoned from the chopper. His arm muscles bulged as he pulled her back, the veins showing blue through the tightened skin. Mary grabbed Martin's arm and investigated his face. His brown eyes danced with glee.

"Wooweee, "Martin yelled over the music and the yells of her team as the helicopter bucked underneath them like a pissed-off bull leaving its holding pen. "Now we are talking!"

"You need some new hobbies," Mary yelled back as she fell into a seat.

The pilot gained control, allowing the Sovereign Guard the first clear opportunity to see what was taking place below them. From the air, they observed a nightmare scenario. An army of at least thirty creatures was spreading out, exploring a way to penetrate the wall of debris. The sand and logs swirled in a barrier that was one hundred feet high, ninety feet wide, and at least twenty feet deep.

Mary was peering through her scope for a target, but the turbulence made it difficult to get a clear shot. The helicopter continued to hover slowly, moving over the attack below. As the chopper approached the home, Mary saw a creature standing on the terrace and lined up a shot. However, she could swear the creature was actively holding back the storm. It looked the same as the others working to breach the mansion from all sides. What the hell? Who were friends and who were foes?

Christine Carlyle stared down at the havoc. "What the fuck are those things," she yelled. Her long hair continued whipping with the wind, looking a lot like the creature crawling out of televisions in *The Ring*. She could feel her West Chicago personality rising as she prepared to engage. Her mother always admonished her for her fits of anger. The armed forces taught her how to take the inner Chicago and turn it into something the enemy feared. A past of dealing with gangs and navigating the dangers of her neighborhood as a child made her fearless. Staring down at the walking nightmares below made her wish for those simpler times, and that was saying something.

Raegan had no idea what those creatures were, but she was confident they were not a welcoming committee bringing over a lasagna. "Mary, what the hell is that creature doing on the deck?" She screamed over the fury of the wind and the fighting helicopter.

"It looks like it is holding that shit storm back. Hang on, wait, I got civilians behind that thing. I can see them in the house. Are they carrying a kid? I think we have a kid in there!"

Raegan called out to the pilot, "That would be Bethany. Get us down there."

The pilot glanced back over his shoulder, "Do you see a place we can fucking land? There is a fucking sandstorm happening down there."

Martin Kyle pointed to a location on the other side of the debris wall towards the ocean, "Over there, you can put us down over there."

Raegan called out to the pilot, "Get us down as close as you can. We have to jump." She turned to the team, "Get prepped.

Get loaded. We engage on contact. Mary, can you place a marker on that creature and the civilians? I don't want any casualties."

"I'll see what I can do. This turbulence is a bitch." Mary engaged the marking device on her weapon. Looking through the scope, she placed the green target on the creature below and fired. The beast flinched slightly. She then took aim at the others, but she could only see one of the civilians clearly, so she tagged her as well. The woman also flinched and looked up to the chopper. "I could only mark two of them, best I could do."

"All right," Raegan pulled her team to focus on her for a moment. "Load those markers and watch your aim. We have unmarked civilians down there."

The pilot navigated the helicopter to the other side of the wall of debris, which was currently keeping the attacking demons out. Logs were beginning to fall from the sky as the wall collapsed. It was now or never. As soon as the chopper cleared the swirling debris, the pilot quickly dropped, getting within ten feet of the ground. The team was going out with limited visuals. This was a bad situation, but Raegan was getting her wish, only the circumstances were way outside expectations. She did not know the Sect meant creatures from another world when the Madame had said outside the usual.

"You gotta go now. I don't think I can hold it for long." The turbulence sent the helicopter reeling left and right as the pilot fought the stick for control. Christ, he was not trained for this. The mechanical beast was opposing his every move. Each time he tried to counter, it was as if the machine knew and railed against him.

The blades on the chopper flung sand grains in a haze, making it hard for Raegan to see. She located a line of dunes twenty feet out and decided to make a stand. "Get your asses to that dune line. They will give us cover to the front but watch your six. There is nothing between us and the water." She jumped, bending her knees, and rolling on the sand to avoid spraining or, worse, breaking an ankle. She double-timed to the dune line, the rest of the team followed, spreading to the left and right. She dove into place while bringing up her weapon. To the left of her was Martin, and to the right was Mary and Christine. Twenty demons clawed and fought against the wall of debris in front of them, working to gain access. The demons did not know they were in position. Raegan hoped it stayed that way.

From the copter, she had seen other demons flank to the left and right. She motioned Martin to begin moving to counter the flank to the left and signaled Christine to go right. Raegan lifted herself from the sand and moved closer to Mary, preparing for a frontal assault. She watched as her two team members disappeared around the debris field, then turned to Mary and gave the signal.

Then all hell broke loose.

CHAPTER 17

Alysia turned to Roland and yelled over the cacophony of noise. "Get them down to the safe room, lock yourselves in, and do not leave until you hear an all-clear."

"And what if there is not an all-clear?" Roland pushed back.

"Then you will have bigger problems to worry about."

Martha shouted, "I'm not leaving you here."

"Then we will all die up here," Alysia yelled, "but I will be damned if I am allowing that. Get to the safe room. If I don't make it, you still need to recover the dagger. Grab the journals and follow Roland down the damn stairs." She then turned back to the front of the house and rushed forward to where Char stood.

The demon, on the other side, was using powerful magic. Char fought for control, desperately pushing against the other. It could hold the storm for only so long before the shield would collapse. Char tried to find Alysia, turning its head left and right then locating her behind it. She was obviously in shock, her mouth ready to catch flies as she stood statue-still watching the chaos unfold around her. Char spoke to her as it prepared itself for one final push, "Alysia, those demons out there, they are more afraid of you than you are of them. To them, you are Demonspeaker. To you, they are only demons."

"There are too many of them. I don't have any blessed weapons to protect myself. We are going to die before we even got started," Alysia said, the sound of self-doubt infiltrating her words.

Char grew hot at her self-depreciation. Maybe it was wrong. Perhaps they all were wrong. She was nothing but a one-trick pony, a dream slayer, nothing more. A weak, petulant human, too quick to give in, to give up hope.

Alysia saw the anger igniting in Char's eyes, its rage boiling under the toil of the power it contained in front of it. The blue in its eyes intensifying, radiating outwards, she could feel the demon's loathing of her. For a moment, she was sure it would cast down the shield and allow the horde to destroy her and those she loved. Locking eyes with the demon, she asked, "what do I do?"

"The sword above the fireplace, I saw it hanging there and touched it. It burned me so it must be blessed. Go get the weapon and cut those creatures down, or they will cut you down, and you, along with all your friends, will become a plaything for Crimson."

THE WORDS MOTIVATED her as she turned and ran to the fireplace. Grabbing the weapon, she yanked it from its mounting. The blade rattled as it unsheathed.

Turning towards Char, Alysia saw him pulse, intensely

bright then fade. The demon used the last of the shield rite to drop a protective spell over what it hoped were allies in the dunes it saw fall from the flying thing. In a sharp outward thrust motion of its hands, Char gave a final shove of the shield. Alysia watched as a massive driftwood log slammed into a demon, throwing it back into the dunes, flattening it. The sand polished another, shredding its form like a floor sander. Two more were buried under logs and rocks, while a fourth was whipped into the air and impaled by what looked to be a car bumper. In the back of her mind, she could not fathom where a car fender could have come from.

IN THE DUNES, Raegan and Mary were ready to move forward and engage when an explosion of heat raced across the dunes and forced them down. Debris began to drop all around them, chunks of wood and rock. New dunes were created as sand fell from the sky. Both should have been crushed, but only sand and light debris fell onto them. Behind them they could hear the maddening whirring of rotors trying to accelerate. Raegan could see the pilot fighting the stick as a large piece of drift-wood shot from the storm directly towards the machine. She grabbed Mary and threw them both over the dunes as the heli-copter exploded. A blade whipped so close to Raegan she felt it tear into her protective clothing. She watched as three more creatures were demolished by the fire and debris. How the hell were any of her team still living while the world crumbled around them? She had little time to ponder that question as the surviving creatures saw their opening and raced towards the terrace where a woman stood alone with a sword. "Protect the asset," she screamed over the increasing warfare. Raegan and Mary began firing into the sprinting creatures.

ALYSIA FLINCHED as the heat from the explosion washed over her. There was no time to react as the first demon jumped onto the terrace and ran directly towards her. She took a fighter's stance, the sword over her left shoulder, waiting for it to get close enough, and then swung. The demon grabbed the blade in its taloned hands and laughed, "Bitch, that's all you got. I'm disappointed."

Alysia panicked, working to pull the sword from the demon's hand when its head exploded in a burst of blackened blood and pus. Alysia was covered in demon filth for the second time in hours but had no time to react as another demon raced in from the left. This time she thrust the sword forward with renewed purpose, catching it in the upper chest. The demon screeched as the blade slid farther into its deformed body and exited the other side. Alysia took all her fear and anger and projected it at the demon. As she withdrew the sword, the monster exploded into millions of pieces, further covering her in the thick viscous innards of the demon. In her chaotic mind, the thought of Innards of Demon on a menu somewhere came sharp and bright before disappearing as other demons gained the terrace.

To her right, two more demons approached, a little slower after witnessing what occurred. Her confidence regained, Alysia ran towards them. As she began to swing, a bullet flew around her and evaporated one of the demons. She slashed down, and the second popped like a firecracker, its insides now outside. Turning to look towards the dunes, she saw two people rushing forward with weapons. Surprisingly one of them fired directly at her. Alysia could not get out of the way. She froze in place. The bullet veered away from her then slammed into a demon approaching from behind.

Glancing left and right, she watched two other soldiers fighting demons, but another demon approached, so her focus returned to her own survival. Her sword slashed through demon flesh while bullets flew around her. A creature sat on top of a weakened Char, ripping at Char's body with talons sharpened to fine points. Char tried to fight back but was powerless. Alysia ran to protect it, but a bullet shattered the attacking demon's back. The hole it created the size of a watermelon. The demon fell forward onto Char.

Martin Kyle turned back to his own problems after dispensing with the creature attacking the other. He could not believe he was protecting whatever that thing was. As he turned, another creature dove at him from the roof. The impact caused him to lose grip of his weapon, forcing him to reach for his knife as the creature's weight toppled him over into the sand. He fell onto his stomach, the creature grabbed his head, pushing it into the soft sand, cutting off his air. He could feel the creature's heat on his bald head. He should have taken Raegan up on protective headgear. Martin struggled to dislodge the beast, the damn thing was heavy. He panicked as he sucked in a mouthful of sand, his throat tearing on the coarse grains. With the hand still holding the knife, he twisted his arm and thrust behind him. The creature's grip on Martin's head lessened, and he rolled, throwing the demon from his body. The knife was still in his hand, so he threw it and watched as it struck the creature in the eye. It imploded, taking his knife with it. "God damn it, I loved that knife," he mumbled.

CHRISTINE FOUGHT for her life on the other side, and even with her hand-to-hand training, the two creatures were testing her resolve. They had come in so fast she could not get her weapon up before they were on her. She would have been ripped to shreds if not for her protective clothing as it deflected their claws. The demons realized this and took swipes at her unprotected face instead. As a creature came from the right, she faked a move to attack but then sidestepped, pushing the creature over her leg and to the ground before turning to face the other. The demon was surprised, and even more so when her knife entered its blackened head. It exploded, covering both her and the other demon in visceral, vile-smelling fluids. She used the distraction to raise her weapon and pop the other one out of existence. She moved to meet up with Mary and Raegan on the terrace, forming a circle to protect each other's backs as the demons raced in from all sides. They were working to reach Alysia when they saw her disengage from the battle and run farther into the mansion.

ALYSIA HEARD screams erupt from behind her, and she vaulted toward the sounds. Running with speed she did not know she possessed, she swept down the stairs towards the basement level. Reaching the base of the stairs, she found Martha and Roland holding back a demon as Matthew struggled to get Bethany into the safe room. The demon grabbed Martha by her skull and lifted her a foot from the floor. Martha screamed as the creature's talons dug into her scalp. The smell of Martha's smoldering hair reached Alysia. Her struggles only made her scream louder as the demon fought to hold onto her. Roland rushed the demon from the side, but the demon brushed him away like a mosquito. He flew five feet in the air and slid the rest of the way to slam against the far wall. The demon turned to stare at Alysia. Both she and the demon's gaze turned towards the sound of another coming down the stairs.

Raegan slowly approached, her weapon trained on the demon holding the woman. The woman must have been in considerable pain, the way she thrashed about. Raegan could see smoke starting to plume from her hair. Mary was the only one with the ability to mark a no-kill target. Unfortunately, Mary had moved out with Christine to assist Martin. Shit, time to improvise. "Let her go. I will not ask you again," Raegan yelled at the creature as she trained her weapon on the its skull.

"Let her go, let her go? You are going to kill me whether I let her go or not. Why don't I just drag her back to Jarapenth with me," the demon screeched with what could only be joy or a at least a demon's idea of joy.

Raegan stepped down two more stairs, keeping the weapon locked on its head, but the demon was oddly smart enough to use Martha as a shield, moving her to match Raegan's position.

"Alysia, I need you to step back. I got this fucker," Raegan said as she tried to move into a better position.

Alysia started to step backward, but the creature pushed a talon against Martha's neck. A little stream of blood began to slide down. "Don't move, Alysia. You stay right where you are, or I will cut this bitch's throat. I told you, I am not going back without a playmate."

As the demon spoke, Raegan saw a green glow appear on Martha's neck. The woman flinched as if bitten. Raegan glanced to her left and caught a swirl of color, a tattooed arm. It was Mary lying flat on the ground, her weapon pointing through the glass. With Martha marked, Raegan gave the demon a mischievous smile.

"What's so fucking funny?" The demon was confused as to when the tables turned.

"This," Raegan pulled the trigger on her weapon, the bullet flew straight but in mid-flight changed direction, going around Martha and struck the demon in the left side of its head. The demons head exploded like a cantaloupe dropped from a skyscraper. The rest of its body falling flat to the floor with a resounding thud. Everyone within five feet was covered in more demon gore.

Martha released collapsed on the floor next to the now destroyed demon. Roland scuttled to her side, checking for a pulse.

"Is she okay, Roland?" Alysia called out.

"I'm not sure. She has a strong pulse, but these lacerations in her scalp are deep. Thankfully, she has a lot of hair, so her head does not appear badly burned."

Alysia saw blood trickling down Roland's forehead, "are you okay?" She pointed to her own forehead.

He reached up, touching his scalp. He felt the cut, but it was shallow, "yeah, it appears to be only a scrape."

Alysia could hear the last pops of gunfire from outside as the Sovereign Guard finished off the demons.

Moments later, Christine, Mary, and Martin came down the stairs, all covered in demon gore but alive. "All clear topside," Martin remarked. "Two creatures made a break for the ocean, but Mary took them out. That creature upstairs is starting to come around. Not sure if we need to have eyes on it."

Raegan looked around the room. "Anyone care to tell us what the fuck just happened, and why I am covered in this disgusting shit and my clothing has burn marks?"

Alysia walked over to Raegan and extended her trembling hand, taking Raegan's in a reciprocated handshake. Alysia was glad to see Raegan's hand suffered a slight tremor as well. "Demons. Don't ask because we do not know how they can be here, but they are. This is the second attack in twenty-four hours. Your arrival saved our asses. We all would have been dead, and those things would have the journals. I take it I have Madame to thank?"

"You do indeed. I am Raegan Marie, that is Martin Kyle and Mary Mueller. The badass who just double-timed up the stairs is Christine Carlyle. The Sect of Light call us the Sovereign Guard, and we are at your service. Before we go further, do you have somewhere we can wash this shit off? It burns a little bit."

CHAPTER 18

Alysia worked with Roland to get everyone set up with robes or garments so they could get out of their clothes and clean up. Martin hosed off the Sovereign Guards' clothing and threw them into the wash for a quick refresh. The clothing would never be spotless, and Alysia would be forced to throw out her washer due to the smell, but fifty percent was better under the circumstances than nothing.

Roland turned his focus to patching injuries. His past included medic training, and in a pinch, he could even perform basic surgeries, something he kept from Alysia, hoping she would never need it.

Roland started with Martha, her beautiful hair now singed or wholly gone in places. He cleaned the wounds and then spread numbing cream on her scalp. After waiting a few moments for the cream to work, he began stitching the lacerations. If they were any deeper, she would have required a trip to the hospital. Roland was impressed with Martha. She only flinched twenty-seven times.

Martin had a reasonably good size cut on his right forearm.

Roland began sewing him up after Martin refused numbing cream. Martin's coping mechanism was to complain. He complained about his knife. He complained about his favorite tattoo and how it was dissected by a large tear from a demon's talon. On top of all that, he had a demon's handprint burned onto his scalp. For someone of such incredible bulk, Roland thought Martin sure did bitch a lot.

The rest of what Roland was now calling the team suffered minor scrapes, bruises and some humiliation at the butt-kicking they received. These could be momentarily solved with band-aids, aspirin, and a prescription of reality.

WHILE ROLAND PATCHED up the crew inside, Alysia and Raegan assessed the damage outside. Raegan was shocked by the destruction. She had seen this devastation in foreign incursions, but only after a bomb detonated. The team was fortunate to be alive and that the home was far enough away from others on the coast that law enforcement did not become involved. Although, Raegan was surprised that a SWAT team was not kicking in the doors.

The Sect of Light was updated and sent in a cleanup crew to remove the pilots' remains and the aircraft itself, or what was left of both. They also began replacing the front windows that were blown out and wash away as much of the visceral mess the demons left behind. Raegan was impressed with the Sect's mobility. They were no ordinary organization, when the shit hit the fan, these people reacted and swiftly. It was the primary reason she agreed to command the Guard when they recruited her.

Raegan, seeing this mission in a whole new light, decided to focus on Alysia. Madame was clear. Alysia was to be protected at all costs. Even if it meant the lives of the entire Sovereign Guard. Madame had informed her that Alysia was to be the chief commander of this mission with Raegan acting as her second. Raegan pointed out to Madame this arrangement would be detrimental to their success as Alysia had no experience running an operation. Hell, she was not even military trained. To be fair, her dossier was an incredible read, and her accomplishments were beyond impressive, but Raegan thought she was ill equipped to deal with the current situation. Furthermore, Alysia's missions were based within the mind, not the real world. Madame listened attentively, but once more, demanded Raegan follow Alysia's lead. Raegan was not one to shirk an order, but she was far from pleased with her boss's direction.

If she was going to place her own life and the lives of her team in this woman's hands, she needed to understand her better.

"Do you need to get seen by a medic? Your scar appears worse for wear," Raegan asked, knowing only the basics of the injury.

"This?" Alysia pointed to her face. "It gets pretty red when my temper elevates or after having my ass handed to me."

"Exactly what happened here, Alysia? What were we just fighting?"

Alysia's voice was soft when she responded, she had never felt so tired, she was barely able to concentrate. "As I said earlier, these are, well, were demons. They are far more powerful here than in the mental world I usually face them," Alysia lightly tapped her head to emphasis the point. "Perhaps they are stronger here on our plane as it is their physical being, not just a mental exercise. This is all new territory for me. Did Madame tell you none of this?"

Raegan laughed, "We work on a need-to-know basis. Guess

we did not need to know, or hell, maybe Madame was unaware of what was coming. To be fair to her, we were rushed to assemble on her orders. You and your friends' dossiers were literally thrown at us as we entered the helicopter, they almost blew right off the building. The paperwork provided some background on your past and the work you do, the rest we were in the dark about. From the sound of it, you are as lost as we are for the moment. I am curious about your work though and this mechanism called transport. What is it exactly?"

Raegan listened, fascinated, as Alysia explained the process.

She was impressed, it sounded unbelievable, but Alysia's dossier was descriptive in her talents and the number of children she had healed. Most would have called bullshit but having worked for the Sect of Light the better part of a year, Raegan had learned the importance of allowing her mind to expand past certain realities. "Sounds like the movie *Inception*."

"Well, kind of, I guess. Never thought of it that way. It's more an image of myself spliced to another's memory during a sleeper's vulnerable time, REM. It is when our minds are most open, willing to accept things outside of its reality.

Unfortunately, my ability to alter a child's path becomes more difficult as they grow older. The brain becomes less receptive, malleable, to interruption. If the child is young enough, I can access the mind. Once engaged, I perform the Rites of Removal. Sometimes violence toward the demon is necessary for extraction. If an infection is caught too late, the demon is impossible to extract, and most times, the person must be eliminated."

Raegan's head shifted to the left, startled. "Eliminated?"

"Yes, and it happens more often than I wish to know. I can't save all the children, a burden that weighs heavy with me. Left unchecked, infected become the worst our society offers, serial killers, murderers, you know, the dredges of humanity."

"Wait, Bundy and Dahmer were demon-possessed?" Raegan was fascinated and she could hear her voice rise an octave, anticipating an answer. If what Alysia said was true, it changed the entire science of psychology. But her response nipped her thoughts in the bud.

"No, demons are not the reason for all violent behavior. We need to take credit or blame for the majority of what happens. Many people claim possession. But most are people with mental health challenges who need help. Infection is a different state. A demon cannot control a host or force it to do anything. It alters behaviors over time by using temptation, manipulation, and emotion, three powerful forces in the young."

"I would argue those three forces are strong in adults as well," Raegan retorted, "tell me about this demon called Char? If the species is born of darkness and hate, what is this one doing helping us?" Raegan asked as they turned around and headed back towards the Rose Mansion. Raegan had not realized how far they had traveled over the dunes as she was lost in the conversation.

"I have no idea. It is beyond anything I have witnessed. For now, it appears to be a friend, not a foe. The thing has saved me twice. I certainly don't understand its motives," Alysia paused and turned to Raegan as they walked. "Raegan, was it my imagination, or did I see bullets curving around me on the terrace and downstairs?"

Raegan lifted her weapon, "These babies are the best technology money can buy. We can tag civies and no-kills with an RFID chip. The ammunition is programmed to avoid the tagged individuals and change midflight, nanotechnology. It's just not for wrinkle-free clothing anymore." A smile lightening up her face as she spoke. Her brown eyes sparkled with a passion for her job.

"I would think our military forces would have access to those."

"Well, at two million per weapon and an ungodly amount per bullet the operational use is outside the reach of the taxpayer funded military. While military R&D are the ones who spent the money to design and test them, the Sect of Light is the only ones who can afford to use them. R&D designed our clothing as well, microfibers are woven with, get this, Golden Orb Weaver spider web filaments. They can withstand a direct knife attack and an armor-piercing round if it is from twenty-five feet out. By the way, don't tell Mary she is wearing a spider's home. We do not want her stripping naked and running through the dunes, it is not a pleasant sight. She is terrified of the eight-legged bastards. What is next? How do we need to prepare?"

"Madame informed you of my parents' journals?" Raegan gave a quick nod of her head, her curls bouncing from the movement. "My team reviewed the journals this morning before the attack, and we found information on a few of the artifacts, but we could not locate any mention of the Kalama Dagger. Time is running short, so I want to pull everyone back together after they clean up and get something to eat."

"Sounds like a plan. I will assemble my team and meet you in the conference room." Raegan and Alysia double-timed back to the house to prepare.

ALYSIA CLOSED the door to the conference room to soften the noise of cleanup crew that had arrived. Work was underway to restore some order. The team found themselves around the same conference room table as in the morning, a little worse for wear and with more participants. Raegan and Mary joined them, but the other SG's walked the perimeter. They would not be surprised a second time.

Alysia grabbed a chair and flipped it around to rest her arms on the back of the seat. "Team, I am giving you the opportunity to back out," She held up a hand in front of her as she could see objections mounting and the look of dedication in her friend's eyes, "Before you say anything, you need to understand this is not going to get any easier. Your lives are at risk, and although we have acquired formidable assistance with the Sovereign Guard, this is still no walk in the park. We just faced a small force of demons, and I can guarantee you, it only gets worse from here. When I brought you together, it was about saving children's sanity, and the risks to each of you were minimal. Believe me when I say this, if you decide to tap out, you will be welcomed back as part of the team when this is over. I will never question your loyalty around what we do. But I will be damned if I am risking your lives without your input."

Martha spoke first, her voice trembling from the attack of the morning, her head hurting from the lacerations and stitches. "I will not abandon you, Alysia. You cannot do this alone. I am scared, scared shitless, but I am even more frightened by what happens if the other side gets the dagger. I am not sure what I am going to tell my husband, but luckily he is on a long haul, so I guess I tell him nothing."

Others nodded their agreements to Martha's sentiments. Alysia wondered if she would have stayed if she was in their shoes? Would she be strong enough to follow this through to the end? The constant body blows over the past hours made her think twice.

Mary Mueller was standing behind Father Tealander and asked the question even Alysia had been wondering. "Speaking of sides, where the hell are the good guys? Angels, gods, spirits, where is our backup? Are we really it?"

Char, distanced from the group, responded, "Maybe they do not know yet. Maybe they do not care. I am guessing the first as they would have to respond if they knew the Council of 120 was seeking the dagger."

"For now, we are the good guys," Alysia sat up straighter in her chair to portray a level of confidence she did not feel.

"Well, I am all in as long as there are no damn spiders. Let me tell you, I can deal with these demons, but if they get eight legs, eight eyes, and attitude, you can count me out," Mary said.

Raegan winked at Alysia and laughed. She did not mean to do so, she knew Mary's feelings on the eight-legged beasts, but it was as if all her tension from the morning released in one sudden burst from her chest. Her laughter sent several around the table into a fit of laughter as well, a welcomed human release after all the destruction and stress. Alysia felt a little of her own tension leave her body as she joined in. Mary's facial response to the laughter caused a further round of fits, her eyes open wide, her arms folding across her chest.

"You all might be laughing, but seriously, my ass is out of here. I have to call the neighbor if I find a spider in my house."

Alysia wiped her eyes, enjoying the feeling of normalcy for a moment. Still, she needed to take control of the conversation. "Raegan and Mary, you were not part of our first scan of the journals. I think we need to scour these again, see if we can discover anything new, something we missed. It would be good to have fresh eyes if the two of you can spare the time."

"Alysia, the Sovereign Guard, is here to support you and your team, so you direct what we need to do, and we will do it," Raegan responded. It was not easy to say, giving over her power to someone she thought less qualified, she felt her jaw clenching and her muscles tighten. But she was starting to see a glimmer of leadership potential in Alysia, a small slice of herself in the way she stood her ground and pulled everyone back to what was urgent.

Char plodded towards the group, a little worse for wear after the attack on the terrace. It had weeping wounds on its body, but they were self-healing at a remarkable rate. Char did not even feel them. During the intense battle, Char had remembered something, something significant that might provide an answer. The demon did not want to forget so was hyper focused on the thought and did not see Raegan's hand move to her weapon, that is, until its peripheral vision caught the movement. Char put its hands out in a show of submission. "I wonder if your parents would have been aware of a substance called Demon's Ink. Or, did anyone see it referenced in the journals?"

The team shook their heads around the table, except for Roland. His face scrunched up, eyes squinting, deep furrows appeared on his brow. "Damn it," he muttered. He picked up a journal and flipped through it, then another, and a third before saying, "aha," slamming the open book down on the table. "I knew it. I knew I read something similar." In front of the group was a black and white photograph of petroglyphs. Along the bottom of the picture, scribbled in a handwriting Alysia recognized as her mother's, *the secret is inked in the blood of demons, once seen, forgotten, written, and remembered.*

"Holy shit!" Alysia exclaimed, "how did you remember that."

"Don't know. I found the statement to be out of place, so it stuck. Char, what does it mean?" Roland asked as he continued to stare at the image in the journal.

The demon stepped closer. Raegan reacted by pulling her weapon. She at least kept it down, not pointing it at Char.

"Let's keep some boundaries," Raegan said while raising a hand to keep the demon from drawing closer.

Frustrated, Char felt its veins beginning to glow as it tried to control its feelings. Signs of aggression and anger were not going to draw this team closer to it, but it was a demon, and those were its core emotions. "As I was laying on the terrace trying to recover from saving your hides from a demon horde, I was thinking about our discoveries this morning. The question that swirled around in this empty head," it tapped its skull, and it gave a hollow thunk, "was, why would there be information about one set of artifacts but not the other? This, in turn, brought back a very unpleasant memory of being flayed in Jarapenth for forgetting to fall to my knees when one of the 120 approached. As they were slowly slicing my flesh from my legs, one of the demons was chatting about how excited it was that it was chosen to learn how to be a scribe for the Council. It required the use of Demon's Ink, a privilege within the demon world as few of us are granted the ability to read or write, to keep us subservient."

The members around the table squirmed as Char nonchalantly described its torture. Even Raegan winced. At the same time, their interest was piqued as maybe this was the answer they were missing.

Roland stood up from his chair, his six-foot form growing taller as he stretched his arms and lifted himself on his toes. An audible crack rang out from his spine as he bent backward to relieve tension. "How would Alysia's parents have known about Demon's Ink? If they knew about it, how would they know to use it? I never once heard them comment on it."

Char shook its head, "Only a demon can teach another the art of Demon's Ink. It is highly guarded, as I mentioned. Demons can only read what is written in the Ink. It would make sense that your parents separated the artifacts into two texts, neither side having access to the other."

Alysia traced the circle on the parchment with her finger as she listened to the discussion, her frustration growing with each rotation. Her desire to find the object increasing every time her finger came full circle to the image of the dagger. Her eyes drifted to her watch, afraid of what she would see. They needed to make a move. She slapped her hands on the table, causing a few to jump involuntarily.

"Okay, let's assume for a moment my parents did find a way to use this Demon's Ink. How would we know? How does one read it?"

Eyes turned to Char, who in return simply shrugged its shoulders. "I told you all I know." Disappointment swept through the room, but the truth was, this was all it could remember.

Conversations erupted as team members spoke over the top of others. Frustrations were unleashed after a hellish morning and still no answers. Mary Muller was the only one who stood quietly looking over the photograph of the petroglyph. She reached over and pulled the parchment closer to her, ignoring Alysia's what the hell gaze as she stripped her of the ability to keep tracing the circle with her fingers.

Alysia watched Mary, turning the parchment left, right, and full circle. Mary thumped the table with her fist, which caused the entire room to grow suddenly quiet and turn their attention to her.

Mary realized she was now the center of attention. "Let's say Alysia's parents accessed this Ink, and let's also say they figured out how to use it. Then, if what Char said earlier was correct and your parents used the Ink to hide information from one side or the other, what if the answer was right in front of us on this parchment?"

Mary waited to see if anyone would see what she saw. After a moment, Mary could not take the silence. "What is in the middle of the circle?"

"The sun and the moon," Father Tealander said.

"Exactly," Mary answered excitedly. "From what I have heard so far, you currently have only been able to discover information about the artifacts of Darkness." Mary waited, but everyone still appeared confused.

"The three artifacts of darkness are under the moon. The three of light are over the sun. What if, and follow me here, what if you can only see the information about the artifacts based on time of day."

"That makes no sense," Raegan spoke up. "If that were the case, we would see information about the Kalama Dagger as it is over the sun, so we would see the object in sunlight."

"Not if your goal were to hide information, to create a distraction. What if it was the reverse? What if the artifacts of light required moonlight and the artifacts of darkness required the sun? Demon's Ink needs moonlight." Mary exclaimed as she flipped the parchment across the table to Alysia.

Was it possible? One read in sunlight, the other in moonlight?

Alysia clapped her hands, excited to have forward movement, even if they were not sure it was forward or backward. "Mary, this is a brilliant observation! Let's see, if Demon's Ink is only readable by moonlight we need to check if we the moon will be visible on the coast this evening. Moclips is not known for clear evenings, the fog starts to roll in around six. Martha, can you please check current moon cycles and weather? Also, would you be able to locate any information regarding this petroglyph. My mother would not have written underneath the picture without it having meaning or a purpose."

Mary nodded her head in agreement.

She turned to Raegan and Mary, "depending on what we discover, I am certain we will need a way to get where these clues lead. Can we get transportation for the team? Weapons might not be a bad idea either. I imagine we are going to confront more demons, and who knows what other horrors will await us."

"That should not be an issue. Mary and I will reach out to the Sect of Light and get the ball rolling," Raegan said as she left the table with Mary.

Alysia placed a hand on Martha's arm as she reached for the journal with the petroglyph image. "Martha, I think it would be best if we relocate Bethany to a new location until we find what we are seeking. No one on this team should know where you are going. Do not reach out to anyone until the end of the day Friday. If you have not heard back from us, assume we are not coming back and do what you can. I will send Roland with you."

"Damn it, Alysia, I can help here. You need me. I am the best research person you have," Martha said, protesting the decision made without asking.

"Yes, you are, and we are going to need those smarts protected. Besides, you and Roland are the best trained to care for Bethany. I will speak with Raegan and see if Christine can travel with you."

Martha hastily grabbed the journal and turned away, pissed at being placed on the bench in the seventh inning. Alysia understood her frustrations. It was not a personal decision. She was thinking logistically of transporting everyone but also protecting the team. A smaller unit would be easier to move and easier to circle the wagons around. She found herself alone in the room as others raced to prepare for wherever this would lead them.

Alysia basked in the silence for a few moments, gathering

her thoughts before exiting the room. The windows were almost replaced, and much of the demon remains cleared. She realized she might never return here, depending on what happened. Although she despised its size and the money spent to complete it, it was also the last remnant of her parents. She feared their legacy would be lost should it pass to another owner. She knew it was a foolish thought to attribute a building, something constructed of materials with no feelings, to those in the past. Her parents were more than this mansion, their legacy greater than wood, paint and concrete, but she felt they still resided here, their ghosts a part of the winter storms and the summer sky. At least she hoped they were here, their energy a part of her surroundings. She dared not think of the two of them in Jarapenth.

She took the stairs two at a time to reach her bedroom to pull together a travel bag. Alysia did not see the person watching her as she walked away, nor did she see the dark shadow in the corner, listening to the person's whispers.

But Char saw it all.

CHAPTER 19

Ispep cringed within Aloc Acoc's head. Crimson approached with Magenta and Yoson on either side, its right- and left-hand demons. Crimson drew its blade and Aloc Acoc fell to its knees and began to weep.

"I'm sorry, I told you they would be prepared. I did what you told me to do," Ispep said through Aloc Acoc's mouth.

Ispep looked up and saw the most wicked of smiles sweep across Crimson's face. "You did well Ispep, you scared them into action. We are proud of you. As your reward, we have created a special place for you in Jarapenth, just a little something to show our gratitude and thanks."

Ispep's cries could be heard throughout Jarapenth as it was dragged by Magenta and Yoson deep into the wasteland.

CHAPTER 20

The call with Madame did not go well. As requested, Matthew kept her informed of developments. On this call, he informed her the water was much too hot for Alysia and her team. They should be viewed as consultants, not as actual doers.

Madame responded by saying Alysia was doing exactly as she hoped. The Sovereign Guard reached the team in time. No one was dead or seriously injured and there would be no pull-back. She was unequivocal. The priority of the dagger was all that mattered, even if it came at the loss of life.

In fifty-five plus years of service to the Sect of Light, he knew they wandered into a gray territory. But this was the first time he saw them go entirely into the dark. They were not only willing to sacrifice him but Alysia's team and their own Sovereign Guard.

Father Tealander did not wish for Alysia to fall into the Sect of Light as he had done. For Tealander, it was a path he did not choose, but one chosen for him. His birth parents did not know how to deal with his gifts, or as they said, "Gifts" in air quotes. Tealander found himself in a boarding school at the age of ten. He had discovered in November, during Thanksgiving break, it was not a school but an orphanage. His parents were not returning. He spent three years going in and out of foster homes. No one understood him and most were terrified of his talents. No one was willing to take the time to understand him until a gentleman named Dennis Geathers arrived. Dennis was not only ready to listen to Matthew but to assist him in understanding his gifts.

Dennis's home was open to Matthew, a beautiful but lonely place on Whidbey Island, overlooking the water. Dennis was not married and owned no pets. The only other humans in the house were the staff who cared for Matthews's needs and studies. Dennis spent a significant amount of time with Matthew, working with him to hone his skills. The two of them would walk the streets of Seattle and Portland, and Matthew would share with Dennis his visions. Dennis would document what Matthew reported in small wire bound notebooks he kept readily available in his back jeans pocket.

Matthews's visions consisted of colors. He could read a person by the colors that surrounded them. Some called them auras, but they were more than an aura. They were a person's fate. Matthew Tealander knew if a person would be a thriving member of society, or someone destined to harm others. His accuracy was uncanny. Dennis, along with taking copious notes, would photograph the subjects Matthew identified. Unbeknownst to Matthew, a private group would investigate the cases he shared with David. By the age of sixteen Matthew unknowingly was responsible for incarcerating ten murderers, three serial rapists, and two serial killers. Each of their colors had shown a brilliant orange-red, flames enshrouding them. It was not until three days before his nineteenth birthday that Matthew discovered how Dennis was using him.

Matthew was preparing his morning breakfast of Mini Wheats. As he poured milk over the cereal, his eyes caught the missing persons' picture on the side of the cardboard container, back when milk came in cardboard instead of plastic. He recognized the face. Six months prior, this child's aura glowed a hotter red than any he had seen in the past.

The red encircling this child was considerably vibrant and intense and for the first time, Matthew had a vision, it was a physically assault. He recalled reeling backward, a feeling of being punched in the chest. The child held a blood covered knife over a woman's body that was strapped to an old plastic folding table. Thick plastic draped the table, the floor, and the walls. The child thrust the knife down into the woman's belly. The child giggled as the woman screamed, blood exploding from each downstroke of the knife like a geyser. Then, the child looked directly at Matthew and smiled, a smile filled with malice. The child knew Matthew could see him and was relishing in his horror. Matthew shared his vision with Dennis. His ward saw his stress and the sessions ended for the day.

Matthew confronted Geathers about the milk carton. True to Dennis' nature, he did not lie to Matthew. He told him the truth. Matthew was playing a vital role in the future of humanity, one soul at a time. Dennis brought him to meet Madame, who never seemed to age, her appearance today much as it was when he met her. She sat with him for hours, sharing his purpose and the importance of his gift. They tried to make him understand his talent was being used for good, but all he could see was the face of that child on a milk carton. Matthew considered the fear the child's parents must feel, the child's friends' anguish, grandparents, aunts and uncles, all suffering loss. He asked Madame where the child was. She told him the child was in a better place and was no longer a threat to those around them.

Matthew found himself turning to the Bible for answers. Could the child have been saved? Were those he identified doomed to follow through with their colors? Were we destined to be what we were, or could we change? Matthew followed his quest for answers with furor, attending seminary and becoming a man of the cloth. During his training, he became close with the Rose family, a couple discovering a world underneath as he discovered years prior. The Sect of Light encouraged them to work together, to use each other's skills to continue learning. When Alysia was born, Matthew was made godfather along with Roland. His heart swelled with his love for the angel brought to them. He interacted with Alysia as often as he was able, learning a new way to value life through this little girl's eyes.

When the Rose's deadly accident occurred, he was shocked to discover he and Roland were made Alysia Roses' guardians. He did not understand why at the time, but on her fifteenth birthday, he discovered the reason. As he and Roland prepared the home for her birthday bash, a delivery arrived, a single letter addressed to him. Within the letter, the Rose's informed Father Tealander of their daughters' abilities to help those in need. When the time was appropriate, he was to assist her in embracing her gift.

Father Tealander spoke to Madame, sharing the letter. He would never forget the look on her face, it showed apprehension, and a deep underlying fear. Madame was ruthless and cunning. Every move she made was purposeful, leading to a future others could not see. To question her motives was to be cast out, removed from the Sect. And when you were removed from the Sect, you did not enter witness protection.

Madame's look was a new one Tealander had never witnessed before, she was worried. He had shared something she had not foreseen. On that day, Tealander made the biggest mistake of his life. He handed his ward over to the Sect. From that point forward, she became another pawn in the great game. The Sect of Light *used* her as they *used* him.

The word *used* stuck with him, as they both were instruments of the Sect. Now he realized that they were only tools for a greater purpose, perhaps not replaceable but necessary. The best that either could hope for was upon their deaths, their names would at least appear on the Who We Lost plaque on the twenty-sixth floor of the Columbia Tower within a secret hallway. Until this week, he had been able to find the balance between right and wrong, good and evil. His faith waned as those around him found themselves in the crosshairs of malevolent forces.

CHAPTER 21

As the team finished preparing, they returned to the conference area to refresh coffee, grab a snack, or simply sit and breathe for a moment.

Martha returned with a massive grin on her face, her past anger wiped away for the moment. "Found it," she called out as she dropped the book containing the petroglyph on the table. "This particular petroglyph is called Atlatl Rock, and it happens to be located within Valley of Fire State Park about an hour's drive outside Las Vegas. Vegas Baby. Where else would you hide an ancient artifact being hunted by demons."

Alysia returned Martha's smile with one of her own. "Well, if the Kalama Dagger is anywhere near this location, it existed well before Las Vegas grew roots."

"Yeah, but is it possible an artifact is so powerful it could shape an area around it? If this is an artifact of Light, what better way to keep it hidden than to have a Den of Sin arise near it?" Mary Mueller mused. She glanced around the table for a confidant. "I'm just saying. We are in new territory here."

"Hard to argue that point," said Alysia. "Martha, were you

able to discover anything other than a location?"

"Not a damn thing. I mean, there is absolutely nothing about this rock or the drawings. The park is full of petroglyphs, many destroyed by asshats who find it humorous to carve their own initials into the stone. The Moapa people are working to preserve and protect as many as possible. This is the most popular drawing in the park," She laid some pictures she printed from Google on the table. "There is a set of stairs which leads up to a platform for viewing. Higher on the rock face are the petroglyphs," she pointed at the image.

"In the short time I had, I cross-referenced the pictures and shapes from multiple research sites. The petroglyphs appear to have no relevance other than one symbol which matched the same symbol found in the Cave of Lascaux in France. This same symbol has been found in other cavern systems around the world. The symbol is this one, a circle, well more a spiral, like a whirlpool." She directed everyone to the image, "but no significance has been attributed to it other than speculations. And those are all over the board and broadly open for inter-pretation."

Father Tealander looked over the images. "Obviously, those are rams, and these are either feet or hands. But what are these bisected circles? They are cut into six wedges --" Tealander barely got his statements out before Mary jumped in.

"What are those figures running from?" Martha pointed to the image. It showed two individuals with their arms raised in the air. The image relayed a feeling of fear, movement. They were running from something. That something had large antlers protruding from both sides of its head.

Alysia continued to look over the picture. The images had no rhyme or reason, squiggles, lines, what looked to be a ladder, people, and animals. Even so, there was a feeling of intercon-nection. "Martha, you mentioned the Moapa people. I would assume they have religious connectivity to the area and these drawings. Were you able to gather any information on them?"

Martha's grin increased in size, if that was even possibl. "You should know me by now, Alysia. The state park exists right on the edge of the Moapa Band of Paiute Indians, once called the Nuwuvi. They were expert basket weavers and adept at irrigation agriculture before contact with the Europeans. Their settlements could be located from Arizona to Colorado. In 1869, they were forced into a small reservation in Nevada with access to the Colorado River and what is now called Lake Mead. Unfortunately, in 1875 they were further forced into an even smaller reservation, one thousand acres. In 1980 they acquired an additional seventy-five thousand acres and have become quite a business-oriented tribe with multiple partnerships in solar farms. Many of these drawings share their ancestor stories."

Alysia looked over to Raegan and Mary, "Transportation?"

Raegan gave a thumbs up. "Transport will arrive at the Ocean Shores airstrip within the hour."

It was time. Vegas was where the team needed to go. Alysia drew the attention of those around the table. "Everyone, listen up. As soon as transportation arrives, we are heading to Las Vegas. It is the closest we have been to a location for the dagger so let's check this out and hope for the best." She turned to Martha. "How about the moon? Are we good?"

"Yes, luckily, we are in the later phases, this evening is a Waning Gibbous, three-quarter moon. We would need to leave Moclips anyway as a major storm is coming in from the Pacific and will hit the coast this evening."

Alysia was way out of her element now. She understood Raegan was following her direction, begrudgingly. Who was she to tell the Sovereign Guard what to do or how to perform? They were highly trained and skilled protectors. If it had been her out in the dunes, well, you could have kissed everyone goodbye. She was being thrown into this leadership role with no real-world or classroom training. Others depending on her to make the right decisions. She was terrified of making the wrong move. Yet, the team trusted and relied on her. They seemed to think she could lead them, so she would perform as best as possible.

"Martha, see if you can contact anyone from the Moapa tribe who can provide guidance on the petroglyph and Valley of Fire. Then, you, Roland, and Christine will locate a safe location to take Bethany until this ordeal is complete."

Raegan lifted her chin toward Char, "What about the creature?"

"That creature saved our bacon, so it is coming with us. We might need its assistance again." Alysia gave Char a wink, startling the demon to receive such human interaction. "Raegan, can you acquire some form of fireproof clothing Char could wear? We do not want the plane erupting in flames when we reach 35,000 feet."

"I'll see what I can do. No guarantees, but I would be surprised if the Sect doesn't have something they can get to us." Raegan excused herself and left the room, trying not to feel like a gopher as she acquiesced to Madame's wishes on relinquishing leadership.

Martin mumbled under his breath so only Mary could hear him, "Great, stuck in an aluminum sausage can with the smell of old sweaty socks and rotted meat. It should be a fun trip."

"It could be worse, you know. Raegan might make us listen to 80's pop music the entire way down," Mary said while patting Martin on the back.

"What is it with her and Culture Club? *Do you really want to hurt me?* Only if we have to listen to that song again," Martin said as the two left to prepare for whatever came next.

CHAPTER 22

"Demon's Ink? How did your team not think of this?" The shadowy figure asked Madame from its customary corner, its orange eyes narrowing.

Although she tried to place lights in different corners, the shadow dimmed all lights before making an entrance. Its edges were always blurry. For a moment, she ignored the question of the shadowy figure and thought about what was known. Alysia was moving quicker than expected, even with the assault on her home. The shadow within Madame's office forewarned her of the upcoming attack. It was the only reason the Sovereign Guard was able to respond as quickly as they did, and even then, they were almost too damn late. She only told Raegan an attack was imminent and had not shared much else. When Raegan discovered Madame knew more than she was willing to share with the leader of the Sovereign Guard, there would be a confrontation.

The genuine surprise to all involved was the acquisition of a demon, this thing they were calling Char. A force of evil suddenly working for the opposing team. She spun a tapestry using all the threads presented within her mind, but the final weave was still unknown. The pattern was unclear. In the past, before the discovery of Alysia's powers, she had been accurate in seeing the future. Alysia's presence had disrupted her abilities, and it created great concern for Madame.

Madame addressed the shadow figure as politely as possible. She had faced its wrath before, and it was an uncomfortable experience. "Maybe a darker force is at work to block our understanding of the journals? There is much we cannot explain of them. I do not understand your concern, we handed the journals to Alysia at your request to decipher." Her tone was confrontational after just telling herself to keep calm, but she was tired of the constant second-guessing and questions. This entity needed to let her do her damn job.

The shadow darkened, its voice intensifying, its eyes glowing like two bolts heated to a fiery orange. Its voice was like razors on Madame's skin, cutting deep. "I would keep your tone respectful. I am tolerant, but my tolerance is waning of late. You and your worthless team were making no progress, I decided to try a different path. We are at the precipice, and yet you treat this as a game. Well, it is no game. We are not kings, we are not even pawns, we are fodder no better than pigs awaiting slaughter. I fear you yet do not see the true disquiet that awaits. Hence, we better hope Alysia Rose can find some answers before our adversaries do." The shadow began to fade, then was gone entirely, leaving her alone once more.

"Go fuck yourself," Madame whispered.

From within her office, the response, a sledgehammer in her already bruised head. "We are all truly fucked if she fails."

CHAPTER 23

C rimson's informant updated the demon on Alysia's progress. The demon lord was well pleased to hear of their continued, rapid strides in discovering the dagger. Alysia was on the move to Las Vegas and a place called the Valley of Fire, a name the demon lord appreciated.

Crimson turned to his left and addressed the demon army standing in wait for his orders. The army consisted of six hundred and sixty-six of Jarapenth's best warriors, each loyal to the Council of 120. It would send them to take the dagger from Alysia Rose. Crimson would not wait for her to bring it.

"When the time is right to strike, you will strike, and you will strike without mercy. You will tear all who interfere into pieces, and you will bring me, Alysia. She will be left unharmed. The rest, I want nothing left of them." As the demon army cheered, Crimson turned back to the front, where its secondary response gathered. Six hundred and sixty-six thousand demons stood before him. If its strike force failed and if Alysia did not hand over the dagger, Crimson would make sure she would forever regret her decision.

Crimson stood ramrod straight in front of its worshippers. Those in attendance roared as their Lord prepared to speak to them personally. Crimson bathed in the admiration for a moment before beginning. "Brothers and Sisters of Night. Creatures of the darkest realms, you will bring pain unlike these humans have ever seen. You shall be the pin that pierces the eye, the razor across the skin, you will decimate hope and seed fear so deeply these pathetic creatures will be unable to recognize friend from foe. The end is coming, and the end tastes of fear."

The cries of its worshippers were deafening. Crimson absorbed them all growing stronger in their admiration.

CHAPTER 24

Char sat in the back of the plane alone. Its eyes followed the team member movements, ever watchful, absorbing information, cataloging, interpreting. Char still carried some humanity, but the longer its sentence within Jarapenth, the more it disappeared. Horrible things it had done in its past were a constant reminder of the suffering it deserved.

Infantmeal, who was now Char, at one point was known as Michael Little, investment broker. He was a husband and a father to three children, two boys and one girl. They lived a good life, but he was never satisfied. He wanted more, more for his family, more for himself. The five thousand square foot home was not enough. He needed a mega-mansion on the water, not just overlooking it. The Tesla was not regal enough. Anyone could get one. He wanted to be recognized when he walked into a hotel lobby. He wanted his name in lights, he wanted women to desire him, and for men to want to be him.

What was a soul worth? Michael soon learned. Surprisingly, there was no deal with the devil to be made. The devil already owned him. He learned quickly how to manipulate penny stocks to his benefit. It started with a few dollars skimmed here and there. Small lies about stocks shared through fake twitter accounts and stock boards. He soon realized that a man's worth was not accomplished with significant deeds, but small ones, building upon themselves, child's blocks stacked one on top of the other. By the time one realized what they had made, it was too late, the cast was set. A web of small lies built an empire. He inflicted maximum financial damage on families that could not afford the loses. He ensnared hundreds. Like a spider, he fed on their financial trust, then casually tossed their carcasses aside after bleeding them dry.

But the devil has its due, and Michael's came when he stole millions from a technically savvy entrepreneur. He was soon linked to hundreds of false social media accounts which he used to manipulate OTC and PINK markets. It had taken him two decades to build his financial image and less than a month to watch it shatter. His final price was his life, taken by one of the many he ripped off and ruined. He was witness to his own destruction in front of the City of Denver Courthouse. The shot echoed off the buildings, and as people scurried like mice, his blood ran freely onto the cold pavement. The woman approached and shot him three more times. As his life faded, his final damnation was watching her take her own life, a bullet through the roof of her mouth. Another life he stole. She was a mother, a wife, a lover, someone who trusted him. She had only wanted what was best for her family. He felt her fall upon his body as darkness swallowed him.

This was Char's hell.

Towards the front of the plane, Alysia faced Char, who was staring intently ahead. When their eyes met, she saw the demon was as deep into its own memories as she, a prisoner of the past. She tried to study the petroglyph, but her mind wandered on to other things. She decided to get the creature's thoughts as she saw something within the image she had not seen before.

Char sat straighter as Alysia approached. She was a mystery, an enemy it now was helping, and it could not reason why it decided to do so. Redemption perhaps? If they were successful, could it receive a second chance?

Alysia sat across from Char, placing the image in front of it. Char did not touch the picture as anything it contacted could be damaged, which was why it was wearing a suit made for fire protection. New technology for firefighters, very lightweight and breathable. Since Char could not control its body temperature, the clothing protected those around it from damage. Raegan acquired the item, and quick modifications were made to ensure it fit. Char was pleased to not be lighting things on fire. At the same time, it felt like being in a toaster oven, its own heat baking its already blackened flesh. Char's hands were currently not gloved so it only looked at the image.

"Tell me what you see," Alysia asked as she pointed to the photograph.

Char stared intently at the image. It focused only on the picture. What was it Alysia wanted it to see? It registered something and leaned closer to the image "The lines. The lines are connected, they are not random?"

"You see that too? What else?"

"Here," it almost touched the image, then quickly pulled its blackened hand back, "Although faint, there are lines here, here and here, connecting." Its eyes grew large, its blue becoming intense. "Are we seeing a faded image of passages?"

Alysia smiled. She saw the same thing once she focused deeper into the image, instead of superficially. They were staring at a three-dimensional drawing on a two-dimensional plane. The animals and hunters above ground, the lines were catacombs below the hunters. There was a lot here not explained, but you could not unsee it once you saw it.

"That is what I'm thinking," she responded, "but I can't find any trace that my parents believed these are passages, so, again, just speculation. I believe your idea regarding Demon's Ink is spot on, and here is why. See this, right there on the image. What does that look like to you?"

"That is a sword or a dagger," Char excitedly responded, "yes, it is. That must be what Crimson seeks."

"I think so as well. This drawing is pointing us toward the answers to our questions." Alysia paused, considering for a moment, then asked, "What was your name before becoming Infantmeal?"

Char shook its head. "I had a name before I became a servant of Jarapenth. I can remember it but am unable to speak it aloud."

"How long have you been damned?"

Char had not been asked this question before. Then again, it had not interacted with humans in the past other than through manipulation. "That is a complex question as time is different in Jarapenth. I left this plane fifteen years ago and found myself in what you call hell." Char looked out of the aircraft window and whispered, "A Biblical hell would have been nicer." It turned back to Alysia and its voice returned to a normal volume. "Anyway, the deeper one travels into Jarapenth, the longer time is stretched. In my hell, a minute equals roughly an hour of earth time. An earth year comprises 525,600 minutes or 1,440 minutes in a day. Therefore, one day on earth is equal to sixty days in Jarapenth. Hence, one earth year is equal to 21,600 days in Jarapenth."

"Holy shit!" exclaimed Alysia, "you have been in hell

for...." She was trying to do a rough calculation in her head when Char said, "Roughly 9,000 years, give or take a few years. We are reminded constantly, so we never forget we still have an eternity left."

Alysia held the demon's gaze, its piercing blue eyes drilled into her skull. How it must have suffered. She wanted to pity it, but she had witnessed firsthand the damage these creatures could inflict on the innocent, it was difficult to feel a genuine connection with the beast before her. Instead, she asked, "How did you know how to do those calculations?"

"Demons still have thought. We possess the skills we learned prior to our servitude. I was good at numbers, so I continue to be good with them. We lose our identity, the ability to speak our name and our ability to read and write, but what we were before we became this is still intact. It is what makes it all the worse. We watch as those we love grow up or remarry or take their own lives. We are never allowed to forget what we were, what we did or who we hurt. For some, it drives them even further into madness. They become creatures of nightmares, the Glebinbytes. The rest of us know it is only a matter of time before we, too, turn. It is inevitable."

"Once in Jarapenth, there is no way out? There is no redemption?" Alysia asked. Her thoughts swirling around all the times she contemplated taking her own life. She confronted demons regularly but never an intellectual conversation about what happens after death. She knew of Jarapenth, Alysia knew of its evil, but she always imagined there was a way to find redemption. In the long nights of the memory monster roaming the halls of her skull, she hoped for some saving moment, the ability to find forgiveness.

"I have never seen a single soul leave Jarapenth. To be fair, there are many of us down there. I am sitting here talking to you so, who knows how many others have found a way to escape."

"As your kind deteriorate, they become worse? More wicked than the evil I have faced?"

"Much worse, and Crimson wants them released to destroy all living creatures, they would become an unstoppable plaque. The Glebinbytes, Deep Demons, live at the heart of Jarapenth, they are feared most amongst our kind. A couple thousand years ago, one of the Deep Demons escaped its bonds and reached a higher level of Jarapenth. It drove every demon on that level insane. They became crazed, turning on each other, slashing, clawing, biting, and tearing. Before Ka could send the creature back to the deep, an entire plane of Jarapenth had been obliterated, it is now known as the Plain of Teeth. You know of this place Alysia. You use it often to threaten us, but you cannot fathom what it means to be sent there, even you would not be so cruel if you understood."

Alysia reached across and took Char's arm in her hand. The demon jumped in surprise, as if she meant to harm it. But instead, she gave it a gentle squeeze. "Then you and I must make sure Crimson does not get the dagger. Thank you for back at the house. I do not understand why you are here, or why you are helping us. I am not even sure if I trust you yet, but you saved me more than once, and for that, I am grateful." She stood up, turned, and returned to her seat.

Char sat quietly after Alysia left, thinking about the conversation it had just experienced and watched the humans. But it carefully observed the one it did not trust. The human turned towards it. Char gave them the nastiest of its smiles. They quickly turned away, but Char continued to watch, its eyes drilling holes into the back of the other's head.

Raegan Marie sat with the rest of the Sovereign Guard facing the back to watch the creature. Raegan and Char's eyes locked again as they had for most of the flight. The creature's crystal blue eyes penetrating hers, its gaze never wavering. She could swear it was smiling, a terrifying thing to see. Its rotting teeth were covered in a black substance she dared not think about. She admitted this thing terrified her. Its deformities were difficult to define somehow both human and alien. Its face, or what you could call a face, shimmered within the burnt outer crust. Its network of facial veins glowed red hot like molten steel. Had she known her war would be against creatures such as these, she wondered whether she would have agreed to lead the Sovereign Guard.

People underestimated Raegan because of her stature. She was born of Scottish and Irish heritage. She was five foot four, pale as a moonlit night with a canvas of freckles playing across her face, stars in the night sky. Her hair was a mass of curls, and no matter what she did to tame them, they always bounced back into the tight bird's nest which rested on her head. Her brown eyes glistened with awareness taking it all in, no matter where she went. Her attitude was upbeat and positive, but her anger was righteous, the sting potent. Scholastically she outperformed, but she did not work hard at school. It seemed to come naturally. Teachers tried to push her into more complex classes, but she was more interested in not being called out and just being a part of the normal flow of things. Her friends considered her the mediator as she always tried to find a win-win situation, and many times, she did. She was quick to care and to love, but when hurt, the healing time was lengthy. From an early age, she found it difficult to connect, to create relationships beyond friendships. She was interested in neither male nor female companionship in a romantic way. As her friends dated, she was just not curious. In the beginning, she thought she was the only one who felt this way. For a time, she worked to fit in, but she was never comfortable. Later she discovered many others felt the way she did, and it was okay. She embraced her asexuality, realizing it was not abnormal. Everyone did not need to find a soul mate, and there was more to a relationship than sex. Her friends could not understand, and Raegan did not feel she needed to explain. She was who she was.

After graduation, she met with a recruiter from the Navy. The Navy saw an intelligent, observant leader. She spent three years at the Monterey Language Institute, consuming her education. Overall, she became proficient in five different languages and sufficient in three others. Raegan's thirst for knowledge caused some confrontations with her instructors, but she was sharp, and her superiors recognized her gifts. Her instructors admitted she was an out-of-the-box thinker who developed brilliant solutions. She was quick to adapt, and upon graduation, she requested to be sent into action. Her superiors desired her to be placed elsewhere, preferably intelligence work. But they could not deny her natural tendency to lead and the fervor in which her teams were willing to follow. No task was too small, too large, or too complex. Her mates called her Doppelganger, as there appeared to be more than one of her.

On her twenty-seventh birthday, her superior approached her regarding an opportunity to lead an elite team for a private organization. Reluctant to leave the Navy, she at first said no. Two weeks later, her superior came a second time, sweetening the pot, and she admitted to being intrigued. She was informed that this group was highly interested in her leadership talents, language skills, and combat training. She was given twelve hours to decide.

The meeting with Madame was short on information. She was told that she would have full authority to choose the team if she were to take on this work. The budget was no issue. She would have at her hands the greatest in technological weapons and equipment not yet available to forces anywhere in the world. She was presented with an over-the-top salary package, a new posh residence in one of the towering condos located in downtown Seattle, personal assistants, and a sizeable open checkbook. Her only constraint, she was limited to three others, the team never allowed to exceed four members.

Madame was good to her word. Not once did she balk. The assembled team was further trained in hand-to-hand combat and weaponry by the most highly skilled in their fields. Looking at her team, she saw the determination on their faces and a deep river of disquiet running underneath. Not one expected what they saw today.

As the pilot announced their approach into McCarren Airport, Raegan once again pondered whether she had signed her team's death warrant in taking this mission. She was constrained by her duty, her desire to help others, but she also had a responsibility to her team. And if self-sacrifice was required, it better have meaning.

CHAPTER 25

The plane landed at McCarren's field five minutes after midnight. During the flight, Alysia received a message from a gentleman named Redstone, a representative of the Moapa. He could meet with them at nine the following morning. He just needed to know where to go. Raegan had acquired short-term accommodations from the Sect of Light in Vegas, a large home with ten bedrooms and a large gathering area. Alysia texted Redstone the address, but she did not receive a confirmation.

Waiting for the team on the tarmac were two SUVs. Alysia directed Matthew to go and get some rest. Raegan sent Martin with Father Tealander as protection and to check out the property and fortify it if necessary. She hoped another attack would not take place soon, but they would be prepared if it did.

As Father Tealander and Martin left the tarmac, the remaining members, Alysia, Raegan, Mary, and Char, stepped into the other waiting vehicle and drove into the desert. The further they could remove themselves from the Vegas glow, the better the opportunity to test the moonlight theory. The night was balmy, and with Char in the vehicle, the air conditioner could not keep the car cool or the smell diffused, so the windows were opened. The warm night air rushed in through the windows, limiting their ability to talk. They sat quietly, staring out the windows in anticipation of what they would discover.

Forty-five minutes later, they pulled off the highway onto a dirt track Mary had located on Google Maps, leading them farther into the desolate landscape. As time was precious, they did not trek far, stopping the vehicle after just a few miles. The team exited and gathered around the warm hood of the car.

Wasting no time, Alysia opened the journal with the petroglyph image. All eyes watched in expectation and were disappointed when no reaction occured. Alysia picked up the journal and opened it as far as possible without destroying the already weak binding. Still, no new information magically displayed on the page, the team was further left unrewarded. She could hear the collective sigh of frustration from the others, but she would be damned if she were giving up. She opened one journal after another, and each one refused to release their secrets. She peered into the night sky. Maybe it was not dark enough, perhaps the moon was not full enough. Too many maybes. Again, she opened the journal with the petroglyph, moving the image around the car, walked the journal out into the desert a little further hoping to gather just a little more moonlight on the page, not a god damn thing.

Returning to the vehicle, she slammed the open journal down on the hood, the noise swallowed by the immensity of the desert. Frustrated, she laid her head upon the journal and closed her eyes, trying to see through her mother's eyes. Alysia felt exhaustion setting in, a feeling of a warm wet towel placed upon her forehead. Her brain was shutting down in need of sleep. A hand touched her shoulder and Alysia's body startled out of its stupor.

"We have done the best we can for now Alysia, stop blaming yourself. You are doing your best with the tools available to us. Give us some time and we will figure it out." Raegan said behind her as she gave her shoulder a squeeze.

"We don't have any more fucking time!" Alysia snapped causing Raegan to take a halting step backwards.

"Wait a minute," Char said as it moved towards the journals trying to tamper down emotions before they became a raging fire, "I want to try something." It pulled its protective suit up its arm, exposing its wrist. With its left hand, it used its talon to cut into its right wrist. A black sludgy substance leaked out. "Do we have anything we can use to absorb some of this," Char asked.

"Holy shit, doesn't that hurt?" Mary blurted as she watched the sticky substance reabsorb into the demon's arm.

"You are joking, right?" Char's blue eyes glittered in the moonlight with just a touch of demon humor.

"I don't know, I just thought it would hurt," Mary retorted with a shrug.

"It hurts, but it is like a mosquito bite compared to the other things done to me."

Raegan reached into the passenger side door and opened the glove compartment, looking for leftover napkins from the previous renter. If necessary, she would get gauze from the medical equipment they were carrying. She would rather not use their supplies on this demon. She located a wad of napkins shoved under an old rental agreement. She pulled them out and returned to the team.

"Alysia, take the napkins, dab them in my blood, and rub the journal page with it." Char pushed its arm out to her and watched as she gathered its blood on the napkins. Alysia was skeptical because all other avenues had failed. Trying to keep the strange smelling demon blood from touching her fingers she rubbed the substance gingerly into the journal page fearful of damaging their only clues. The team were stunned to watch as Char's blood became translucent. She dabbed a little more blood and continued working it into the page. As before, nothing changed, the secrets remaining out of their reach or never there in the first place.

"Fuck!" Alysia yelled into the desert, throwing the soiled napkins on the sandy ground. The dry desert wind caught the stained napkins and dispersed them into the darkness. As she stepped away from the vehicle, infuriated that all possibilities had failed, the page was exposed to the full light of the moon.

Char stepped backward as the page glowed, growing brighter. Images began to appear above the petroglyph image.

"Holy shit," Alysia exclaimed softly.

"What?" Raegan shouted as she pulled her weapon.

"It's Demon's Ink," Char chortled, its excitement making its laughter sound like shattering glass. "Your parents mastered the art of Demon's Ink."

"Raegan, you don't see this? Mary?" Alysia danced left to right as her wide eyes took in the images.

"I don't see shit, just the journal," Mary said as she too moved left then right, mimicking Alysia's movements.

"Are you two fucking with us?" Raegan asked, perturbed. Like the others, she was too tired to deal with any more bullshit, the pressure to protect Alysia already a heavy burden after the events of the last twenty-four hours.

Raegan and Mary might not see it, but Alysia certainly did. The page projected a hologram, an image above the journal. As she watched the image brightened, its colors becoming sharper. The images began to move like a holographic motion picture.

Alysia turned to Char, "how did you know that would work?"

"I didn't?" Char responded. "I was just desperate for an idea and demons blood has some interesting properties in Jarapenth."

"You need to share ideas more often. So far, you are batting a thousand," Alysia said with a little awe in her vice, elation replacing the sodden sound of earlier fatigue.

"What the hell are you two talking about?" Raegan was waving her hand over the top of the book. Each time her hand swiped across the hologram, it wavered and shuttered. "There is nothing here."

"It is most definitely there," Alysia replied. The hologram continued to expand, unfolding hidden secrets, riddled messages, and diagrams. Alysia had been correct on the flight. The petroglyph was a three-dimensional drawing on a two-dimensional wall of rock. She could see hunters holding spears and advancing on rams in a rock-strewn landscape. Trees, and grass swayed lightly in the wind. Children chased one another in open fields. Below them were the passages, hidden catacombs. She reached up to touch the shifting image and the hologram responded. She could move the image left and right, up and down, backward and forward. Each movement changed the picture, displaying more critical details. She reached into her pocket, grabbing her phone. She took a photo, but when she tried to pull it up on her phone, the image was only the vehicle windshield.

Every time she glanced away, she immediately forgot what the image showed her. Glancing down at the picture in the journal, her eyes were drawn to her mother's handwriting. *The secret is inked in the blood of demons, once seen, forgotten, written, and remembered.* To remember, they must write it down. It could not be held in their memory Alysia ran to the back of the vehicle and gathered notepads and pens.

"Mary, you and Char pair up. Char, you describe everything you see to Mary in as much detail as you can. Raegan and I will do the same. I will only move the hologram once we both agree we have captured as much detail as possible. Nothing should be missed. Capture every twist, turn, climb and drop in these passages. We will compare notes when we get back to the rental."

"This is some crazy shit," Mary said as she began to take notes.

CHAPTER 26

The team arrived back at the residence a little after four in the morning. Martin met them at the door providing Raegan an assessment of the home and the security equipment he had stationed outside to warn of a potential assault. Raegan decided the team needed rest. Martin's early warning system would suffice for the short term. The team was thoroughly exhausted so a couple of hours rest would be beneficial to all. Besides, Raegan was unsure when the next opportunity for rest might present itself. They were awakened a few hours later by Father Tealander to prepare for the meeting with Redstone. Each showered and put on fresh clothing. They reassembled with the rest of the group in the great room overlooking Red Rock Canyon.

As they awaited the rest of the team to shower and put on fresh clothing, Martin, and Father Tealander, read through the notes the team captured in the desert. The cave's location and entrance remained a mystery, but its passages were well documented by the look of their notes. It showed as one long single cave system and appeared to have no branches, just a single trunk. The passage opened into a series of more extensive caverns, large rooms. The first cavern's walls were covered in square holes. The second was dissected by sharp lines. The third consisted of two six-sided wheels toward the front of what appeared to be a dead-end chamber.

Father Tealander was focused in on a set of riddles,

Rare beauty, sirens sleep, beware the whispers of those who creep.

Words have weight, a guided hand to seal one's fate.

Thread cut bare blade of knife, hastily cut will cost your life.

Wheel cannot exchange, start from beginning, mornings change.

Blessed be thee who touches light, placed within a demon's plight, handed down the world ignite.

"What do these mean?" asked Father Tealander.

"I have no idea," said Alysia. "I am hopeful Redstone has an idea and can show us where this cave system might be located. Look right here," she pointed to an image on the paper, "that is the same icon as the dagger in the parchment showing the six artifacts, which means it is hidden within these chambers."

"I'm sorry," Raegan said, shaking her head, "I am still confused as to why you and Char could see the images but no one else could? How do we know this is not all some ruse to confuse us, to get us chasing shadows? Char even said no one knows how Demon's Ink works except for a small group of demons. What if this is a trap?" Raegan's voice rising as her doubts surfaced.

"Excellent points," Mary backed her boss as her eyes wrinkled incredulously. "I mean, everyone else is affected by the journals and their abnormal properties, but you. Yet, you can see Demon's Ink, and we cannot. You must admit, this all seems, well, peculiar?"

Alysia wondered why only she could see the hologram but could not feel the differences in the journals as well. They were all mysteries the team would need to work out later. Doubting each other would only create rifts which in turn could turn them against each other. Alysia needed a team that trusted each other even when trust was hard to come by.

"I understand your frustrations. I understand your doubts. Hell, if I were in your shoes, I would question all of this as well," Alysia said through pursed lips. She stood ramrod straight, and her hands became as animated as her voice when she spoke. "Right now, our focus needs to stay on the Kalama Dagger. We need to put aside our disbelief, doubt, and distrust. We need to recognize we might face things that make us uncomfortable or sow doubt. If our emotions are allowed to take over, then we will question everything. For now, let's try to stay together and afford ourselves some grace."

"I don't disagree, Alysia, but understand all my training is tripping alarms in my head right now," Raegan said as she paced the room. "What are our next steps?"

Alysia nodded to Raegan as thanks for backing her decision. Even if it was only for now. "To start, it appears we are going to need caving, safety, and sleeping gear, including enough water and food for at least a couple of days. We need communication equipment which will work underground. Can you contact the Sect of Light and see what you can do?"

Raegan returned Alysia's nod and called Martin over to assist. He was the outdoor survival expert and could pull together a list of necessary supplies. She was still unhappy with what she thought were relevant questions not being answered and although she appreciated Alysia's rah-rah speech, the unknowns were mounting. In her line of work, unknowns were disasters in the making. Now everyone was depending on a demon and a woman she barely knew to decipher information only they could see. Raegan feared the two of them might have missed crucial information, or the found information was a ruse to lead them into a kill zone. Her job was to protect this team and she did not want the Sovereign Guard eliminated before the artifact was even located.

As Raegan and Martin retreated to a corner, the doorbell rang. Mary Mueller escorted Alysia to the door, her shoulder-length brown hair bobbing to her steps. Her tattooed arms holding the weapon as if it were a part of her body.

"You will have to tell me the story of those tattoos someday," Alysia said as they walked. "They are beautiful. The one that appears as stitch work is amazing. I have never seen anything like it."

"That one is my favorite as well. Get us out of this mess, and I will tell you anything you want to know." Mary gazed through the peephole. A gentleman stood on the stoop. "I think this is our Moapa representative, but open the door slowly. I will cover you from behind."

Alysia unlocked and opened the door, "Good morning." She said as her eyes squinted trying to adjust to the bright Nevada sun.

"Good morning, I am looking for an Alysia Rose? Martha Ortega contacted my council with a request to meet regarding the Atlatl Rock petroglyphs. My name is Redstone." He was a tall, handsome man. His skin was weathered by sun and time, tan and worn like a leather belt, his hair jet black and straight falling just to his shoulder blades. He was a few inches over six feet tall, dwarfing Alysia.

She opened the door wider and offered her hand. Redstone's handshake was firm, the palm of his hands rough and warm. His hand dwarfed Alysia's, she could feel him pulling back some, but not in a condescending way. Alysia felt like she was equal in his eyes, which shone with an underlying intelligence. His voice was rich and deep, and when he spoke, it was as if each word was being weighed for importance. Alysia made a silent bet with herself that this guy was a professor, or someone required to do a lot of speaking.

"I am interested as to why you seek my counsel. Are you writing a paper, a doctoral thesis, perhaps? Mrs. Ortega was a bit stingy with her reasons for meeting with me, other than to say it was urgent. Most times it is business professionals looking to use our land." Redstone asked as he continued to stand on the front stoop, his head tilted slightly, trying to see around her.

"Unfortunately, I'm not writing a paper. I think it would be better if we could talk inside. Care to come in?" Alysia stepped away from the door while also trying to hide Mary.

"Depends on whether or not the young lady behind the door is going to jump me the minute I walk in."

Mary stepped from behind the door, her weapon pointed towards the floor and held at waist level. "Sorry about that. We cannot be too careful right now." She offered her hand, and he took it. "Name's Mary."

"Redstone," he answered with some alarm as he gripped the hand not holding a deadly weapon. He watched her eyes as they shook hands and noticed her grip was firm and assertive. There was definitely a military presence here. "Agree, one can never be too careful. What assurance can you give me I am not walking into a mugging. We are in Las Vegas," he asked, but this time with just a hint of a smile to his voice.

Alysia answered, "Best I can give you is my word. I promise we are not here to kidnap or harm you, but we really need your help if you can provide it."

Redstone stepped through the threshold and followed Alysia and Mary into the air-conditioned living room connected to a kitchen and separated by a floating island. His wife wanted an open floor concept, but living on his college career paycheck, a remodel was not yet in the cards. He noticed others sitting in chairs as he entered.

"From the looks of this group, I am assuming this is more than a simple history lesson?" Redstone said as he continued to observe the people in the room. He quickly identified two more potential military individuals. One built like a brick wall, the other with the curliest head of dark red hair he had ever seen. Both exuded dominance in the group, like the one who had been behind the door. He could feel the tension in the air. He sensed this group had been thrown together recently and were still figuring each other out. Alysia appeared to be in charge, but the red-haired woman standing next to the island could just as easily have been the leader as well. Alysia interrupted his thoughts as she began to make introductions.

"Let me introduce you to our group. Raegan Marie is the head of a security group called the Sovereign Guard. To her left is Mary Mueller, who you already met. To her right, the guy with arms like Schwarzenegger, is Martin Kyle.

This is Father Matthew Tealander. When I was younger, he was my co- guardian and, well, he continues to be rather protective of me." She said and flashed a knowing smile to Matthew. Redstone registered a pseudo-father-daughter relationship between the two.

Each shook hands with Redstone, Martin matching Redstone's pressure pound for pound until Redstone grimaced and released his grip. Martin released his hand with a knowing grin. There were some definite dominance issues in this group, Redstone thought as he moved towards the island.

"Before we begin, can I offer you something to drink, Mr. Redstone?" Alysia asked as she continued to walk to the kitchen.

"Please, just Redstone, and yes, some water with ice would be appreciated. May I sit?"

"Of course, please, make yourself comfortable. Sit wherever you would like." Redstone sat on one of the stools at the island. Something about the smell of the place was bothering him. Either these people did not bathe, or something dead was rotting in the house, which did not make him feel at ease. He was about to comment on the smell when Alysia slid a glass of ice water across the granite countertop. He took a drink, enjoying the coolness of the water. It was early in the morning but already in the upper eighties outside.

Alysia sat next to him. "Thank you for coming here on such short notice and with so little information. The best way to explain why we need your assistance is to start at the beginning of this week and bring you up to speed." Alysia paused for a moment gathering her words. "What I am about to tell you is going to sound unbelievable. I ask for your patience and to listen with an open mind if you can."

Redstone considered this request and nodded his agreement, his curiosity piqued at this point.

Alysia told the story of what had occurred up to this point. She shared with Redstone the attack on her home, the journals, and the discovery of the mysterious Demon's Ink. At first, Redstone glanced around to see if he was being filmed. Was this some sort of bad joke, was this one of those Internet pranks? As he listened, he lost his incredulity and became further intrigued. That feeling, however, disappeared when Alysia showed him the parchment with the six artifacts circling the sun and moon and attributed them to the petroglyphs at Atlatl Rock. His heart rate increased, and a lump formed in his throat. He stood to try and settle himself.

Redstone took another sip of water, trying to relieve his newly formed cottonmouth. "The parchment with the six artifacts circling the sun and moon is very close to an artifact of my people." He reached into his shirt pocket, removing a pen, and pulled a small wire-bound notepad from his back pants' pocket. Redstone quickly drew out the parchment Alysia showed him and then added images of his own above each. "You are aware of the four elements, Earth, Wind, Fire, and Water. Two others provide balance. They are Aether which is space, and Darkness. There can be no life without these six elements. We are bound to them. In the middle of your parchment is the sun and moon, but it is the North Star in ours. The North Star is of great importance to our people. It is a constant, true north. He is called Qui-am-I Wintook Poot-see." He stopped for a moment and took a drink.

"One of our spirits, Shinob had a son, his name was Na-gah, the mountain sheep, and he traveled on Tu-weap, the Earth." Redstone picked up the petroglyph image and pointed to the image that represented the characters in the story.

"Na-gah was an explorer, always climbing, always seeking. That is what this ladder represents on the petroglyph. He discovered a great mountain and climbed, wishing to climb higher than any other before him. While he climbed, he found a crack in the mountain and ventured into it. At first it traveled down then would level off, only to once more go down. His journey was long, and he was faced with many strength and knowledge tests within the cave, each challenging his ability to go forward. He became exhausted and wished to go back, but found his way blocked. He was forced to continue forward. Na-gah was filled with a gnawing fear, one deep within his soul, this fear was doubt. He was convinced he would never see his home again, the sandstone cliffs. He continued forward, until he saw the light above him and climbed. Upon reaching the light, he discovered an object of intense power. He was certain it must never leave this cavern, for it would destroy all it touched. He left it and was able to squeeze himself out of a crack beyond the object. He found himself on a peak of such height he could not return to his home. His father Shinob rewarded his son for not being swayed by the object and turned him into the North Star."

Redstone once again took the pen and drew the object Nagah had located. After it was completed, he lifted it and showed it to the group. All of them gasped. It was the exact image they found in the hologram and on an expanded image of the petroglyph.

"It's the dagger. That has to be the dagger." Alysia shouted as her hands clapped together in front of her. Her excitement radiating throughout the room.

"I would tend to agree," said Redstone. "It is of great significance to our people."

"Has anyone ever seen it?" asked Alysia.

"No one but the North Star. Although many have tried to find the object because it is believed that to hold it would grant them dominion over worlds. Those who have entered the passages have failed to return, lost in their hunger for power."

"The caverns exist?" Alysia leaned closer to Redstone, engrossed in the story.

"Yes, but my people blocked the entrance many decades ago to stop others from entering the cavern and losing their way. An object of such power must not fall into the wrong hands, including yours. I believe it would be best if you and your team left it where it sits and your team finds another treasure to steal." Redstone said, putting the picture down and crossed his arms in front of him. He leaned against the island, a stoic figure with an emotionless face.

"We cannot do that," Alysia looked deep into Redstone's eyes. "I respect your concern, but I have seen what these creatures are capable of, and should one of them retrieve this dagger, they will have one of the six artifacts and that might be all they need to conquer or destroy our world. We need to enter those caves, and we need to acquire the artifact before a more dangerous nemesis secures the dagger."

Redstone's stance did not change.

Alysia sighed deeply, afraid of what she was about to disclose, fearing his reaction. "There is something we have kept from you up to this point, but I believe you need to fully understand our situation. I know you think we are here to steal this object. I think you believe we are treasure hunters, but you are wrong. Char, can you come out and greet Redstone?"

Redstone soon discovered where the underlying odor of rot and decay was emanating. What came from the hallway was something out of a nightmare. It stood on two legs, bony formations protruded from its shoulder blades and around its knees. Charcoal black with red embers glowing within its malformed frame. It reeked of death and decay, dried blood, and rotting flesh. Redstone stepped sideways, trying to move away from the island to not be pinned in. He stumbled backward, nearly tripping over another stool. Alysia reached out to steady him, but he pushed her arm away. Redstone was paralyzed with a raw fear he had never felt before, the creature before him a terrifying presence.

"I am terribly sorry. I cannot help you." Redstone gulped air, trying to breathe as he pitched forward towards the front foyer and the exit.

Char's voice, glass under feet, grating on Redstone's ears. "If you turn away now, if you do not help these people, not only will they perish, but you and your people will suffer as well. Imagine hundreds of thousands of my kind doing as we please with those you love."

Char approached Redstone and watched as the man continued to dodge its advancements, trying to keep as much distance between them as possible. But Char refused to relent. "I do not know your history or your suffering but understand me when I say you cannot comprehend true suffering. Look at me." Char stepped forward again, its voice rising, "Look at me. Do I seem like a creature that knows pity? We feed off your pain, we cannibalize your anguish, we feast on your fear. Imagine what we will do to your kind. Imagine what this planet you call Earth will become once we cover it in eternal night. Are you still willing to walk away?"

Redstone froze for a moment, his gaze leaving the demon, being drawn to movement behind the creature. Redstone witnessed three prairie dogs standing and watching him through the large glass patio doors leading to the back yard, their gaze matching his. In his culture these animals were forebearers of death, a warning of what was to come, an omen of bad fortune.

Redstone stammered as he turned and opened the door, "I cannot help you. I am sorry. I will not help you."

He fled the home into the blinding sun, the heat of the day slamming into him after the coolness of the house. Redstone opened the door to his jeep and barely started it before his foot hit the gas pedal. The Jeep flew down the driveway, gravel peppering the lawn, to escape the nightmare behind him.

"WELL, THAT COULD HAVE GONE BETTER." Mary sighed as she stood from the couch, stretching her limbs. Her body sore from sitting too long, she craved a decent run to loosen up. "Now what?"

"Maybe someone else can help us," Alysia said though her voice did not sound confident.

"I will reach out to the Sect and see if they have any fresh intel on the caves. I doubt it, but not sure what else we can do now," Raegan said as she grabbed her phone from the island.

"Damn it!" Alysia slammed the journal with the petroglyph down on the granite, the sound of a firecracker in the room. Her frustration a mounting storm just under the skin as she tried to calm herself. They needed Redstone.

REDSTONE OPENED the driver's window and allowed the hot breath of the desert to flow over him. He drank deep the smells of sand, limestone, and dry earth. He questioned his reasons for abandoning the group. The sight of the creature nearly knocked him to his knees. Such creatures were only legends, stories told to memorialize morals. To deny what he witnessed was to deny his own eyes. He clearly had seen a demon walking on Earth. His thoughts wandered to the legend of one coming forward with the ability to not only acquire the dagger but to wield it as well. Was Alysia the one to do so? More importantly, would she do so for good? What if the object was too powerful for her, consuming her, turning her from good to evil? What if one of these creatures, like the one they called Char, was to acquire the object?

Back in Black by AC/DC blared from the Jeep's speaker system, startling Redstone from his thoughts. The steering wheel jerking to the left as he tried to turn down the volume.

A deep voice came from the backseat, "Don't mess with the radio. This is one of my favorites."

Redstone looked in the rearview mirror and saw a shadowy figure sitting in the middle of the bench seat. He began to turn his head when the jeep jerked to the right.

"I would rather you keep your eyes forward. A heart attack in the middle of the Interstate would do neither of us any good.

Actually, why don't you let me drive for a while. You can listen."

The wheel was ripped from his hands as the vehicle leaped across three lanes of traffic, the Jeep's speed accelerating. Redstone watched as the speedometer went from seventy-five to over one hundred in seconds. *Back in Black* grew louder, and he could hear the shadow behind him belting out the lyrics as the car careened down the freeway. Drivers laid on their horns as his jeep flew missing other vehicles by mere inches.

"Don't you just love good old fashion rock music, Redstone? Tell you what, we have some of the best rock music where I am from. These bands just can't keep out of the cocaine, so damn, do we get some greats down there."

"What are you?" Redstone shouted over the music and the hurricane-force winds blowing through the open window.

"Me? Hell Redstone, I am nobody. Well nobody you want to know. Listen, I am going to need you to help Alysia acquire that dagger."

"What, so she can give it to the likes of your kind? No, I will not help. You can kill me if you must, but I will not help you retrieve the dagger."

"Well, that is just plain rude, Redstone, already judging me, and you don't know a thing about me." The radio changed from *Back in Black* to *Highway to Hell*. The shadow sent the car over one hundred and twenty miles per hour, swerving around semi-trucks with inches to spare. "What if I say please?"

"What if I tell you to kiss my ass, and we plow into one of those trucks you keep aiming at?" Redstone shouted with confidence he did not feel.

"See, I am not fond of this attitude, Redstone, especially after I said please. That is humanity's problem, zero gratitude. Since you want to be a dick about it, let me tell you what will happen if you do not help Alysia. Oh, better than that, why don't I just show you."

Redstone found himself no longer in the Jeep. He was tied to poles in an X within a barren wasteland. Cries of misery filled his ears. In front of him were his wife and two children, tied to their own poles. Next to each stood a demon, like Char, each holding sharp instruments that looked like knives but were thin and transparent. He could see they were razor-sharp.

The shadows voice was quiet, Redstone felt his skin crawl as it spoke. "Those are skinning knives, Redstone. So thin they just slide right under your flesh and remove it from the muscle and tendon. You have skinned a deer before. This is the same thing. Who do you want me to demonstrate on?"

"No! I will do what you want, please, don't hurt my family, I am begging you, I was wrong, I can help!" Redstone pleaded as he watched a creature move towards his nine-year-old son.

"It's a little late for that now. We could have talked, but you wanted to be a dick, and I can be a bigger dick. So let's start with your son."

Redstone's face grew pale, his lips quivered as the demon placed the knife on the back of his son's hand. "God damn it! He is only nine years old, skin me instead, teach me!"

Redstone fought his bindings, but every move he made only tightened them. His arms and legs were pulled apart, a wishbone waiting to snap in two. The knife pierced his son's hand, the sound of his screams assaulting Redstone's every nerve. He closed his eyes, begging for mercy he could not find.

"No, no. You open your eyes and watch this Redstone. You wanted to be a badass, you wanted to play strong. You be witness to what that does for you." The shadow said behind him.

His eyes were forced open. He watched as the flesh was peeled from his son's arm. He could hear the sickening wet sound of his sons' flesh being scraped from muscle. The demon was slow and exact in its flaying, removing the flesh in one long, perfect piece. His wife and daughter were forced to watch. Their screams added to his begging pleas. His son's eyes bulged out of their sockets, his tiny body bucking on the poles. The demon moved to the other arm, the knife stopping inches from his son's flesh.

"Here is the thing, Redstone. By the way, I love that name. It just rolls off the tongue, Redstone, Redstone. Anyway, Redstone, I can do this for eternity. Flay your family over and over again, day after day. Oh, and the days are long in Jarapenth. When I grow bored, I will allow my minions to have their way with your family, and if you think skinning is bad, WOWEEE, are you going to be surprised." The shadow cackled from the back of the Jeep, needles in Redstone's already shattered mind.

Tears streamed down Redstone's face. He was embarrassed to give this entity the pleasure of seeing him break, but the screams of his family were too much. His son's butchered arm a screwdriver in his eyes.

"Redstone don't be embarrassed because you love your family. It makes torture so fine. The pain it causes others is much worse than the pain it causes the one being tortured. Let's stop this and talk."

Redstone found himself back in the Jeep as it continued to hurtle down the interstate. "You help Alysia get what I want, and I promise your family's safety, well, until we take over this worthless world, but that could be a while. Do we have a deal, Redstone, or should we return to our previous program?"

"No! I will help. I will help Alysia get the dagger if I can."

"That a boy Redstone, I knew I could count on you. Now put your hands on the steering wheel so when I leave, you do not go crashing into a guard rail, you have been under a lot of stress. I can't have you dying just yet." The shadow left the vehicle like the sound of air leaking from a tire.

Gaining control of the Jeep, Redstone steered it toward the emergency lane, where he brought it to a complete stop. Placing the vehicle in park, he laid his head upon his hands at the top of the steering wheel. His entire body shook uncontrollably. Sweat poured from every pore in his body. He sat in the silence, only the sound of cars whooshing past. Redstone began to take deep breaths, working hard to lower his heart rate. After a few moments, he opened the driver's side door and stepped out. His legs like jelly, forcing him to use the car door to hold himself up. The wind deepened his chill, pressing his sweat-soaked shirt against his back, causing him to flinch from the cold, despite the Nevada desert heat assaulting him.

Redstone looked up and down the freeway, amazed not to see the state police pulling up behind him. Had no other drivers reported his erratic behavior? The more he stood, the less real it all felt. Was it a dream? Had he dozed off behind the wheel? Did any of what he thought just happen really happen? In answer, the Jeep's engine started with a deep-throated rumble and *AC/DC* once more blared from the stereo.

"No, no, no!" he shouted. "I will help, I swear." The Jeep once again grew quiet.

In that moment, Redstone realized he would never be able to listen to *AC/DC* ever again, which was a damn shame, because he enjoyed rocking out to Angus's solos.

Redstone reached back into the vehicle and grabbed his mobile phone from the center charging station. Pressing contacts, he looked up Alysia Rose and pushed the icon for an audio call.

"Very well, I will bring you to the cavern entrance tomorrow morning," Redstone said after Alysia answered her phone.

Alysia stammered, "we cannot wait that long."

"You will have to, as the entrance is sealed, and it can only be opened when the sun's light touches the locks to the cave. I need to speak to the elders to access the keys and get the rituals to use them. I need time to convince the elders to hand these items over to me. The way was blocked for a damn good reason. You and your team will meet me at the trailhead tomorrow morning, at four o'clock. It is a four-mile walk to the entrance so give yourself plenty of time to arrive, we cannot be late, not even by a minute. The trailhead for the Firecaves is within Valley of Fire State Park. You can locate it on Google."

"Thank you, Redstone," Alysia said, a tremble in her voice she could not control. All the stress from the past few days trying to find a way to escape. She was close to tears but tears of relief because if Redstone had refused, she had nowhere else to turn.

"I warn you, once we enter the caves, there is no turning back. It will seal behind us, and we will be forced to complete the journey. There will be no one to save us, no one to help us. We will be alone. My people will not sacrifice others to rescue us, and they will not disclose the location to search and rescue. Your team needs to understand, if we become trapped, we are as good as dead."

"You are coming with us?"

"Yes, you do not know our legends. These might be of great importance to complete the tasks and find the dagger. Bring your journals and the parchment. I am truly hopeful members of your team are trained to protect us. I do not believe we are going to gain the dagger easily."

Redstone hung up the phone and stared into the desert. How would he explain to the elders why he must enter the cave? Would they believe him if he simply shared the truth? Stepping back into the Jeep, he turned over the engine and gently patted the dashboard. "Let's hope we can behave for the remainder of the trip home." When no response was given, he placed his foot on the gas pedal, turned on his signal, and reentered traffic.

CHAPTER 27

Alysia put her phone down on the counter. She could see the team awaiting news, many leaning forward, trying to hear the tinny conversation through the phone. "Redstone is a go, but we cannot access the caverns until morning. He did want me to warn you all that we are on our own once we enter the caves. No help will be coming. The entrance will be sealed, we either find the dagger and hope an exit exists, or the caves become our tomb."

"Well, that sounds terrifying," Mary said over a soda she recently grabbed from the refrigerator.

"Question," Martin said as he leaned forward. "Do we have any choice, really?"

Alysia turned to Martin. "We could choose not to go. Maybe all this is some elaborate hoax, a despicable game set to see just how long we will play. But I think it is more. My parents died believing it was more, so I must finish the game. I need to know where all this is heading. I would not blame any of you for stepping out. If these journals belonged to anyone but my parents, I would probably choose not to continue especially if my life was in jeopardy."

"Bullshit," Raegan said from the other side of the island. "You are stronger than that. You see what's at stake. You and I, we are not all that different. I cannot believe for an instant you would bail on this. You might be able to convince someone else, but don't try and con us."

"Understood," Alysia said, as it was all she could think to voice at the moment. Overwhelmed with gratitude to Raegan and the rest of the team. "Well then, let's get our gear in order."

As team members began to engage in the work of preparation, Alysia wrapped an arm around Matthews's shoulder and pulled him aside.

"I want you to stay behind, Matthew. This is going to be extremely dangerous. We don't know what the terrain will be like, let alone what we will be expected to do to acquire the dagger."

Matthew violently shook his head, his hands clenching in front of him. "I have to go, Alysia, and please, do not ask me why because I cannot explain it. This is the moment my life has been building towards. I feel it deeply. I know I will be a burden. Hell, at seventy-five, I should be on a cruise ship heading to Alaska, but instead, I am here. Alysia, I must continue this mission."

Alysia moved her arm from around him and took Matthew's hand. Her love for him was profound. He had always been there for her, no matter the situation. She was deeply disappointed he did not share with her all he knew about her parents or the journals, but she could understand the circumstances he was placed in. She felt the roughness and the frailty of his thin skin under her palm, the soft tremors of palsy beating a tempo she could not hear but feel. She looked up into his brown eyes and saw them pleading with her.

"Very well, I understand, Matthew. If this is where you were meant to be, I don't want to be the one to dissuade you from coming. Please, do not overstress yourself down there. When you grow weary, you must inform me, deal?"

"Deal," he said, and with a gentle squeeze of her hand, he walked away and back to his room to lie down for a while.

REDSTONE WALKED up the stairs to the building housing the offices of the Moapa council. His steps were hesitant, and the heat was an anvil on the back of his neck, pummeling him, trying to turn him into a puddle on the sweltering concrete. He was sweating profusely, and he recognized it was from more than the damn sun. He was nervous going before the elders.

As he opened the building doors the airconditioned air made the hairs on his arms stand at attention. The change from scorching sun to chilled air a slap in the face. It did not help that he realized his good standing was at stake. He was respected in the tribe, a professor. A voice for the protection of the land and its meaning. How would the council see him now coming to them with lore and legend?

"Good day, Redstone," Wendi said from the front desk. "The council awaits you in conference room B. Do you know where that is?"

"Down the hall to the left, correct?"

"Yes. Redstone, might I suggest you stop in the men's room and throw some cold water on your face? You are dripping in sweat. It must be sweltering out there," Wendi said as she returned to her work on the computer.

He agreed it was hot. However, he did not agree the beads of dripping sweat were a cause of it. He stopped in the men's room and splashed cold water on his face until his skin felt numb. Standing before the mirror, he gazed at his image. His face was deeply lined with fear. His eyes still red from his earlier tears. He could back out, say he was crying wolf. Those thoughts vanished as the shadow appeared in the mirror, its eyes menacing, and one shadowy finger slowly went back and forth, a silent chastising. He gave the shadow figure a one finger salute of his own watching as it slowly faded from view leaving him with only his haggard face staring back at him. He wiped his face down with a handful of paper towels then left the bathroom and continued to the conference room. Arriving, he paused, took a large breath and then knocked on the door and awaited permission to enter.

Entering the room, he found seven of the nine council members sitting behind a table. There was a single chair in front of them. Redstone walked with what he hoped looked to be a well thought out purpose and then sat on the hard plastic chair facing the council. Elder Raven was directly in front of him. He was head of the committee, all others waited for him to start.

"What is the purpose of pulling the council together on such short notice?" Elder Raven asked, a tinge of annoyance in his voice.

Redstone found his hands were jumping around in his lap. He clasped them together and answered the elder. "I must request access to the Firecave. I have been summoned by a spirit that cannot be ignored. It has instructed me to assist in locating the dagger."

Not one of the council allowed their eyes to leave his. They did not turn to each other, their gaze intense, boring into him. Elder Raven frowned, furrows appearing above his gray eyebrows. "No one has been allowed to enter the cave for decades. You are aware of the dangers. What spirit would send you to your own death?"

"I believe the one the stories speak of has arrived, the one who can retrieve the dagger and bring balance to Tu-weap." Redstone leaned forward and told them of everything which had occurred. He spoke softly while he shared the torture of his son, he held nothing back, they needed to hear the truth. He would allow them to decide whether to believe it. The council of elders grew quiet as Redstone completed his story. Elder Raven's eyes had not left him, not once since he entered the room. He felt judged, guilty of asking something he knew he should not ask.

Elder Raven stood. "Allow us a moment to speak amongst ourselves. We will call for you."

Redstone nodded. He stood and left the conference room.

An hour passed, and then two. He was growing weary of sitting on these hard chairs and pacing the same hallway. He walked down to the vending machine, but it was out of order. The drinking fountain water was warm and tasted slightly of minerals. It did not quench his thirst.

He was confident their answer would be no after such deliberating. Would he, if he were to ever sit on the council, answered any differently? He could imagine them sitting in that pale yellow conference room, windows covered to keep the heat out and the cool air in. He was certain the decision had been made thirty seconds after he left, but the elders were spending the remaining time discussing what to do with Redstone and his imaginary spirit.

As the third hour grew closer, Redstone was getting ready to just get up and walk away. Maybe that is what they were hoping for? Looking at his watch, he felt ridiculous sitting here for this long. As he began to stand, the conference room door opened, and Elder Raven beckoned him back in.

Redstone followed the elder into the room and sat once more before them. The elders continued to watch him as he awaited their decision. If it were no, what would he say to Alysia? How would he protect his family from the shadow figure?

Elder Raven stood and spoke. "We have agreed to provide you access to the cave."

Redstone sat stunned before the council. He was sure they would deny him.

Seeing his dismay, Elder Raven continued, "Yes, we will allow this. The spirits have spoken to you. Although we are unsure if this spirit is for the good of our people or will bring great sadness to us. We must trust it is what must be done. Perhaps the one called Alysia can provide the balance we have sought for so long. But Redstone, she might also bring destruction. We entrust you to make the right decision when the time comes. You have always been a constant voice of our people." The council awaited his acknowledgment.

He was still in shock of their answer, so his voice carried a hint of disbelief when he agreed. "I will."

The elders rose from their seats. Elder Raven nodded towards a fellow elder to his left. "Elder Fisher will assist you with the ritual and provide you the objects necessary. One other thing, you will take the keys to the lock with you once the ritual is complete and destroy them. Do you understand?"

Redstone nodded his head. Yes, he understood. The elders were sealing the cave. If he failed to retrieve the dagger, there would be no way for anyone else to access the weapon.

CHAPTER 28

Alysia's team awoke early, packed the SUV, and pulled out of the rental's driveway. Fifteen minutes later, they merged onto Interstate 15, leaving downtown Vegas, and heading out into the desert towards Arizona.

They exited Interstate 15 onto the Valley of Fire Highway. They rode in silence, not even the radio played, as each focused on the upcoming mission. Alysia had initially been disappointed that the team would have to wait for the following day to act. But, at the same time, she recognized the need to decompress and absorb everything up to this point. The delay allowed the team to review the diagrams drawn from the Demon's Ink and get some much-needed sleep.

Raegan and Martin acquired the necessary gear, including some newer technology for underground communication based on TTE, Through the Earth signaling. The Sect of Light sent reinforcement weapons for the rest of the team. Before the team retired last night, Mary brought the new team members out into the desert and taught them how to shoot with the high-tech gear. It was a quick class. Alysia hoped everyone remembered, including herself.

Alysia watched the sky begin to lighten as the day approached. The black sky was turning a deep navy blue with hints of purple. She was lost in thought when Raegan announced from the driver's seat that they were arriving. They passed the pay station too early for a ranger to be in attendance. Raegan instead pulled the vehicle over, placed fifteen dollars in a self-pay envelope, and put it in the yellow box. The landscape changed as they entered the park. Although it was still dark, a touch of light allowed her to see the formations thrusting from the dry desert ground, reaching towards the sky. Raegan turned down a gravel road two miles into the park, leading them past what Martin informed them was Aztec Sandstone. The stones were pocked with holes and weirdly shaped shelves, Tafoni, Martin called it.

Approaching the trailhead, the passengers saw Redstone standing next to a yellow Jeep, his backpack lay on the front hood. Standing beside Redstone was a park ranger. Raegan pulled up next to the Jeep and Redstone approached with a parking permit to place on the dashboard. The team stepped out of the SUV and into the early morning warmth. The daytime temperature would reach over one hundred and ten degrees, but for now, a cool desert breeze brushed against them, making the upcoming trip tolerable. The sky turned a hazy shade of blue to the east as the sun worked its way over the low peaks on the horizon. Everyone was thankful to get out of the vehicle, as Char was particularly ripe this morning.

Redstone introduced the ranger as a friend who would be watching over the trailhead for the next few hours, allowing them time to access the cave system and keep tourists at bay. Redstone did not tell them the real reason the ranger was here. To remove the vehicles from the location should they not return within forty-eight hours. The Ranger was already tasked with scrubbing the video feed from the entrance point. One way or the other, they were never here.

Packs were handed out from the SUV back, Father Tealander receiving the lightest while the Sovereign Guard carried the bulk. Alysia was responsible for the journals. She was the only one not affected by the shifting physics of the manuscripts. Redstone led the team up the trail, the sienna sandstone lifting to the right and left until they found themselves walking in the middle of a slot canyon with walls thirty feet high. The canyon so narrow if Alysia reached both hands out to her sides, her fingertips could scrape the sides. The ground was pale orange sand, difficult to walk in as their feet sunk into the soft surface. The smell of dry earth, limestone, and a hint of mesquite filled Alysia's nose. It smelled clean and pure.

Redstone acted as a tour guide, pointing out petroglyphs high within the canyon, some over two thousand years old. Alysia wondered how they reached such heights to create this amazing art.

She increased her pace to catch up with Redstone at the front, "why did you change your mind?"

Redstone raised his eyebrows. "Let's just say a shadow of doubt filled me with dread as I was returning home. What if you were right? Would I be a complacent witness to the end times?"

"Well, the getaway driver is as guilty as the one holding the gun in the bank. But I would have understood if you said no after all you had learned."

"Bullshit," Redstone said, which made Alysia laugh, Redstone following suit.

"What's so funny up there," Raegan shouted from the back.

"Nothing, just blowing off some steam," Alysia shouted back.

Alysia and Redstone continued in silence. Their footsteps echoed off the narrow walls. Redstone glanced over at Alysia. "Something possessed my Jeep yesterday, nearly slamming me into the back of a semi-truck at one hundred and twenty miles per hour. As I fought for control, a shadow spoke to me from the backseat. It told me I would help you or it would butcher my family. Its exact words were flaying my family repeatedly. Then the shadow decided to show me what would happen. It tortured my son in front of me. Only after I swore to help did the force return control of the vehicle to me. I have never been so terrified in my life and I have been on the front line in the past. After I gained control and pulled over, I called you. I realized then that I would need to tell my family something, an explanation as to why I would be gone."

"Oh my god. I am sorry. I did not want your family wrapped up in this."

"We never mean to include others, Alysia, but you must have realized, after all you have seen and been through that none of us are safe."

Her face said all she needed to say, her embarrassment tattooed on her cheeks as they turned four shades of red. She never dreamed the demons would go after anyone but those involved. She knew better. They were masters at leverage and deceit. It was stupid to think the opposing force would not use all tactics possible to win. "What did you tell your family?"

"I told them I was taking a group of college students on a trip through the park to visit religious sites and petroglyphs. What else could I tell them? I may never return home? I gave my kids long hugs and my wife an even longer one. The Council Elders will inform her if I do not return."

"Speaking of the elders, how did you convince them to give

you the keys?"

"I told them the truth," he said, turning his head to face forward and toward their destination.

"I am sorry, Redstone. It was just unfortunate luck you were the one sent to us. Well, unfortunate for you, fortunate for us." Alysia tried to give him a smile, but it failed. This was not the time to make light of the situation she had put him in.

The silence between the two was not uncomfortable. She expected him to be outraged, but he took the punches and continued. Redstone carried himself with such self-assurance, she could not help but feel she could be herself around him.

Across the path, a small lizard ran, trying to avoid the feet of those stomping on its territory, unwanted invaders. She could see herself as the lizard, the demons destroying her home. Alysia, was so focused on the little lizard darting across the sand she jumped when Redstone spoke.

"John."

"Excuse me?" Alysia glanced over.

"John is my first name, John Redstone. Thought you should know, seeing we might die out here in this beautiful landscape."

Alysia smiled. "Well, John, when you aren't out hunting demons with us, what do you do with your days?"

"Entomology, the study of insects, specifically desert species. Currently, I am a professor at the University of Las Vegas. I was brought onto the faculty last year after we discovered a new aquatic species which can only be found in the Mud River Thermal Pools. They can only live within waters that are between 85 – 106 degrees. Fascinating little creatures."

"Well, if you say so," Alysia said as she looked up at the changing sky. She was worried they would not make it in time, but Redstone did not seem concerned, so she tried to settle her mind.

"And you, Alysia, what do you do when you are not out

hunting ancient artifacts to save the world?"

"It is a long story. My life is rather boring."

"Bullshit," Redstone repeated, which started them both laughing again.

"Seriously, it's hot as hell out here. You could bake a tin of muffins in my cleavage, and we are walking to our death. Share the damn joke already," Mary said as she traipsed up the sandy trail, complaining about the dust getting into her nose. Which only made the two of them laugh all the harder.

THE SLOT CANYON bent to the right in front of them. As the group came around the bend, they were awestruck by the natural structure. The sandstone wall to their left crested over like a tidal wave, thirty feet tall, forming an open tube. The right wall disappeared, replaced with a half wall sitting four feet high.

Alysia felt like a surfer as she followed Redstone into the tube of the wave, the sandstone worn smooth by thousands of years of wind and occasional rain. Millions of visitors running their hands over the course stone also assisted with wearing it down. It truly felt as if they were being swallowed, the back wall curved and crested overhead with formations that looked like sea foam at the curve of the wave. The floor added to the experience. A river of ripples comprised of different colored sandstone flowing into the distance. In the middle of the tube, a slight arch separated the tube into two sides. A few of the team walked underneath the small arch, letting their hands brush against the pillar holding the structure in place, awed by the stone's power.

The tube came to a dead end. Set within the sandstone back wall was a series of strange holes and shelves of different sizes and depths. Something you would see in an art deco home around a fireplace or the nest of an alien hornet. Redstone announced they were at the opening to the Firecave. Everyone looked around for an entrance but only found solid walls bathed in deep red, violet, and orange tones, muted by time but brightened by early light reflected from the stone.

Redstone beckoned everyone over to where he stood. He spread a woven blanket on the ground, its colors muted but somehow almost glowing in its vibrance. The colors flowed and changed as the early morning light touched the weave. Redstone stood tall, straight, and proud and began the ritual to open the sealed passage. His hands moved in time to his voice. His voice undulated up and down, rhythmic, mesmerizing. The team were captured by its cadence.

"It was not only the Moapa, Paiute people, who wished this passage to be sealed. Our friends and enemies also wished it to be so. The legend of what was hidden within these passages brought people from around the earth, some with good hearts, many with bad. The Elders of seven tribes, Koso, Paiute, Panamint, Shoshoni, Walapi, Washoe, and Ute, united to find a way to protect the object hidden within these passages. One evening as the elders sat at a fire in animated discussion regarding how to protect the dagger, a bright star fell from the night sky. It bade them follow. The elders tracked the star and were brought here to the opening of the passage. Before the elders stood the North Star. The Star instructed each to bring a precious token from their tribe within a fortnight. The North Star would then assist them with barring entry into the cavern. The elders dispersed, returning at the time of the Stars request, each carrying an object of importance."

Redstone reached into his pack and removed a smaller drawstring bag. He began to carefully remove objects and display them to the team.

"A vessel, filled with the waters of Quitobaquito, a sacred spring. The Everglow, a Gypsum Crystal which continues to produce light after thousands of years. The gold Anch, brought to these lands by strange people who taught us many things. Vulcan's Flame, a stone that burns hot yet never ignites. The tooth of a Thunder Lizard. A piece of the North Star which led the elders to this location."

Redstone gently removed the last item from the bag, a dark object pulsing obscenely within its vessel. It phased from solid to liquid to steam, then started the process once more. Alysia watched the object. She could swear it was drinking in the light, sucking it in. She could see light being absorbed through the glass vessel.

"This is a death stone. When the ceremony begins, you must not touch this stone. It must only be held within its protective vessel. Should it touch you, your soul will become foul."

"I know of this," Char said as it leaned in closer. "This is Hellspread."

Mary bit, "What's Hellspread? Is it like Vegemite"?

"It's a liquid secreted from the backside glands of a Hospherdrom." Char patted his well crisped ass to solidify what he meant, "They are one of the largest creatures in Jarapenth, it has a mouth a ship could fit into."

"So, demon shit."

"You could call it that. It is a delicacy in Jarapenth, exceedingly rare. A Hospherdrom only secrets the liquid every three thousand years. There are herders who wait for this secretion to receive a reward. They must follow the creatures continuously, because if the secretions touch the ground, they become worthless. It is Ka's favorite. Of course, once you eat it, your breath smells like, well, Hospherdrom shit. If that vessel breaks, don't touch it. It does not infect your soul, but no one will come to your house for dinner ever again. I wonder how you got this?" Char asked as it continued to watch the object change form.

"I do not know. It has been with us for a long time. I am unsure how any of the elders acquired these objects, it is lost from the lore of our people." Redstone said as he carefully laid the last object on the blanket completing a circle. The blanket changed from muted colors to a brilliant orange, glowing brightly in the shadows of the stone structure.

"We are ready to begin. "Once the keys are in place, and we enter the cave, we are committed. We cannot turn back. We must complete our quest or--"

"Or what?" Martin asked.

Redstone paused quietly. His response was unsettling, "I have been instructed to bring the keys with us, to lock the cave permanently behind us."

"No shit, there is no way out but forward?" Martin shook his head. "Guess I should have finished that will I started ten years ago. Who is going to take care of my Blu-ray collection?" Martin was miffed. No one laughed at his joke, but then again, they were walking into a cave system with no exits. Bad timing should have been Martin's middle name. It certainly would have been better than Gregor. Who names their kid Gregor?

Redstone continued to speak. He no longer sung, his words more focused. Each word held gravity and the team could feel his intensity. "I do not know what we will be required to do, but I know we are not coming back out this way. We have searched for other entrances and have never found one. The story from our ancestors claims the cave climbs and exits on the top of a mountain or ridge. We have been unable to locate the exit. The elders were clear. When we go, we go, and there will be no rescue party."

Father Tealander spoke with conviction in his voice, even though he did not quite feel it. "I will gladly accept my fate if it means saving the world from creatures such as that." He pointed to Char, "no offense."

"None taken," the demon responded. With its burnt flesh crackling in the Nevada heat, it sounded like rain against a metal roof. Char was incredibly uncomfortable, not because its protective suit was baking it like a tin of muffins, but because it realized, at this point, it was an actual traitor. There would be no turning back, no quarter given. The best it could expect was to become the cellmate to a Glebinbyte. The demon shuddered just thinking about it.

Alysia looked to the rest of her team and held each of their eyes for a brief second. Fear and doubt resonated from each, emotions she clearly understood. But behind that fear and doubt she saw resolution, a desire to get moving and be done with this. "Then it is decided," she said her voice echoing off the walls.

Redstone picked up the first object. "As I hand you an object, you must first take it and place it next to your heart. Then place it next to your forehead and then move it over your head, as high as your arms can reach. Finally, bring the object back down, press it to your lips, and say these words, Tu-weap is good. My trust in Qui-am-I Wintook Poot-see is unwavering. Guide my heart, guide my head, guide my spirit, guide my words, guide my hands to do what is right. Once you complete this, you must pass it to the next person in line. Do not drop any of the objects. If any should fall and break or touch anything but ourselves once the ritual begins, the door will not open."

"What about Char?" Alysia asked.

"No need to worry about me. Redstone, is the cave behind that wall?" Char said as it walked towards the end of the cresting wave.

"Yes, of course."

Char disappeared.

"Well, holy shit," Martin yelled, his voice carrying out into the desert. He rushed over to the rock and placed his hands on the cool stone. He pushed, looking for a secret entrance, a hidden doorway, but the stone did not give.

"I guess that demon is committed. Actually, we should all be committed after this," Mary replied as she prepared herself for the ceremony.

Martin Kyle returned to the circle as Redstone picked up an object and demonstrated what each of them needed to do. As an object completed its circuit, Redstone gently placed the object in either one of the holes or on a shelf. The last object was the Deathstone which he put on the last shelf then stepped back. Everyone waited with anticipation.

Minutes passed, the team's anxiety growing. They watched Redstone, who in turn kept his eyes towards where they entered the wave. The sun's light slowly slid across the rock. As the light touched the back wall, the solid mass disappeared, and they were staring into the mouth of a cave, at least twenty feet in height.

Char stood within the cave. "Welcome to hell," it cried out as the others stared into the mouth. "I have always wanted to say that but never could get on the welcoming committee."

"In we go," Redstone encouraged individuals into the coolness of the cave. As the sun crossed over, the cresting wave and its light intensified the items which unlocked the cave glowed with increased brightness. Redstone removed each item from its location and placed them in the shape of a triangle.

"Cover your eyes. This is going to be bright," Redstone cautioned as he placed the last object into the middle of the triangle. An explosion filled the space with a flash of light so intense it burned its orange image into Alysia's retina even with her eyes closed.

"Holy shit, Redstone, you could have warned us to cover

our ears as well." Raegan yelled, "I am not going to hear right for a frigging week."

"You could have at least given me the Hospherdrom's secretion," Char lamented, disappointed in losing a rare treat.

"Get real, you smell bad enough without eating shit," Mary said as she passed the demon.

"Fair enough," Char responded as it stepped out of the way of the others.

The Sovereign Guard pulled flashlights and headlights from packs. The lights reflected off the red sandstone walls. Since light had not dulled the color, the inside of the cave was as red as blood with deep orange streaks. It was simply stunning.

"Okay, no turning back now," Alysia said, trying to sound courageous but feeling petrified, locked in an inescapable cave system. She had set in motion what might be the last mission for some individuals on the team. She did not know what lay ahead but if the past few days taught her anything, it was to expect the worse than double it. She took a moment to look at her friends and memorize their faces, to capture them in a photo within her head. If they could not escape, if they found themselves entombed within these red walls, she wanted to remember them at this moment.

"All right, you heard Alysia. Let's get moving. The clock is ticking," Raegan said as she pulled her weapon forward from her shoulder and glanced down at her watch. "Alysia and I are on point. Martin watches our six. The rest of you speak up if you need to take a break. Drink water down here. You will dehydrate fast."

Alysia and Raegan set the pace, the team following closely behind. They walked in silence each grappling with their own questions and fears for what was to come.

CHAPTER 29

Christine Carlyle, the newest and youngest member of the Sovereign Guard, drank Chai tea as she stared out at the Pacific Ocean from the windows of the home Roland had acquired through Airbnb. If that guy had not been some type of special intelligence agent in his past, then her mother did not make the best damn hushpuppies this side of Chicago. Crap, now she was hungry.

She was not pleased to be on babysitting duty. Raegan assured her this was an important role, but she felt sidelined. What was the point of being one of the best hand-to-hand combat personnel in the unit if you simply spent your time staring into the vastness of an ocean? Maybe she could head outside, and karate chop some dune grass, since it appeared to need a good mowing.

The drive to this location was not difficult, but it set everyone's nerves on edge. Christine did not blame them. They transported a child across state lines without permission from the child's parents. Kidnapping was Roland's word. Christine drove the entire trip while Roland and Martha monitored the child strapped to a hospital bed in the back of the van. Christine should have written Free Candy Inside on the side of the vehicle, or played some creepy ice cream truck music from a speaker attached to the top. It would have felt less suspect. Every police officer she passed and each that approached from behind set her teeth on edge. Christine was a West Chicago girl. She was used to law enforcement giving her the once over but the thought of being pulled over with the child in the back sent deep shivers down her spine. The Sect of Light was powerful, but were they powerful enough to pull her ass out of prison?

Making matters worse, Roland contacted Bethany's parents, who lived in Spokane, WA, and informed them all was well. It was just taking longer for Alysia to repair the damage. As they should be, her parents were concerned and wanted to fly over, but Roland convinced them to wait a few more days and allow Alysia the time she needed to help. A lie built on top of another lie, Christine felt nauseous.

As she continued to stare out the window, she saw a line of dark clouds on the horizon and watched as they started to make their way toward the shore. A storm was moving in, and from the looks of the shadows, it was going to be a doozy. The wind blew in from the ocean. The dune grass waving frantically like one of those balloon dudes at a used car lot, flopping left, then right, then standing straight up. Watching the storm roll in returned her thoughts to Roland and his past. She had seen him book this location and unbeknownst to him as he stood to go get his credit card, she glanced over and saw not one, but three fake IDs. And they were damn impressive. The guy was good.

Christine caught Roland's reflection in the glass as he approached from behind, holding a cup of coffee. The smell made her wince. She could not stand the smell of coffee. It smelled like cat piss to her.

"Christine, what the hell is that over there? By the tree?"

Christine turned to where Roland pointed but could not see anything, just the tree limbs blowing in the breeze. "Just the storm coming in, the wind is starting to kick up."

Roland's head turned swiftly to the right, "oh shit."

Christine captured a glimpse of what Roland witnessed in the dunes. But it moved swiftly, barely seen, disappearing behind a clump of trees. Her weapon sat on a chair next to her. She found herself reaching for it.

Her fingers tightened around the weapon as dark black objects began to rise from the dunes. These were not the demons they faced at Alysia's home. Roland and Christine watched as more of the creatures appeared, forming a line of at least twenty beasts. One of them stepped forward. Christine felt her bladder loosen but controlled her emotions, trying to remember her training.

The creature stood on four legs, but they were not legs. They were human arms. The human components had human hands, but the fingers ended in claws which must have been at least twelve inches in length. The arms supported a body the size of a small cow if that cow was burnt to a crisp like an overly toasted marshmallow. Christine could see no eyes. Hell, the only thing she could see on the creature's head was a perfectly round mouth. It was a huge mouth with a whole lot of tiny teeth jutting out, like a giant sea lamprey, getting ready to suck its dinner. The beast continued forward, its pack stepping in time with it until it reached the back lawn of the rental house, where it stopped. The creatures created a perfect V formation. Oddly mesmerizing in its perfection.

"How did they find us?" Roland asked as the creatures

continued to stand, watching with malice or what he thought was malice as all he could really see was that gapping mouth of razor-sharp teeth.

Suddenly, the television on the wall above the fireplace to their right turned on. White noise blared from speakers while the TV showed static snow. Christine and Roland slowly turned towards the television as an image appeared behind the snow, enormous and terrifying. It was impossible to focus on the picture. It was too transparent like a watermark. A voice boomed in the home, not from the TV speakers but from the very walls, driving both to their knees, hands pressed firmly to their ears.

"Make no attempt to contact the outside world, or I will release the War Hounds to feast on your flesh and drag your soul to me. There will be no further warning. Perform as told, and they will stay where they stand. Try and thwart me and my vengeance will be fast and true."

The television turned off, and the house resumed its quiet nature, with only the sound of the wind and the ocean waves.

Martha stumbled from the back of the house, her ears bleeding. "What the hell was that?"

Roland rushed over to her, "Martha, you're bleeding. Come into the kitchen."

Martha reached up and touched Roland's ear. "You're bleeding as well. What was that?"

Christine spoke from her location next to the window, wiping blood from her neck with her sleeve "It was a warning."

Martha slowly walked to the windows as her vision caught sight of the creatures standing outside. "I take it those are the War Hounds? I wonder if they would be interested in a Milk-bone, what the hell are we going to do?"

"Nothing is what we are going to do. And pray the other

team is in a far better place than us right now," Christine said as she watched the coming storm gather strength. The wind begansmashing into the windows, rattling the panes, reminding her just how thin the protection was between those in the house and the hellish creatures outside. She wished she could take back her complaints of earlier boredom.

CHAPTER 30

"We might have a problem," Martin said as he looked down at his watch. "Either time is different down here, or our tech is failing. I have nothing but gibberish on my watch."

"It's more than our watches," Mary responded with concern as she checked her weapon. "Our weapons are live, but tech is not functioning. GPS is down, and the marking system is offline. When we get into a firefight, the bullets are going straight, no fancy stuff."

"Are communications still functioning?" Raegan asked. The team performed a com check through earpieces and mics. Communications were working, at least for now.

"Let's keep moving, not much we can do at this point. If anyone has issues with their communication lines, speak up."

Raegan glanced over her shoulder to see where Alysia was and found her towards the back, helping Father Tealander. Raegan was uncomfortable with the shifting situations, one issue compounded by another. The Father should never have been allowed to be part of this quest, or mission or whatever this was. His body was too frail for a journey of this intensity. He was slowing the team down, and he would be challenging to protect in a fight for survival.

Raegan was trained to adapt and improvise, but it became a more difficult task when six humans needed protection and there wasn't much room to protect them. They could not go backward. They were forced to move forward. The cave was also fucking with her senses. At times she heard moans or soft voices, no more than a whisper. When she asked Redstone, he simply said it could be the wind or the ghosts of those before them. Normally, she did not believe in the supernatural, but her mind was changing after fighting a demon horde. To be fair, the idea of being trapped in a small space with the spirits of those who failed to make it out did not increase her confidence. Her frustration grew with every step.

"Martin, how are we looking back there?" She called out to get her mind off her escalating anxiety.

"We are good back here," Martin replied, not even using his communication system, just belting it out down the tunnel.

Martin's adrenaline pumped freely through his body when they had first entered the cave but now, he was excruciatingly bored. He had been primed for action the minute the team entered the passages but all they were doing was walking, and a lot of it. When Martin grew bored, he tended to flex his muscles, and at six foot three inches tall and weighing in at two hundred and seventy-five pounds, he had a lot of muscles to flex. As he walked, he stretched his arms, tightening his biceps, flexing his pecs and then let them go slack. It helped keep his mind occupied.

Where the hell was the action or some unique findings within the passage? The confrontation at the mansion had shaken him, but he was exhilarated to be alive. He was looking for that next hit. That next endorphin rush. Martin was an explorer at heart, an adventurer who spent most of his life scouting new locations, unseen wilderness, and uncharted rivers. His explorations usually had a purpose. He was a rare earth and gem hunter with three master's degrees under his belt in geology, organic chemistry, and cultural studies. Geology and chemistry were a direct result of his father's passion as a hunter of rare earth minerals. Martin's mother was the reason for cultural studies. Before meeting his father, she was a member of an indigenous tribe in the Amazon. His father won her heart through his stories of exploration and his wonderous views of the world. Soon they were married. She moved with him to the city but could not acclimate to an urban lifestyle. Her only happiness was found at the city zoo where she would spend hours watching the colorful birds of her native land. She missed her people and her way of life, a more straightforward way, the jungle way. A place without loud cars, too many people, and the ground too hard underfoot. When his father was attacked and killed by a Puma during an expedition, she returned to her home. He was fourteen when she left, leaving him with his grandparents.

Unfortunately, Martin did not belong in either place, the city or the jungle. His mother's clan did not accept him, and although she loved him dearly, she loved her way of life more. He attempted to visit her as often as he could but the trip into the interior was difficult, and he found that as time moved on, their connection grew weaker and his visits to her home grew farther and farther apart, his last visit three years prior. The loss of both his parents was a weight he carried but rarely shared.

When Raegan approached him about joining the Sovereign Guard, he emphatically said no. Once she showed him the salary, the new digs, and promised him adventures outside of the normal, he said hell yes. But, when she said outside the normal, he did not expect giant demons, sand tsunamis, and dark passages potentially leading to even bigger monsters or whatever madness existed down here. He was deep in thought and nearly ran over the top of Tealander and Alysia as Raegan brought the group to a halt. He knew the rest of the team was on edge, so he kept it to himself that he absolutely loved the shit out of this.

"Martin and Mary to the front," Raegan called out from the front of the procession.

Martin hustled forward, anything to get out of the doldrums. As he approached the front, he discovered why Raegan called a temporary halt. The passage turned into a narrow chute. Its circumference more like a waterpark slide, large enough to sit down and not hit your head, but relatively tight. One could stretch their arms out to either side and touch it with ease. He flashed his light down the dark passage and could only see about fifty feet down as the chute curved towards the right and disappeared. The tube floor was smooth and shined like freshly polished granite. If he stepped into the tube, he would find himself barreling down the tube like a child in a waterpark. Trouble was, at the water park, there was water at the end. Who knew what they would find below? Martin had explored many caves in the past and knew that you never trusted a chute. They could either lead to bigger chambers or to small crevices that ran several hundred feet deep. He recalled several tragedies where cavers had become wedged into what started as open passages and quickly squeezed down in size. One of them not far from here in Utah at the Nutty Putty cave system, now sealed due to the tragic death of an explorer.

Mary stooped down next to Martin and pulled a quarter from her pocket, which she rolled down the chute. She could hear it rolling as it made the turn, but then the metallic clink disappeared. Either it stopped or the sound was dampened withing the tight space. Standing up, she turned to the other members of the team, "Alright, who is ready to take the plunge? What? No takers? This is going to be one sweet ride surprised everyone is not pushing to the front of the line."

"I don't know about everyone else, but I think I will wait to hear for a splat or a scream before I take this ride," Raegan joked back with Mary, a wry smile on her face. Raegan straightened up and put on her serious face. Both Mary and Martin knew she meant business when she came to attention, and her voice became one of a drill sergeant. "Mary is right, we are going to take this ride, but we will take it safely. Let's get ready to rope up. We knew this might be necessary." She did a quick assessment. Each team member, minus Father Matthew, and Char were carrying two hundred feet of PMI 11 rope, which meant they had one thousand feet of rope. She hoped it would be enough to reach an end to the chute.

"Hand your line to Martin. He is going to be our anchor," Raegan said as she began to remove her coil from the pack she carried.

Martin threw up his large arms in frustration, visibly upset by the decision. "Raegan, you know it needs to be me going down that chute. No one here is a caver. Hell, I am not a professional caver, and I will tell you, it is too dangerous to send someone with no experience. If someone gets caught in a squeeze, there is no room for a rescue."

"I get it, but you are the strongest of the bunch. You can arrest a fall if necessary or pull someone up if they do get in a jam. How the hell do you expect us to pull you out if you become stuck? There is no way we could get you out. You are massive. Someone needs to play clean up and retrieve the rope and cams on the way down, without support from above. That is you." Raegan paused for a moment to let this sink in while keeping her eyes locked on Martin, "Christine would be the best choice as she is the smallest and lightest on our team.

Unfortunately, she is not here," Raegan said, trying to smooth Martin's ego.

Alysia moved next to Raegan. "It has to be me, Raegan. I got the team into this. I need to go down and check it out."

"Love your spirit, but we cannot afford to lose you. Currently, you are the only one, other than the demon, with the intel we need to get through this cave. Sorry, but I am not ready to put my team's lives in the hands of that creature." Raegan pointed to Char as she spoke. The demon flinched with each word she punctuated, but she did not give a damn. She turned to Mary, who was standing next to Martin and flashed her a smile.

"Oh, come on. Really, Raegan!" Mary huffed as she stared down the chute. "There could be spiders down there." Her hands waved in front of her face like she was brushing cobwebs away.

Raegan and Martin laughed as Mary ran her hands through her messed-up hair. "Hey, you were the one chomping at the bit to go down the chute commando-style a few minutes ago. We have not seen any spiders in here since we started." Raegan said through her laughter.

"Seriously, you are worried about spiders after yesterday?" Martin quipped.

"Fuck you, Martin, maybe we can find a few scorpions in here to keep you company." Mary shot back as she dug through her pack to retrieve her climbing harness.

"Hey, don't joke about scorpions. Those things will mess you up, no joke." Martin slapped Mary on the back as he helped her into her harness.

"I don't suppose you could perform a little of that magic you did earlier at the opening and tell us what the hell we are sliding into?" Martin asked Char while he finished securing lines.

Char moved closer to the opening, staring down into the darkness. His presence made Martin gag involuntarily. "I need to know what is on the other side, or someone needs to be able to clearly tell me what is there so I can picture it. Otherwise, I will end up embedded in this rock and sent back to Jarapenth. Which I would like to avoid."

"Don't blame ya," Martin offered, "after seeing what you bastards topside can do I'm not interested in finding out what happens below." Martin gave Mary a measured glance, checking her gear one more time, tightening ropes. "All right let's do this. I am ready when you are."

"Let's go before I chicken out. Don't drop me, Martin." Mary warned with an accusatory look as she sat down on the ground and prepared to be lowered into the chute.

"I dropped you once Mary! Do we need to continuously bring that up? It was a damn training exercise." Martin huffed out exasperated.

"Yeah, it was a training exercise, but it was a twenty-foot drop. You are lucky I ended up only with a sprain. Wait, what if communications fail?"

"If you pull once, it means to hold. Two pulls signal danger. Three pulls you have reached the bottom, or you have reached a point you can no longer keep going," Martin calmly said, "If I give three pulls, we are out of rope. Now if the rope abruptly goes slack, we will assume something devoured you," he said chuckling at his own humor.

Mary looked up at him with a WTF look on her face. Martin could not help but laugh, a deep booming sound echoing off the walls. The laughter took the edge off, which was good.

Raegan patted Mary on the shoulder. "Watch your back."

"You watch my back. I will be too busy pissing my pants and watching my front."

Mary slipped into the chute and began her descent. She felt tight, tensed as an overwound toy, ready to take off the minute she was let go. She let Martin lower her slowly into the chute. His light helped to shine the way forward until she arrived at the bend. As she slid around the corner, the light from up top disappeared, and she found herself alone with only her light to guide the way. She began to hum *Heathens* to get the thought of spiders out of her head, or something much worse.

THE FIRST TWO hundred feet of rope disappeared with the chute offering no surprises. The floor was slippery as ice. Mary was forced to use her feet against the sides of the pipe to slow down. It was an uncomfortable stretch for her legs, doing the splits while gravity tried to pull her down. Several times her feet slipped but she caught herself before plunging down Now she searched for a crack in the wall to place the first cam, but the walls were unblemished and smooth. She finally located a minuscule crack she could wedge the cam into and secure her rope. Upon completing she once again started downward. Mary tested communications. Thankfully, the team could still hear her. It was a good thing because the only noise keeping her company was the sound of her heartbeat, her breathing and now that song repeating itself over and over within her head. Tired of the silence, she asked Martin what he thought about how the floor could be so smooth, polished like a granite countertop.

His quick and witty response, "Thousands of years of water rushing through the tight tube at ridiculously fast speeds. Water moving that fast would shoot you out like a bullet from a pistol."

"Thanks, that makes me feel better. If it isn't spiders, then a flash flood could wipe my ass out in here. You are uplifting," Mary mumbled under her breath.

"That's the spirit, Mar, you are my glass half empty yin to my yang." Martin replied in his best Jim Carrey impersonation, which sounded more Australian than Carrey.

"God, you suck and don't call me Mar. Reminds me of my dad, asshole."

Her fucking dad was the last thing she wanted to be thinking about in this damn hole. Her dad's warped sense of punishment was her mother's cedar hope chest. The level of wrongdoing determined the amount of time spent in the chest. As a child, the trunk was large enough. She did not fear the interior and had enjoyed the smell of the cedar. She would curl up and sleep until her time ended. However, as she grew older and taller, the chest became tighter, the timeouts longer. She feared running out of air. During the summer it became a heated locker, her sweat pooling, staining the beautiful yellow boards. She always knew when she had pushed her father too far, his tone would change, and her name would shorten to Mar. At those times, the chest was not far behind. Mary was not claustrophobic, but the sudden bombardment of memories of her time in that fucking chest filled her with dread. Goddamn him. She slapped herself in the face making a loud smacking sound in the chute.

"Mary, you okay?" Martin demanded, hearing the sound through his earpiece.

"Yeah, fuck, just claustrophobic as hell in here." Mary continued down. Another two hundred feet of rope disappeared as quickly as the first. She was approaching the six-hundred-foot mark when she saw something ahead which made her stop to reassess, "Hey, Martin, hold up a second."

"Copy that, holding up. Everything all right?" Martin tightened the slack in the rope.

"Yeah, but there is a turn ahead. An orange glow is reflecting off the stone. It's shimmering. I also hear gurgling like water over rocks. Wondering if this is the water you were talking about Martin?"

"Could be. Or it might just be water leaking in from up top or from the sides of the chute," Martin responded.

Mary pulled a pistol from the holster at her waist and checked to make sure it was ready. "Martin, I'm going to turn, so I'm on my stomach, head facing down. It will be easier to get a shot off if necessary." Mary contorted her body to readjust herself in the chute. Facing down, she asked Martin to begin lowering her once more.

Raegan spoke to Mary through her earpiece, "Watch yourself Mary, we have no idea what's down there."

"No shit," Mary murmured through her open mic.

"I heard that," Raegan responded back.

"Sorry, a little tense down here," Mary said distractedly as she reached the bend in the chute.

She allowed Martin to lower her, using her hands to negotiate the sharp turn. The sudden change in brightness hurt her eyes momentarily. The brilliance of the orange glow was surprising. She blinked her eyes several times to adjust to the change. The gurgling noise increased as well. Mary exhaled sharply, "Oh my god."

"Mary, talk to us?" Raegan said with a touch of worry in her tone. She did not like sending one of her team into an unknown situation with no way to provide backup so she focused on keeping Mary calm in an unknown situation.

"You guys are not going to believe this shit," Mary's voice filled with a wonder Martin had never heard from her before. She never got flabbergasted about anything. Everything was a joke to her. Martin instinctively drew the line tighter in case he needed to react swiftly.

Mary's eyes felt as if they would pop from the sockets. She had never seen anything as beautiful as what she was seeing before her. Covering the chute walls and ceiling were bright orange flowers, illuminating the darkness. Surrounding them was a luminescent fungus, shimmering a deep vibrant blue. Turning her light towards the sides of the walls to see them better, the flowers disappeared back into the stone, like tube worms on a pier, only to return when the light no longer shone on them. As they reappeared, the bizarre gurgling noise returned, never above a whisper. The sound was intense in the small space with so many flowers. Mary did not sense an immediate threat, so she rearranged herself back to a sitting position.

"Mary, we need you to keep communicating with us. What is going on down there?" Martin asked through her earpiece.

"Yeah, I'm here. This is unbelievable. There are glowing orange flowers down here, covering the walls and ceiling. They are surrounded by a blue fungus or lichen that is also luminescent but not quite as bright."

"Mary, it's Redstone. Can you describe the flowers to us?"

"Yeah. The stem is narrow, the bloom looks like some of the orchids my mom grows back home. The colors are spectacular. I never thought oranges could be so vibrant. The flower has the classic lady slipper shape, with a fleshy tongue down at the bottom, and tonsil-like structures towards the back. The flowers colors fade in and out, from bright to pale. They are gently swaying, but I cannot feel a breeze or any airflow down here. They do not seem to like the light. Anytime it hits them, they retract back into their holes."

"Mary, listen to me carefully. Do not touch those flowers, leave them alone," Redstone said over her earpiece. She was mesmerized by the slow pulse of color and the calming sounds they made. Just water over stone, the gentle sound causing her eyelids to droop, desiring a nap. She wanted so badly to touch one. They looked downy soft. She was sure they would feel silky smooth. Redstone's voice became a whisper, a nagging mosquito in her earpiece. The orchids slowly waved back and forth. Such a soothing pleasant motion, she felt all the stress leave her body. She could not remember feeling this relaxed. Her hand raised to touch one, her finger slowly stroking the flower. The colors began to pulse faster and under her finger, she felt the blossom tremble.

She screamed, the sound echoing through the chute, resonating off the stone, thrown back at her with high velocity.

Her trance crumbled. The tip of Mary's finger had disappeared into the blossom. Panicked, she pulled, the pain intensifying with each forceful pull. Electrical currents flowed up her arm. She watched in horror as the bloom pulled more of her finger into its form, the goddamn thing seemed to be eating her finger. Her finger disappeared further down the throat of the flower. It had taken hold up to the first joint. The other flowers reacted by swaying faster, their colors a strobe of intensity, her retinas felt afire. The flowers no longer gurgled. Instead she could hear her own screams mimicked back at her. She pulled, the pain a white-hot lance slicing her body. She screamed again.

The rope tightened as Martin worked to pull her out of danger, but the flower would not let go, its stem strong and secured. Martin yanked, and Mary screeched as fresh pain radiated from her finger. "Jesus Christ, stop, stop," she yelled at both Martin and the bloom consuming her finger.

"God damn it Mary, tell us what to do!" Martin's frantic voice yelled in her ear as the pain radiated up her arm.

The orchids registered her stress and reached out to her, their stems much longer than she expected. Mary tried to lay flatter to avoid the reaching mouths, but any movement sent waves of pain straight to her heart, tightening her chest. She was not sure how much more her heart could take before it failed from the intensity of the pain. Either Martin would pull her lifeless body from this damn chute, or just cut the damn rope and let her dead body drop to wherever this fucking chute went. Maybe it just kept going, deep into the bowels of the earth. Her body sliding for all eternity. Mary was unwilling to accept any of these outcomes so sprang into action. Frantic, she unsheathed the knife at her waist, next to her holstered pistol, and chopped at the flower's stem attached to the rock holding her finger. The blade could not cut the fleshy stalk. There wasn't even a tiny slice, not a nick. *"Were these things composed of Titanium"*, Mary thought as she frantically hacked at the stem with the razor-sharp blade. The orchid retaliated and sent a new form of pain through her body, its intensity so vibrant she nearly passed out. Mary dropped the knife and heard it slide down the chute as she reached for her pistol. She pulled the gun and placed the barrel where the stem met the stone. Firing the weapon, the stem disintegrated along with her eardrums. The pain immediately decreased, but Mary looked down and found the entire tip of her finger was gone, bone and all.

"Fucking thing ate my fucking finger!" she cried out. *But the damn thing also cauterized the wound,* she noted silently. *Efficient little shits.* Removing her water bottle, she poured a little over the damaged digit. The pain reduced to a throbbing sensation instead of the full-on tidal wave of pain.

"It did what?" Raegan's voice yelled through the earpiece.

Mary thought that if the flowers did not consume her, then she was sure she would be deaf from the gunshot and the loud concern from her teammates above.

"I'm okay! Give me a damn minute to sort this shit out."

Mary responded to her team, her voice filled with frustration and pain.

The flowers continued their dance and Mary felt compelled to touch them again. The pain a distant memory. They were beautiful, the colors so inviting. She just wanted to feel the silkiness again. She reached up with her uninjured hand. A new flower stretched out to reach her. It sang to her, telling her she was safe, not to worry, all would be well if she just touched the flower. Somewhere in the far reaches of her mind, alarm bells rang as jarring as a fire alarm. She flinched and jammed her injured finger into the wall involuntarily, dragging the digit across the sandpaper texture.

"Fucking hell!" she screamed. "Pull me up. Pull me the fuck up!" The rope tightened, and Mary was yanked backward around the sharp turn, catching her elbow, and smacking her funny bone. "You have got to be shitting me," she screamed, grabbing her elbow. "Hold up, stop pulling for fucks sake!"

"Are you out of danger?" Martin called.

"Yes. Those fucking flowers are carnivorous. The bastard ate the tip of my damn finger. It's fucking gone."

"I told you not to touch them," Redstone said with a little too much admonishment in his tone. "Based on your description I was afraid the flowers might be a subspecies of *Aracamunia*, a carnivorous orchid discovered in a remote area of Chile. The only carnivorous orchid discovered to date, well, until now. How badly are you bleeding?" Redstone added.

Around the bend, she could hear the flowers screaming obscenities in a decent mimic of her voice. "I know what you told me professor," Mary's reply was snarky, but fuck them, they had not lost a fucking finger, "but the little fuckers hypnotized me. I am bleeding a little. I had to smash my injured finger into the stone. Hey Redstone, can the orchids in Chile talk?"

"I would think not. They are simply plants," Redstone replied curiously.

"Well, these will not shut the hell up. They do not like light so shine your flashlight on them when you get here. I also suggest you close your eyes as you slide through or keep your light directly on them as you pass. Their reach is greater than you think so don't be fooled. The little fuckers are hungry."

"Do they perform a decent *Mean Green Mother from Outer Space?*" Martin asked not able to resist dropping a *Little Shop of Horror* reference.

"Honestly, Martin, how many movies can one man watch?" Mary said wearily through her mic.

"Mary, you sound tired. Are you able to continue?" Raegan asked, keeping the group focused.

"My finger throbs like a son of a bitch, but I think I am okay. I am a little drowsy. My guess is the damn things hypnotize you. There is something in the flower which makes you tired. I don't think they were able to get enough into me. I can keep going Raegan, what choice do we have?"

"None," Raegan remarked. "Okay, let's get you past those flowers."

Up top, Tealander shut off his microphone, "These flowers must be related to the first riddle from our notes, *Rare beauty, sirens sleep, beware the whispers of those who creep.*"

"Guess we better start paying better attention to those riddles moving forward," Alysia said.

Down below, Mary wrapped her injured finger as best she could. She called up to Martin and told him she was ready to start back down. Mary slowly slid around the corner but kept her light focused on the flowers, forcing them into their holes as she passed. The little bastards reached out behind her, she could feel them trying to attach to her clothing, but they could gain no leverage. She hoped the little shits starved. Out of danger, Mary set a new cam and continued down.

At roughly nine hundred feet of line, Mary exited the slide and entered a cavernous space. The drop to the floor was fifteen feet so she used the rope to descend and settle on the ground. When her feet touched the sandy surface, they crunched through something brittle. Glancing down she saw a pile of bones at her feet, a crushed skull under one foot. *Well, here is at least one of the poor bastards that tried to come down here,* she thought. Next to the pile was her knife, which she grabbed and held at the ready. The chute dropped her off at the back of a long cavern. She shone her light and looked for any movement but saw none.

"Anything in here?" Mary yelled. "I'm already pissed off and tired, if you want to bring something, bring it now." She waited a few moments for a new terror to appear out of the dark, but when no new fresh horrors presented themselves, she gave an all clear to her team and disconnected her harness. She administered first aid to her damaged finger while she waited for the others to descend. Trying desperately to ignore the darkness that tried to swallow her within the cavern.

CHAPTER 31

Progress was slower than expected due to the inexperience of the group in arresting slides. Martin waited for each team member to reach the four-hundred-foot mark before sending the next person down. He was more of a coordinator at this point, with cams in place for security.

Martin descended last. He found Char knocked out cold on the chute floor within the flower chamber. The flowers kept trying to connect to the creature but would burst into a quick flash of flame. They must have pumped enough toxin into the demon to make it pass out before bursting into flames themselves. Martin could hear the flowers mimicking Mary and several others from the team. Blended in was the sound of their own pain as they tried to feed. A small, exceedingly small, part of Martin felt terrible for the little guys, too stupid to realize they were trying to feast on a festering lump of rotting meat. Martin lowered Char down in front of him as he continued to progress through the chute, removing cams and coiling ropes. He lowered Char to the floor of the cavern and then dropped out himself.

With the team reassembled they agreed to take a break, eat some food, and give Mary and Tealander proper time to rest. They also could not go anywhere until Char woke. The demon lay unconscious on the sand.

Alysia felt the pressure of time. How long had they been in here? How much time was left? Would Crimson be forgiving if they arrived a few hours late? The quiet and darkness of the cave only intensified her dread and fear of failure.

As the team dug into some energy bars and nuts, Alysia approached Redstone to try and distract her anxiety ridden mind. "How did you know about the orchids?"

"One of the botanists who discovered the orchid in Chile gave a lecture at the university. My mother loves plants and it has become a hobby of mine as well. We both attended."

"Do the ones in Chile eat people?" Alysia said with a smirk.

"No, not as far as anyone knows," Redstone returned the smile with a tired one of his own. "I wish I could have taken a sample of this species. What a discovery. Of course, no one would believe me as I could never show them where I found them."

Between bites of her second peanut butter crunch bar, Raegan began to laugh, "Was it just me, or were those plants swearing as I passed by them? They sounded exactly like Mary."

"All this shit is just berserk," Mary said through a mouthful of cheese. "I can understand the whole meat-eating plant gig, plenty of those out there. But talking plants? Not just talking plants but ones that can mimic someone's voice. Crazy shit. Add to the list of stuff I do not want to see again." Shaking her head and staring at her half devoured finger.

Alysia tilted her head in thought, "Reminds me of a film. I think it was called *The Ruins*. A bunch of teenager's trespasses onto sacred land and climb this temple in the jungle. A weird ivy consumes them, and then it would mimic them to coax the others into the ruins. I loved that film. Maybe not so much anymore."

Redstone stood and stretched, shining his light down the new cavern. "Anyone interested in a little recon while others rest up?" Alysia and Raegan volunteered. All three gathered their weapons just in case some new creepy crawly slithered from the dark.

"This has to be the cavern of holes from the riddles," Raegan pointed out as they continued to survey the space.

The cavern was the size of a football field both length and width-wise. The walls averaged roughly ninety feet in height. Along the side and back walls, squares, a foot wide and deep, were evenly spaced every three feet in perfect rows and columns, floor to ceiling. Alysia cautiously let her hand slip into one of the squares while Redstone and Raegan held their breath in anticipation. The stone was perfectly cut, smooth to the touch. Alysia's hand-scooped a small handful of sand out of the hole and let it filter between her fingers to the floor.

Reaching the front of the cavern, they found themselves at a dead end. The front wall did not have the squares cut from the floor to the ceiling. Instead, six squares set up like a tic-tac-toe board were carved into the wall. Within each square, perfectly centered was a lever, or what they thought to be levers or switches.

In front of the squares, floating four feet off the floor was a round stone with a hole cut from the middle. A donut stone, the hole in the middle large enough for an arm to fit through. The stone sat six inches from the wall. Raegan ran her hands along the top and bottom of the giant floating rock, searching for wires or anything that would hold it in place. She found no such objects. She pushed down on the stone, and she felt it shift just a little. She could feel the resistance.

She tried to push the stone towards the wall and felt the same opposition.

Redstone watched as Raegan inspected the floating stone. "Interesting," Redstone said under his breath.

"Are you thinking the same thing I am?" Raegan said working with Alysia to move the stone.

"If you are thinking opposing magnets, then yes, we are thinking the same thing," said Redstone. "But if these are magnets, they are the strongest rare earth magnets I have ever encountered. I would love to get Martin's take on them."

As Raegan continued to try and force the stone to move, Alysia investigated the levers within the squares. Her hand slid behind the floating stone. She could reach one of the levers with just a bit more oomph. A loud snap filled the space along with a bright blue spark. Alysia awoke to Raegan gently slapping her face. The floating stone sat ten feet away.

"What the hell just happened?" Raegan asked as she helped Alysia into a sitting position.

"I don't know. I reached out to touch one of the levers, then you were slapping me in the face," Alysia said, rubbing her now numb arm the second time since the shotgun battle in her bedroom. It was not a pleasant feeling.

"It threw you back about ten feet. I'm guessing we should not touch them. Can you stand up?" Raegan asked, offering her hand.

"My arm feels like I touched a live wire, but I can stand." She grabbed Raegan's offered hand with her working arm and lifted herself up as she pulled. Standing, they returned to the floating stone.

Alysia continued her observations. "What are these symbols on the top of the stone?" Alysia traced her fingers across the etched icons. There were four of them in all.

"No idea," Raegan replied. "I think we are at a point where

more brains and a look at that riddle from our notes might present a clue to figuring this out. We are not solving this ourselves."

As they returned to the group, Redstone paused. "Is it not strange to you that there are no footprints in here but our? Even if some others became plant food, someone would have reached this cavern, yet only our prints are on the sand. There is a skeleton back there. Where are their prints?"

"It has been a long time since anyone has entered these caverns. You said so yourself. Maybe water got in here and washed them away, or maybe those bones are the leftovers from the orchids," Alysia said.

"Maybe," Redstone squatted down and shoved his hand into the red sandy surface, lifting a handful and allowing it to flow from his fingers. He could not help but feel nervous. It all felt wrong.

CHAPTER 32

Returning to the group, they found Char revived and looking well rested. As well rested as a demon could look. Martin was giving the creature shit when they returned which was causing the others to giggle uncontrollably.

"You can hold back a wall of debris, but a bunch of fairy flowers knocks you on your ass?" Martin said shaking his head.

"Well, it is not as if I can hold a flashlight, it would just melt." Char said with a level of embarrassment that was humorous coming from a being that looked like a nightmare.

"Still, the little bastards knocked you out. I have to say Char, I lost a little respect for your species back there," Martin said, obviously fucking with the demon.

Alysia saw Char's veins begin to pulse a violent shade of red, its emotions beginning to take over. She walked over and patted the demon on his fire suit protected back. "Martin is just messing with you Char, he does not mean any harm. It is how humans connect."

"Oh," the demon's veins cooled, and it smiled a hideous

smile of black rotted teeth. "Would it then be appropriate for me to tell Martin to fuck off?"

Martin looked shocked and Alysia laughed out loud, her body bending over as she tried to catch her breath. "Yes, by all means!"

"Fuck you Martin," Char said with a giddiness that was at the same time repulsive as its voice sounded shrill and unnerving.

"Wow," Martin replied. "That is a new sound I never need to hear again."

The team repacked their gear and moved to the front of the cave. Raegan wanted to make camp and approach a solution after resting. With no way to know how much time had elapsed, Alysia wanted to keep moving. Raegan was concerned after the recent trauma, they needed more downtime, but she also understood the situation's urgency.

Members of the Sovereign Guard played with the floating stone, but it moved only inches even with all three of them pushing and pulling. Father Tealander had read the riddle he believed was associated with this cavern, *Words of weight, a guided hand to seal one's fate.*

"What does that mean?" Martin grunted as he continued to push. His muscles bunching and veins popping as he tried to force the stone to move. The forces holding the stone in place were powerful, refusing to give any lenience.

While Raegan and Martin continued to force the stone to move, Mary stood at the front of the round behemoth reconsidering options. She stooped down, surprised to find she could look through the hole and see the lever in the middle square. It could be accessed. She reached through the circle and could touch the lever. "Hey, I think I got it," she said excitedly as the tips of her fingers curled around the lever pushing it backward.

"Mary, wait," Alysia called out, remembering the snap she received from the mechanism.

Pulling her arm from the circle, Mary turned to the anxious eyes of her team. "What's the fuss? I got it. The lever was right there." Mary wiped her dusty hands on her pants.

"Well, that was pointless excitement," Char's graveled voice echoed within the cavern when they were rewarded with no reaction. The silence within the cavern broke as a grinding noise, stone on stone, filled the large space. A new noise followed the grinding like the sound of sand sifting through an open hand.

"Oh shit," Mary remarked as her light flashed across the left wall. Sand was spilling from the top rows of the cavern walls ninety feet up, resulting in a waterfall of red. Everyone pointed their lights to the walls. The top two rows of squares were open with sand sifting through at a tremendous volume, like watching water flow over Snoqualmie Falls.

"It's an hourglass!" Alysia cried out.

Frantic, they worked together to push the stone to another lever, but it would not budge.

"We are fucked," Martin called out through grunts of exertion. He damned himself under his breath for desiring more excitement. Next time Martin would be more explicit. He wanted something he could fight or kill, not an escape room straight from the underworld.

Father Tealander yelled over the sound of sand. "The answer is in the phrase. We need to figure out the phrase, *Words of weight, a guided hand to seal one's fate.*"

"What the hell does that mean?" Alysia asked as she grabbed a cloth to put across her mouth and nose as dust from the sand reached them.

"I don't know," Matthew said, "The answer is here but we need to figure it out," his voice echoing the panic of the team.

Others, beginning to couch and gag from the accumulating dust, dug into their packs to find anything which could be used as a makeshift mask.

Father Tealander reacted as he watched Alysia pull the journals from her pack, looking for a shirt to hand to Matthew.

"Words of weight," Tealander murmured, "Words of weight!" he said louder. "Alysia, the journals, bring them here."

"What, why?" Alysia asked.

"*Words of weight,* Alysia. The journals, that is why they have those weird properties. They are the key to unlocking the puzzle."

"I can't tell the difference. They all feel normal to me," Alysia said as she removed the rest of the journals from her pack.

"Exactly, we need someone other than you to pick up the journals and tell us which ones have unusual weight."

Martin left the stone and grabbed the books, placing those aside that were physically heavier than the others. Redstone checked and verified by picking them up as well. Five of the nine journals were identified as being unusually heavy. The dust was thickening in the air, making it difficult to breathe even through face coverings. Their eyes began to burn from the silica in the sand.

"What do we do with them?" Raegan yelled to be heard over the echoes of falling sound and anxious team members within the space.

Alysia stared at the stone, drawn to the flat top while the rest of the stone was round. "Balance them on top of the stone!"

Raegan reached down to the stacked journals but was unable to lift them. "Son of a bitch," she grunted as she tried once more. "I can't lift them," she tried to raise only one but to no avail. They were welded together.

Martin pushed Raegan out of the way. His muscles bulged,

deadlifting the stack. This was embarrassing, first the stone, now the books. "Oh man, we are in deep," he said, glancing at the side walls where sand dunes were forming, the excess sand sliding into the middle of the chamber.

Char cried out, "Alysia, you have to place the journals on the stone. You are the only one not affected."

Alysia used her body to push Martin out of the way. She bent down prepared to deadlift the journals and nearly toppled backwards as the journals lifted with ease. Righting herself she carried them to the stone and placed the stack on top, balancing them upon the flat surface. Immediately the rock shifted towards the bottom left and aligned with another lever.

"Hot damn," Mary cried with excitement keen to get out of the sand filling room. She reached in and pushed the lever. The grinding noise began once more. The team watched as the next two rows of squares from the top opened, the cascade of sand flowing even faster.

"Fuck, fuck, fuck," Martin yelled as he kicked sand under his feet. Looking like a toddler throwing a tantrum in the grocery store.

"Goddamit! Calm down. We need to stop and think," Raegan scolded Martin as sand flowed like water into the chamber. Raegan could no longer see the back of the cavern due to the dust that was billowing from the falling grains.

Alysia blocked out the noise, focusing only on the balancing journals. What were they missing? Her hand moved to the symbols on the stone, her fingers running across the carved glyphs. She scanned the journals, their pages browned with age. A memory scratched at the ridges of her brain, there and gone. She turned the journals so the bindings were facing her. Sitting in the Sect of Light conference room, she saw the symbols on the bindings of the journals but was too focused on Madame's story. Now, she looked at the journals and the marks on the stone. She removed the journal whose symbol did not match. The stone moved towards the upper right. Alysia, too short, called out to Martin for help. Martin shoved his arm through the hole and pushed the lever.

The following two rows of squares opened, the stream now a flooded river, banks overflowing, sand rushing in mad torrents. They were moments from being buried in the cavern. Gear was moved against the back wall as sand pushed towards them. Alysia, unphased, stared at the journals. The answer was here. She would be damned if her friends were going to die in an hourglass.

"Yes," she yelled, the answer right in front of her. She rearranged the journals to match the symbols on the stone, top to bottom. The stone shifted to the bottom right. She reached through the hole and pulled the lever. The grinding of stone on stone overlapped the sounds of cascading sand. Alysia gave in to her despair. The sounds of celebration, however, pulled her back. The stone squares were closing bottom to top, the avalanche of sand ebbing. The cavern floor shuddered under-neath them as sand escaped through one-foot squares that were buried in the floor underneath them. The sand dispersed, the holes in the base closed, and the remaining sand filled the voids, hiding the openings once more.

Alysia bent over in exhaustion and tilted her head towards Redstone. "Mystery of the footprints has been solved." Both of their faces covered in dust with rivulets of sweat interspersed, their faces lines of light and dark. Alysia's white teeth shone through the dirt as she gave him a tired smile.

"I would have waited to pull the lever a few more moments. Built the tension to its maximum," Redstone said, leaning over, trying to catch his own breath, and remove a cramp shooting through his side from holding his breath.

A sharp crackling sent the team scrambling. Behind the

group, a crevice appeared, running from top to bottom of the wall behind the floating stone. Alysia shone a light through as dust settled around her. The crack was fifteen feet deep showing an opening on the other side. Alysia grabbed the journals and her pack, sliding through the gap before the Sovereign Guard could stop her.

SHE EXITED the narrow opening finding herself in a cathedral. Not a real one, but the semblance of one. The perfectly shaped walls were overtaken by stone which flowed from the stone like melted plastic. Majestic columns of yellows, reds and milky whites held the ceiling in place. Stalagmites formed castles throughout. The space was enormous, magnificent in its formations.

"All clear," she yelled through the crevice and then followed the sound of water, her gaze cautiously looking for orchids or other potential threats. She discovered a terraced pool with crystal clear water flowing over blue, green, and orange terraces. Reaching down with an open hand, she scooped a handful of water bringing it to her nose. A slight smell of sulfur lingered, but she drank it anyway. It was cool and crisp against her sand tortured throat. It tasted like bottled spring water from the store, minerally but fresh. Alysia knew she was taking a risk by drinking water from this cavern, but her thirst was overwhelming. The cool water washed the grit from her throat. If she dropped over dead, at least her thirst was quenched.

She followed the terraces to the largest pool at the base. Kneeling, she scooped handfuls of water and splashed it on her face, scrubbing the dirt and grime free with her hands. Standing, she watched as the others slipped from the tight crevice, their faces showing the same tired awe she felt. How could something this beautiful be found in a place so dangerous? Char was last to slide through the crack, and as it came out the other side, the crack slammed shut, sealing them in.

"That's it, everybody," Regan called out, "we are going to stop here and get some rest."

"Absolutely not. We keep moving. I know everyone is tired, but we must reach the dagger," Alysia exclaimed as she prepared her pack to move on.

Raegan had reached her boiling point and stepped into Alysia's space, coming toe to toe with her. "Not open for discussion. I thought we were clear. One of my team checks out any new terrain. You nonchalantly walked in here after we nearly suffocated in a sand trap and were nearly eaten by a goddamn carnivorous flower. You are not thinking as part of a team. You are thinking only about yourself. You, or anybody dying in here is not going to get us to the dagger faster."

Alysia knew she was not processing her emotions well at the moment, she knew she was about to make a mistake. She knew it, but the built-up pressure found a release and she could not stop it from exploding. She responded by using both of her hands to forcibly push Raegan out of her space. "You work for me last I checked."

"I work for the Sect of Light," Raegan stood her ground, "and I say we are pausing and resting. Look at Father Tealander. He can barely stand. The entire team is worn down. If you wish to move on without us, I will not stop you. But the rest of us are resting, and we will move out when I am god damn ready to do so. Last," Raegan said while jabbing her finger at Alysia, "you touch me in anger again, and I will give you a beat down which will make you wish you were dealing with the damn demons."

Raegan sharply turned and left, leaving no chance for

Alysia to respond. Alysia's hands were balled into tight fists, ready to fight. What would it gain her, other than the distrust of the Sovereign Guard? Besides, Raegan was right. Alysia needed to check her ego. She looked at the team through fresh eyes. They could barely stand, exhausted and dirty, gulping down water like camels away from the oasis for too long. She was embarrassed by her actions. A leader did not act this way. It showed her immaturity. She could feel Raegan's team watching her, waiting to see her next move.

Alysia went to where Raegan knelt by the lower terrace washing the grim off her face. "I'm sorry," She said, her voice echoing the embarrassment she felt.

Raegan looked up. "Hard words to say, aren't they?"

"At times. Listen, I know I am hardheaded. I lack experience and was thrown into this as much as you and your team. I am terrified that I led us into a trap. I am terrified of making a mistake, and I am terrified of not reaching the dagger in time to save the children. But my fears are no excuse for taking it out on you. I should not have shoved you." Alysia reached her hand out, and Raegan took it. The tension between the two an ember once more.

"To be clear, I could totally take you," Alysia said with humor as she helped Raegan stand.

"You could try," Raegan replied, a smile crossing her face. Her eyes became serious. "We cannot battle each other, Alysia. I have not been as open as I should be. I have my own worries, such as protecting you while keeping my team alive. I should have gone down the chute instead of Mary, I am just thankful her injury is not worse. Losing a team member is soul-crushing, I hope we don't experience it. We must work together to reach the end, or if we don't get out of here, at least we did all we could. Can we agree to at least try?"

"Absolutely. I need you and your tea, Raegan. Not just for

protection, but because I trust you," Alysia said, her feelings washing across her face.

Raegan nodded, then turned and walked back to where the group was huddled. "We are going to settle for a few hours. Grab some sleep if you can, or at least rest. If that was our first test, I am worried about what awaits us. Guard, check and clean your weapons, we cannot afford any jams from all that sand and dust."

CHAPTER 33

Roland and Martha ate as they watched the War Hounds. Neither were hungry but forced food down in case they needed the energy to fight and protect Bethany. Their concern for Bethany's health continued to grow as her vital signs grew further erratic with each passing hour. Thirty-six hours were all that remained to return the dagger to Crimson. No word from Alysia built their anxiety. That, and the creatures watching over them.

The War Hounds remained at their stations, just as the voice said. Christine ventured into the backyard and walked ten feet from the front creature in what could only be called a fit of madness, tempting it to attack her. Its eyeless face followed her every move. When she lifted her weapon, all the beasts screamed, a loud shrill sound.

The storm outside worsened. Rain and wind thrashed the blackened figures, but they did not move, other than their heads. The mist continued to swirl around them as the rain evaporated on their molten bodies, the wind blowing it away like shredded ghosts.

Christine returned to stand watch at the window, a sandwich in her hand. She tossed a slight wave at the other two sitting in their chairs. Like Roland and Mary, she had no appetite, but she stuffed the rest of the peanut butter in, chewing as she tried to breathe through her nose. If those things rushed the house, she would do everything she could to protect her wards, but Christine knew they would all be dead in a matter of minutes. There was no way she could kill them all.

As the three watched the War Hound's lamprey teeth began to whirl, each circle going opposite the other, one ring clockwise, the next counterclockwise. Christine could hear the teeth clattering even through the storm. They sounded like a chainsaw losing its chain.

It was the sound of building carnage.

CHAPTER 34

Alysia admitted the rest was good for her, and for the team. Her sleep had not been dreamless, the clown in the mirror maze returning front and center, but her exhaustion won over, and her brain shut the nightmare down. Awakening, she found everyone was eating and prepping to move on. Alysia reached into her pack and found an energy bar. She completed it in three quick bites. She wanted more as she listened to her stomach growled. Instead, she drank water, worried about their supplies.

As team members stood preparing for their continued march, Alysia took a moment to observe the remarkable structures within the cavern. Formations of flowstone and drapery filled the space, the constant drip of water, a soothing backdrop. The longer she stared at the shapes, the better she felt. In moments of doubt and fear, beauty could still be found. Nature was a healer, its soothing properties giving in to moments of reflection.

She recalled a conversation with her father. They were in the yard, watching her mom plant flowers in the raised beds.

Her father reached down and picked a red rose and handed it to her. The smell was lovely, a heady perfume filling her lungs with its rich scent. They sat on the edge of the raised bed her father next to her with a loving arm around her back.

"It is beautiful, isn't it Alysia? Just like you," his warm smile shining down on her.

"It is daddy. I love it, thank you."

"Take a moment and really observe the flower, Alysia. The shape of its petals, the shades of red. Take a moment to understand the complexities of the organism. Few people take the time to truly observe. This flower is no different than you or me. It might not have a brain, and we do not attribute thought or pain to it, but it is a complex system. From its stem to its stigma, this flower has a purpose. You and I have a purpose. Some might not understand it, just as they do not understand the purpose of the rose. I ask you to take the time to observe instead of just look. See deeper than others. Reach deeper, try to understand what lives, and grows around you. Do the same for those you interact with. Embrace their flaws and see the beauty within."

Raegan's voice of authority drew Alysia out of her memory, saddened to see it disappear.

"All right team, drink as much water as your stomachs can hold, then refill your water bottles in the pools and let's move out," Raegan said as she walked amongst the group checking to make sure they were ready to go. "Martin and Mary did some forward recon. This cavern continues for some time. We need to walk a distance to reach our objective."

Alysia threw her pack over her shoulder and watched the others. The Sovereign Guard looked rested and ready, but even they were dragging butt. Redstone continued to impress her. He was much like the Guard. He appeared tireless, prepared to go, hiding any pains he might have behind his smile, and reassuring words to others on the team. His black hair was now a dull tan from all the dust. He was a valued member to this team, not only because he gave them access to the cave, but he also held a wealth of knowledge that had assisted them tremendously so far.

She looked over to Char. Char was Char. Never needing sleep, it sat in a corner and just watched. It was nerve-racking to fall asleep with it staring at her, but unlike it, she needed rest. Alysia knew Raegan had zero trust for Char and had the demon under twenty-four-hour surveillance by her team.

Alysia searched for Matthew and found him in the corner of the cave, away from everyone. He was as tired as she had ever seen him. Her guilt at dragging him along resurfacing for the two hundredth time since they entered this place. He seemed to be mumbling to himself. Concerned, she called out. "Matthew, are you okay? Need any help? The team is moving out."

Matthew jumped at her voice but regained his demeanor. "Yeah, had to, you know, take care of business. Be right there." His voice still sounding tired even after resting.

"Okay," Alysia shouted back. She failed to see Char's unwavering watch of Matthew's every movement.

THEY PICKED their way through the cavern structures, working to avoid delicate straws of stone reaching up from the floor. Alysia weaved her way around others until she was next to Mary, who was eating an energy bar. "What brings you to these parts, stranger?" Alysia said in her best cowboy drawl. Mary burst into a fit of laughter, bits of half-chewed energy bar flying out of her mouth. Mary took a drink of water, continuing to laugh and choke at the same time.

Alysia patted her on the back, trying to help. "Didn't mean to make you choke on your breakfast, or lunch, or whatever the hell time it is." She paused for a moment gathering her words, "I'm sorry about what happened back there earlier with Raegan. I let my temper slip. I really do appreciate you and the others for protecting us."

"Don't stress about it. This is the shit, and we are in the middle of it. Tempers are going to flare at times, tensions must be released at some point. Raegan is a big girl. She can handle herself better than most I have met." Mary took another bite of her bar.

The two were silent for a few moments, both watching the colors of the cave change as lights touched upon the surfaces. Alysia glanced over at Mary, "What's your thoughts on all this?"

"Got to tell you, this is the weirdest experience I have ever taken part in. I am paid to protect my assets, but this is messed up, I mean, really fucked up. First, I am flying on a helicopter, fighting crunchy demon motherfuckers. And now here I am, journeying through a cavern system no one has ever escaped from. I don't know about you, but every movie I have ever seen shows this will not bode well for any of us."

Alysia agreed. "I have seen those same movies. I'm hoping for an ending with a bit of a miracle, like *Cabin in the Woods*."

"You do remember the giant hand coming out of the earth and smashing them, right?" Mary said through a mouthful of the bar.

"You never actually see the hand smash those teenagers. They might have made it."

"You know, if you had told me when I joined the army at nineteen, I would be searching for a dagger with mystical powers ten years later, I would have laughed. But this is a sight better than being at home, and that is saying something."

"Bad home life?"

"I don't want to say it was bad. My parents love me, I love them. My father had a unique way of punishing me, which I will not delve further into due to our current circumstances. You do not want to see this lady have a panic attack, just saying. Dad punished me far into my teen years. I rebelled and did exactly what my father had told me not to do. I joined the Army. Frankly, the army and I were like two peas in a pod. I discovered I was a natural when it came to weaponry. I trained to become a sniper and became a damn good one, until I also found out I had a conscience. I knew the work I was doing was to protect others, but the thought of killing people placed a heavy burden on my soul." Mary stopped for a moment to take a drink. Alysia did the same.

"One day, I am sighting this lady in, a big-time drug dealer who put kill orders out on at least twenty people. How many others she had already killed no one knew. I am a hair breath away from pulling the trigger when a young boy and girl come running into the bedroom, they had to be twins. I watched through the scope as this lady picked both up and I could see the giant smile on her face. She genuinely loved those kids. I thought about pulling that trigger and the brain matter that would spray across those little kids faces. The trauma it would cause them, years of psychological damage.

Then she turned around to face the window and she must have seen something. A glint of light on my scope, a shadow or something, because she stared directly at me, a look of terror on her face, her eyes pleading. I knew what she did was wrong. I knew what she was selling was killing people back home. I knew she was a ruthless bitch, but I could not pull that trigger. I broke down, my superiors frustrated with my inability to react. I was too be reassigned but Raegan allowed me to leave the game and join a new one, which was fantastic until about forty-eight hours ago." Mary looked up dry eyed, but the pain was visible by the slight quiver in her lips.

"Tell me if it is none of my business, but how exactly did you get tied up in this shit, and I gotta know how you got that badass scar across your face? Seriously, it has to be a great story." Mary asked as they carefully climbed down a flowstone structure of golden brown, trying not to create any more damage than necessary. Both silently wondered why they should care when no other living human would ever set foot within these caverns again. Alysia decided in her own mind it was an acknowledgement that much time had been spent by nature to create these works of art, and it was not her place to destroy such masterpieces.

Alysia's hand reached up and traced the scar on her face, unaware she was doing so as she spoke. Her scar did not embarrass her or lower her self-worth, but she was always conscious of it. Not only because it was right there on her face, unable to be hidden by the best makeup but it constantly burned, never enough to drive her crazy, but enough to remind her it was there. "I wish I had a better back story about this scar than the truth. I received it from the car accident that killed my parents and left me in a coma for six months. I was ten when it happened."

"Oh shit. I am sorry. Your dossier did not provide much of the backstory." Mary said.

Alysia turned to her, "No, it's okay, it was a long time ago." Both grew quiet for a moment, both captured in their own thoughts. "Mary, have you ever felt like what you thought was true was starting to fall apart, and you began to question everything you believed in?"

Mary let the question linger for a moment. It was one she had been thinking about since they entered the cave. "If you asked me before the events at your home, I would have said no.

I am not a religious person by any means. My parents were not churchgoers, but after joining the military and seeing all the death and mayhem in this world, I fell into an agnostic position. Never certain if it's yes or no. The last several hours are making me question what faith is. Where is the good? Shouldn't we be getting help from some angels or something? This battlefield is feeling a little lonely."

"Exactly," Alysia agreed. "You asked how I got here, and I thought I knew, but now, well," Alysia halted and turned fully to Mary. "The Sect trained me to perform what is called transport. Matthew has a power that allows him to identify people infected by a demon presence. I say infected because that is what it is, it's not possession. The demon enters a young child's mind and begins to manipulate the part of us that is evil by nature. I understand we all have evil within us, but most of us balance it with the good we also carry. We might tell a white lie, cheat a little on our taxes, pad our resume, or find the store did not charge us for items under our cart, and we keep them. Most times, it is little bits of evil. Matthew's powers were used when he was younger to identify adults who were unstable, truly terrible individuals, and the Sect of Light would remove them from society. Basically they were trying to balance the equation." Alysia took a breath and released it in a sigh. "When they discovered what I could do, the Sect decided to remove the infection early from the child. Through transport, we discovered it was possible to re-balance the good and evil within the infected child. It was not always successful, but enough to continue to perfect the art."

Alysia stopped talking and drank some water her throat dry from talking so much. But it felt wonderful to talk so openly with Mary.

Mary's head was tilted slightly to her left. "You know that is some crazy shit you just told me, right?"

Alysia smiled at Mary, "You know, you use that phrase a lot?"

Mary's laugh was light. "Yeah, hell yes I do, because this is some crazy shit, and life is filled with crazy shit. It is a strong phrase, but tell me I am wrong?"

"You are not wrong, crazy shit is how we ended up here. I was performing a transport on a young girl named Bethany, whom you have met. Her parents brought her to multiple doctors and psychiatrists. Neighbors reported missing pets for months, and her parents began to wonder if their daughter was the reason. Multiple doctors told the parents their child did not test out on any scale for sociopathic behaviors. She was a perfect angel. Great grades, supportive friends, member of the drill and debate teams. She was just a gem to have in the classroom her teachers would say.

One day her father followed her into a wooded area behind their house. He had seen here journey back into the space multiple times, but when he inquired why she simply told him she was playing. On that day he followed his daughter along the trail deep into the forest. For a moment he lost sight of her but caught the whisper of a dog whimpering. He followed the sound and came into a small clearing amongst the trees. He watched as his daughter tortured and killed the neighbor's new Bichon puppy. You might be asking why the hell he did not stop her? He claims he was frozen, unable to move or even speak. His daughter turned to where he stood behind a tree and smiled, placing a bloody finger to her lips while stripping the dogs' organs from its fresh carcass. Bethany's father claims he could not move or close his eyes, forced to watch as she eviscerated the dog and then his daughter ate its heart."

"Holy shit!" Mary exclaimed.

"Father Tealander visited the hospital she was being kept and found her to glow the brightest reddish-orange he had seen in years. Her evil is righteous in her mind, the demon manipulating her in new ways we do not understand. The Sect convinced her parents that only I could save their daughter. On Monday morning, I completed my first transport to discover who was infecting her. I thought it was Char. It turns out it is a demon called Otrebo. Char was only a messenger. During the transport, my memories meshed with Bethany's and a force accessed my memory monster."

Mary interrupted her, "Memory monster? What the hell is that?"

"It is what I call these memories that want to break free but cannot. I have dreams, wicked dreams that wake me in cold sweats, but I cannot remember them. My memory monster wants to break free of its chains. But at the moment it almost escapes, it shrinks back in fear, because it does not want to be released. I do not know if my subconscious is trying to protect me from truths I cannot yet process. I believe the memories revolve around Santa Cruz, California."

"Why Santa Cruz, did something happen there?"

"I don't know, that is the thing. I remember going on vacation at a young age with my family, but the significance is lost. I have never returned to the boardwalk. A part of me wants to, but each time I decide to face my fear, the memory monster takes hold and pulls me back. What happened in Bethany's transport felt deliberate, as if Crimson were manipulating me."

Mary glanced over to Alysia as she had suddenly stopped speaking. She gave Alysia a few moments before she responded. "I find, sometimes, these feelings are early warning signals. In my training, I was taught to pay attention to those feelings. If I felt I was being followed, watched, or the situation was turning sour, those insights told me to listen and prepare to react. Our brains are much faster at processing data than our other senses are in reacting to the data. Don't ignore what you are feeling, but also, don't dwell on it."

Alysia gave Mary an inquisitive look.

Mary shrugged her shoulders. "Think about it. Suppose you are trying to find your car keys and you are concentrating on where you put them. The more you think about it the more frustrated you become because your brain has stopped everything and is now one hundred percent focused on the keys. Which means, it is accessing those file cabinets and remembering everywhere you have ever set your damn keys. The minute you turn your focus to something else, bam," Mary clapped her hands, startling Alysia, "you remember you left the damn things in your other coat."

Both grew quiet as the cave floor presented new obstacles for them to avoid. These looked like small stone penises, erect at attention. Mary started to giggle like a teenage girl as she stepped over the structures.

"What's funny?" Alysia asked.

"Sorry, I was thinking about these weird stone dicks under us and how embarrassing it would be to die from being impaled by a stone dildo. How would Raegan explain that to Madame?"

Alysia and Mary laughed as they picked their way through the formations, they both needed a moment of ordinary. It would be the last taste of normal for either of them for some time.

CHAPTER 35

R aegan's light caught what appeared to be the end of the large cavern as the passage narrowed, the walls coming together to hem them in. Approaching the narrow path, she shone her light through. It was manageable without removing packs. She couldn't see a ceiling. It was a deep chasm with them at the bottom. She moved her light along the walls. A sudden movement drew her light back. Raegan continued to stare into the dark chasm above her, seeking what had drawn her attention. Her light glinted off thin strands' way above, too far to see clearly. She lowered her light after a few moments, sure it was her mind playing tricks in the tight space.

Raegan was growing weary of being on point but felt it necessary. She was concerned they had missed something along the way. No new challenges presented themselves. Either they missed another cave opening, or the shit was going to hit the fan, and soon. She lined the team up, with Mary taking the rear. Raegan was not claustrophobic, but this tight rift was not increasing her comfort. An attack within the confines of this space would be disastrous, their bones left to disintegrate over time into the sandy ground the team traveled through. At one point, the team was forced to lie on their stomachs and belly crawl for at least fifty feet due to an ancient rockfall that filled the gap above. The larger stones lodged lower in the rift, holding back the rockslide from closing the crack completely. Raegan could not stop thinking about the millions of tons of rock resting on the larger boulders scratching against her back.

Crawling from under the tightest squeeze, Raegan stood and stretched, waiting on the rest of the team. Her focus was on assisting the others to their feet, so she completely missed Redstone stepping behind her and shining his light into the next chamber.

"Oh hell," Redstone's voice echoed. His baritone an octave higher and filled with dread.

"Oh hell, what?" Raegan asked as she finished helping Mary to her feet and turned to see what Redstone was concerned about.

Redstone stepped forward, staring into the massive hall. Strands ran from the cavern floor to what he assumed was the ceiling which was not visible. The same tethers were attached from wall to wall, parallel, perpendicular, at all angles. He turned to the rest of the group, "Don't touch those lines."

Mary stumbled backward with a look of pure horror on her face, "Tell me that is not a spider web, please tell me it is not. I am not getting devoured by some Shelob *Lord of the Rings* spider in here. I hate spiders, I mean fucking hate them!"

A faint sound of scurrying filtered from above. Redstone recognized this sound as millions of tiny legs walking over and through each other. He had heard this same sound when he traveled to Africa to witness the migration of Siafu Ants, also known as Driver Ants. The colony consisted of nearly fifty million ants, and as they moved across the ground, the same sheeshing noise was made. It was unnerving, no way to explain the chills it presented up your back. He was getting those same chills now. "Martin, any juice left in that high-powered flashlight of yours?"

Martin removed his pack and reached inside, grabbing the powerful light. He handed it to Redstone, who pointed it into the darkness. Hundreds of thousands of giant spiders were moving across the ceiling. Hanging among the moving mass were cocoons which could only be other spiders. Redstone knew of spiders turning cannibal when food supplies were short. Every square inch of the ceiling was covered in arachnids. From leg tip to leg tip, they were the size of a soccer ball, abdomen mustard brown, and after his light left them, they glowed with an eerie green iridescence. Adding to their terrifying appearance were two large red fangs.

"You have to be joking," Mary's hands tightened on her weapon as she stared at the ceiling. If she had not recently relieved herself, she was sure a waterfall would be running down her leg right now.

"Why aren't they attacking us?" Alysia asked.

"Why would you ask that?" Mary quipped back.

Redstone continued to stare up at the massive horde. "I'm guessing we are not a threat, and we are not food as we have not triggered their web yet. They are probably sightless and most likely unable to hear, using other senses to capture their prey in the dark." Redstone found himself lapsing into the professor roll, standing before the lecture hall, "These appear to be a member of the *Califorctenus* species or the Sierra Cacachilas wandering spider. They were not discovered until 2017 in an abandoned mine. Of course, those are only the size of a softball."

"A goddamn softball, and those are out in the real world? Once again, professor, thank you for scaring the living shit out of me," Mary said through gritted teeth.

Alysia's neck was kinking from the constant staring upward, but she could not take her eyes off the shifting horde. "Are they venomous?"

"The recently discovered species is not, its bite more akin to being poked by a cactus, a little inflammation of the skin, and mild irritation. These I do not know, but would it even matter if several thousand were to ascend upon us?" He turned to look at Alysia.

"*Thread cut bare blade of knife, perform hastily will cost your life*," Father Tealander said as he stared upwards.

"What?" Raegan asked.

"That is what was written on the pages of the hologram. The cavern of lines," Tealander said, his head drifting down to look at Raegan.

"We do not want to cut these strands, and we most definitely do not want to touch them but we need to get to the other side. How the hell do we do that?" Alysia asked.

"Carefully," Raegan responded. "Take off all hats or gear which could accidentally touch one of the threads. We cannot afford any accidents. Guard, be ready in case we need to go on the offense. Hopefully, if we are careful, we can avoid a confrontation. Let's break into two teams, Alysia, Father Tealander, and Redstone, you are with me. Martin, Mary, and Char, you come up behind us, watch our six."

"Better idea, how about I hang back here, make some coffee, and when you all find the dagger, I will be waiting for you with something warm to drink," Mary said, continuing to stare into the luminescent moving bodies.

"You could be here a while, as the way is shut, the dead keep it," Martin said as he made a fist and hit her shoulder.

"Damn your movie quotes, Martin." Mary looked down, rubbing her shoulder.

"Hey, you brought up Shelob first, I simply rode in on your coattails."

Raegan navigated through the maze of webbing. She felt like a cat burglar avoiding a laser system in a museum or bank, except a mistake here would turn her into lunch. She ducked, belly crawled, rolled, and shimmied on her back. Turning, she watched as the other team members followed suit. Her light caught the opposite wall, a hundred or so feet away, still a ways to travel.

Mary's eyes watched above, looking for any behavior change. Her light was not bright enough to see the moving masses, but if they stayed up there away from her and she could not see them, she might make it out of this chamber sane.

Alysia traveled with Matthew. She took his hand and guided him through the maze. Helping him to get back up when crawling on hands and knees or belly crawling was necessary. His hands trembled from exhaustion, and although he would not admit it, she knew he was in tremendous pain. Each time he had to get down or back up, it was slower than the time before. Redstone followed Matthew, helping him from behind when he could.

Char brought up the rear. Its eyes could see the massive organism above, at least three deep, many more of these creatures than the rest of the team realized. It was not worried. Char had seen much bigger spiders in Jarapenth, and their fangs were the size of elephant tusks. Still, it did not want to find out what these were capable of doing. As it shimmied on its belly under a particularly low strand of filament, one of its horns caught the silk thread. With a loud twang, the strand snapped, the noise echoing throughout the chamber. Char halted mid-belly crawl.

Martin was belly crawling in front of Char when he heard

the loud snap. "What was that?" he exclaimed, turning his head to see behind him.

"Martin," Char growled, "we have a problem."

Nearing the end of the spiderweb maze Raegan's enthusiasm was growing. Her team was thirty feet from the exit of the cave, and the spiders remained above. When she heard the snap and the change in noise from above her confidence fell to the pit of her stomach. Caught in the middle of her own belly crawl, she twisted to flash her light upwards. She witnessed hundreds of spiders marching down the filaments towards their prey while others dropped from strands attached to the ceiling. "Oh my god," she exclaimed under her breath. The sheer number of arachnids descending could not be processed in her brain. Their milky eyes and red fangs shining in the light of her flashlight were terrifying. The first landed on the ground scurrying towards her team, its size more significant than it appeared from a distance. They were built for maximum damage. More struck the floor and scurried towards Matthew. Raegan found her voice and yelled, "They are coming!"

MATTHEW PANICKED as the scurrying soccer balls with fangs rushed towards him. He leapt from the floor and tried to run forward. He had no desire to be a portable smorgasbord. His tired body tried to force its way through the sticky strands but with each movement it sent silent shockwaves through the web further exciting the beasts above. Matthew, unable to free himself, called out to Alysia in front of him. Alysia rushed to Matthew's side and went on the attack, thrusting her knife forward, piercing the arachnid climbing down the filaments toward Matthew. It popped like a massive zit. Its insides bursting in a greenish-brown goo, entering Mathew's open mouth and covering his face in the thick slop of the spider's insides. "Holy hell, that is disgusting!" he cried as he tried to spit the sticky mess out.

Alysia could hear the cries of her friends as gunfire filled the cavern with a deafening roar. She cut Matthew free of the webbing and moved towards Raegan, who was firing into the air. Spider parts and bodies fell like hail from the ceiling, hitting the floor with loud splats, turning a chaotic scene even worse as the floor became as slick as an ice rink.

Behind Raegan's group, the bedlam intensified. They were stuck in the middle of the cave, creepy crawlies approached from all sides and from above.

Mary's nightmare became a reality. Time slowed, noises became muffled. Fight or flight left her standing still, eyes wide, watching the massacre around her. Only ten feet away but sounding a million miles from her, Martin yelled as he opened fire into the dropping swarm. The memory of the cedar chest, the punishment chest, filled her with dread. The wolf spider was closed in with her by accident. She pounded her fists on the locked top, desperate screams to be freed. The spider frightened by her fear, scurried to escape. It crawled up her side, its eight legs resting on her chest in the tight quarters. She did not realize it was terrified for its own life, frozen in its own tiny fear. It did not move. They were both frozen in time, staring each other down. Neither moved for hours, her eyes becoming dry from not blinking. When the chest opened, her father found her and the spider in the same position, both wrapped in a blanket of terror, afraid to move. Her father reached in and removed the spider, but not her. She would never forgive him.

Mary was thrown from memory as time-warped ahead the sounds of gunfire and screams crashed against her eardrum, a sonic boom in her moment of silence. Spiders surrounded her, trying to separate her from the group She was easier pickings.

She turned and fired to the front, her bullets tearing through soft bodies, screaming at the top of her lungs as spiders exploded in masses. Behind her, Martin and Char were fighting a wave of spiders. The sound of gunfire peppered the cave, ricocheting back and forth off the walls. Mary was surprised no one had been shot by the friendly fire occurring all around. She thought being shot right now might be the best thing to happen to her but only if it was a headshot. She did not want to be wrapped in a cocoon and drained.

Mary heard Martin gasp in pain as a spider bit into his leg, its red fangs gnawing into his flesh. She watched as he stepped down on it with his other foot, squashing it, the entire time continuing to fire into the river of movement. Spiders were everywhere. An army of eight-legged soldiers crawling over the backs of the dead and the living to reach a meal.

Martin moved toward Mary's position pressing his back to her. Char joined them to create a circle, making sure its body did not touch theirs. Burning them would not assist the current situation. They moved as one towards Raegan, circling and firing, Char igniting the mass as they touched the demon's smoldering body. They were going to run out of ammunition well before they killed all these fuckers, Martin thought as he slapped in a new clip.

As Martin and his team fought to reach the front, Alysia, Tealander, and Redstone reached Raegan and were firing their weapons into the bore of forward-moving creatures, trying to clear a path for the others. Father Tealander used his knife to stab the spiders as they approached. His weapon was lost when he became entangled in the web. The spiders hauled Matthew's gun to the ceiling, beyond their reach. Tealander became overwhelmed, covered in a pile of legs, crying out in pain as their red fangs stabbed into his exposed arms. Raegan dropped her gun as she turned with her knife and hacked at the soft bodies, Alysia and Redstone covering her. The bodies of the arachnids were hairless, smooth, and slimy, like a slug. Her knife pierced their squishy bodies, each one an explosion of guts and ooze, releasing a smell almost equal to the odiferous Char. She cleared the spiders from Tealander and pushed him forcefully towards the exit. She heard him fall to the floor with an oof. She did not have time to check if he was okay as the spider horde pressed forward relentlessly.

Raegan reached down to pick up her weapon and continued firing into the never-ending wave of teeth. The damn things darted across the ground with unusual grace. "Mother-fucker," she cried out as one fell from the ceiling and bit into her back. Reaching behind her, she grabbed it by one of its legs and pulled it around. She squeezed it between her hands, its legs frantically scratching her to escape. It ruptured in a tremendous pop releasing its warm insides all over her hands. Spider innards as slick as vegetable oil was making it extremely difficult to hold her weapon. She glanced up from the merciless wave of creatures to see where the rest of her team was in relation to her position.

Martin rallied his small group, moving them across the slippery floor and the constant riptide of spindly legs working to swallow them. As the damn things continued to drop on them, Mary fired upwards while Martin and Char worked to clear a path.

Mary fell to her knees as one of the arachnids launched itself at her and bit into her chest. Great, they could jump as well? These suits could stop a bullet, but these fuckers' fangs could pierce it like butter. Her chest burned as the spider chewed into her flesh. She slapped the creature with an open palm. The spider ruptured and fell to the ground.

Martin reached down and yanked Mary up, "Keep moving, god damn it!" He propelled her forward and shoved Char along. His body was hurting from the hundreds of spider bites, as well as the continued kickback from his weapon. Christ, they were going to die in here. Martin drove forward, kicking spiders, stepping on the bastards, shooting them, screaming at them, basically anything that caused the little shits pain. They were almost to the forward group when he saw Alysia fall in front of him. Neither Raegan nor Redstone saw her fall as they were covering their own asses.

Martin yelled into his mic, "Raegan, Alysia is down, the asset is down!"

ALYSIA WAS ASSISTING Tealander when she stepped backward and tumbled over a small mountain of dead spiders. As soon as her back hit the ground, she felt her feet wrapped like a Christmas present. A small army of spiders hauled her away from the group. Alysia screamed for help as she was lifted into the air, hoisted towards the ceiling. She tried lifting herself up to cut the webbing with her knife but was too exhausted, scolding herself for all the hours spent working out. Below her, the two teams rejoined, firing into the converging mass of quivering bodies.

"They have Alysia," Martin called out again over the rustling of legs, gun chatter, and general mayhem around the team.

Redstone shined the powerful light towards the ceiling and saw Alysia quickly approaching the swarming mass of bodies. How the hell could there still be so many of them? They were working well together, like ants, a coordinated team to take down prey. Redstone was scared shitless and at the same time, he could not stop watching the way they moved. Everyone thought it was a mindless mass of flesh moving in the cave, but he saw their patterns, their ability to quickly adjust to changing situations. They were working within a hive mind.

"Shoot her down," he called out, watching Alysia squirming in her wrapping, trying to free herself.

"I could end up fucking hitting her. The damn fall alone will kill her," Mary called out.

"They are going to kill her if you don't. Shoot her down," Redstone demanded enunciating each word.

"Mary, get her down from there," Raegan cried out over flailing spider bodies.

Mary pulled her aim towards the thread holding Alysia and fired. Spiders exploded on the ceiling sending a rain of muck onto the team below. "God damn it," Mary screamed, took a breath, and fired again, this time hitting the thread. Alysia fell, but Redstone was ready and broke her fall. He quickly untangled her by slicing through the sticky strands, then lifted her up and carried her to the group.

"I am running out of ammunition," Martin called out. The spiders' advances did not slow, continuing the onslaught, rushing over the bodies of the dead, wave after wave, with a desire for sustenance.

The tide forced the team against the wall, the exit a taunting dream directly to their right. To turn their backs and run would be signing thier death warrant. Knifes stabbed outward and down, the last remaining clips mowed hundreds of soft bodies, only to be replaced by hundreds more. The shouts of pain from the continuous bites had grown quiet. They were weary of wasting much-needed breath. Alysia heard the empty click of weapons. The team had nowhere to go. The spiders quickly overpowered them stopping any attempts of the team being able to protect themselves, forcing them to their knees. Weight crushing, fangs piercing spiders everywhere.

Alysia was pulled under the tide. She had failed her team,

Bethany, and herself. The bites of a thousand fangs pierced her skin, needles pushing through tender flesh. The spiders, sensing victory, piled onto the squirming mass, their spinnerets throwing thread, working to contain a meal to sustain them for a short time.

Alysia felt the heavy carpet lift, peering to her right, she saw Char stand, spiders igniting around the demon. It released a high-pitched wail. Alysia was sure her own brains were going to rupture and leak from her ears as Char's pitch intensified. The spiders stopped their assault and ran, tripping and falling over themselves. They shuddered and danced across the floor. As one, hundreds of bodies seized and splattered. Guts flew in all directions, slathering the team in a thick sticky soup. Char closed its mouth. The remaining spiders scurried up the sides of the walls to escape.

"Damn it, Char, why didn't you do that at the beginning?" Mary said as she wiped the smelly mess from her face. Her body, and all those around her, a pincushion of bite marks.

"I didn't know I could. I felt it rise in me. It just happened," Char responded as it looked at the battered team.

"Well, thank Christ it did," Raegan said as she assessed the damage. The ammunition was dry. Their only protection would be hand to hand and knives moving forward. She was amazed everyone was still intact. Bruised, bloodied, and battered, but alive. The odds of survival decreased with each encounter. Raegan hoped the Kalama Dagger was worth it.

"Let's get the hell out of this cavern before they decide to come back." She led the battle-weary team through the exit and into the following passage. The group followed, dragging their damaged bodies through the opening, silent prayers raised, hoping they were not going from the frying pan into the fire.

CHAPTER 36

"We are going to provide no assistance?" Madame asked the shadow figure. "We know the enemy has a force awaiting Alysia and her team should she acquire the dagger. How can we ignore this information?"

The gritty voice replied from its darkened corner, "We cannot intervene, it is vital Alysia and her group, works this out on their own. Our involvement will come later."

She shook her head in frustration, her hands falling to the desk like a bird shot down from the sky. "That is if they make it out of the cavern with the dagger. We have received no updates as to their progress. The minute they entered the cave, and it sealed, we lost all ability to communicate with them. What if they survive but are too weak to defend themselves?"

"It is all part of the risks they assumed when they began the search. It was not forced upon them. They decided to take on this quest themselves."

Madame stood in frustration and moved to the window. "Of course they did, because we scared the living shit out of them by sharing the stories of our true creation and the upcoming storm. What did you expect them to do, cower, run away?"

"I did not know what to expect," for once, the voice sounding unsure of itself, "I find your kind interesting, your willingness to sacrifice for a perceived greater good. Alysia does not even know what these objects signify yet, or the power they possess. Still, she went into harm's way, dragging friends into danger. I continue to be intrigued."

"Glad we can be of amusement to you," Madame responded sardonically.

The creature laughed. She despised it when it did, the sound jarring.

"You are not amusement. You are more like pieces to a large puzzle. Your kind thinks of themselves as the great inventors, tamers of nature, builders of empires. Still, you have not come to realize humanity is simply only a piece of a larger, grander scheme," the shadow speculated with further delight.

Madame was growing weary of its bullshit. She turned from the window and took a step toward the shadow, her ire raised. "Yet here you need our kind, the table scraps, to locate the dagger for you and yours. Interesting, wouldn't you say?"

"If two children had not decided thousands of years ago to go against their creator's wishes, we would not have needed your kind for anything. Their insolence and hiding of the artifacts created ripples the two could not understand. Furthermore, if Alysia's parents had left the scrolls where they were hidden, we wouldn't be in this situation. Both sides would have stayed oblivious, and we could have avoided this for a few more millennia," its voice rising in frustration. "But," the shadow breathed deep, calming its presence, "it is true your partnership is needed at this time, and as we agreed, your kind will be spared in the great war, as long as our agreement is met."

Madame pondered the agreement quietly. She wondered,

sometimes deep into the night, if the Sect of Light had part-nered with the right side. She supposed they would not know until near the end. And even if the right choice had been made who was to say these greater powers would hold up their end of any agreement? Why should they? A simple flick and the Earth could careen into the sun. Humans were not even ants to them. And what of Alysia and her gifts? She was an active piece on the chessboard, a powerful one neither side understood. Madame believed both sides considered Alysia to be no more than a pawn. However, Madame was starting to feel Alysia might be the queen. Alysia the wildcard. She was young, strong-willed, and determined. The dagger was just a test, the real work would begin in the location and acquisition of the other artifacts. If she survived.

Madame turned to ask the shadow its thoughts on Alysia and her future roles in their success but only the sound of empty space reached her ears. Once again, she stood alone.

CHAPTER 37

Alysia knew she was still in shock, as were the others. She even saw Martin shaking from head to toe as the thrill of the battle wore off and shock took over. It was like watching a mountain rumble. After a brief rest everyone tried to clean up as best as possible, but the grit and grime of the cave, sand, and sticky offal from the spiders left the team itching and uncomfortable. Mary said it best, she had more sand down her crack than a towel on a nudist beach.

The team trudged forward, weary and beaten. Each quietly fearing what the next task would force them to do, or what terrors they might have to battle. The soft floor of the cave did not help with their exhaustion. Feet slipped into loose sand like old slippers. Each lift sent little puffs of dust and silicon into the air, making it difficult to catch a deep breath.

Raegan turned to monitor the team, feeling concerned that Alysia and Tealander were falling farther behind with each step. This entire situation was totally FUBAR, fucked up beyond all recognition! Her team was ill-prepared to protect the assets under the current circumstances. Put her team in the real world, actual events, she would bet her life on their success. Her team was trained for almost every contingency. Except the nightmares of the past few days. How does one prepare for millions of soccer balls with teeth flanking and trying to eat you? She was even more pissed that she had been saved by the demon yet a second time. She felt her face grow flush with anger and embarrassment. She needed to take a moment. The team needed a moment. She called out for a twenty and placed Martin on watch.

Everyone groaned as they sat down with their backs against the cool walls of the passage. Bite marks itched and burned red. Some were seeing slight reactions to the spider bites including mild headaches, dizziness, and small pimple like pustules around a few of the worst chew marks. But it was the itching that was driving them all mad. The itch was deep like the ones you got in the palm of your hand. Sometimes you just wanted to bite the flesh off to get to the damn itch. Raegan encouraged people to eat and drink, but no one had the energy to dig through their packs to locate sustenance. Several team members lost their bags during the battle, which meant that supplies would run thin if they were stuck down here for too long. So far, the only win was Martin locating six clips of ammunition in his pack, which the SG distributed amongst themselves. It would be their last-ditch effort.

The twenty-minute rest ended faster than most of the team wished. Alysia and Mary helped Matthew to his feet, his old bones creaking and cracking as he stood. His face was puffy from spider bites and Alysia was unsure how much farther Matthew could go. Her stress and worry for him showed as Matthew grabbed her hand, squeezed it reassuringly, and shuffled forward, following the team.

Mary took the lead while Raegan monitored the team, moving from person to person, checking hydration and pain levels. This passage was just one round tunnel much like at the beginning, almost perfect with no cracks, crevices or pock- marks, just smooth dark red sandstone. This was okay by Raegan. It meant nowhere for beasties to hide. The group stum- bled through the extended passage in silence until Mary called a halt. Raegan worked her way to the front, leaving Martin to watch their backs.

CHAPTER 38

"New chamber," Mary said as Raegan approached.

Raegan and Mary shined their lights into the open cavern. This was the smallest of the spaces they had encountered so far. The walls were about fifteen feet in height the ceiling showing a slight curve in the middle. At the front of the cave, their lights captured two large stones sitting side by side.

"Why are there rows of holes in the floor?" Mary hesitantly asked as her light followed a row to the opposite wall. The holes were spaced maybe four inches apart, and each hole was perhaps a quarter inch in diameter. Each row was spaced about two feet from each other. The rows continued to the front of the cave, going around the two stones.

Redstone came up from behind and moved beside Mary and Raegan. "Perhaps another sand trap, like the first puzzle? Although these holes seem too small in diameter for that purpose."

"My guess is, no damn good is what those holes represent," Mary lamented, reaching down to run her hand across a row.

Raegan guided the team into the chamber, warning

everyone to touch nothing. Alysia approached the front and the two stones. Each stone was six-sided and stood three feet high with a circumference of six feet. A funnel-like hole in the middle of each stone radiated six grooves extending out to the six equal square sides. They had seen these on the petroglyph picture. On the wall to the left of the stones was a shelf holding six glass vessels, within each container a colorless liquid-filled halfway. The right wall had six holes, each aligned with one of the vessels on the other side. She returned to the others in the middle of the room.

Alysia stepped into the beginnings of a conversation with Raegan and Matthew. Raegan was asking Father Tealander if there was any riddle or phrase that went with this cavern, and he was flipping through the notebook as he could not bring it up from memory.

"Yes, here it is, *wheel cannot exchange, start from beginning, mornings change*. It is the phrase associated with the two stones upfront, I am sure it is the correct one. Father Tealander said as he pointed to the words.

Raegan was hesitant to begin this test without some much-needed rest. At the same time, the spiders were still behind them, which concerned her. How long would they stay within their space knowing a free meal was simply down the passage? How long would their fear of Char hold them back? They were low on food and water and the last set of batteries had been distributed to keep the lights on. If they failed to find the dagger soon, they would be up shit creek without a paddle.

Raegan let her stress go by stretching tall, then bending from the waist and touching her toes. Her entire body complained as she felt the bites reopen, releasing blood and pus to leak down her body. She was so covered in mire and things she dared not think about that the thought of her own bodily fluids mixing in did not phase her in the least. But the very act of forcing her body to flex made her feel better mentally. "Okay, let's all take a few moments to decompress and think about what this means. We cannot afford to make the same mistake we made in the sand room."

Alysia was to wound up to sit. Time was slipping by. She feared they would not retrieve the dagger in time, if at all. Bethany's condition weighed heavily on her mind as she wandered the cavern finding herself back in front of the vessels sitting on the shelf. She reached out to touch one of the vessels, and as her hands approached the glass, she saw a faint glow begin within the liquid. She noted the longer her hands stayed in front of the jar, the brighter the color became. As her hands moved away from the glass vessels, the light would dissipate and then disappear. She moved from vessel to vessel. The first vessel glowed yellow, then in sequence, amber, orange, vermillion, red, and magenta.

"What did you find?" Martin asked from behind her, his bass voice close to her ear.

Alysia jumped. Startled, her voice came out louder than she meant. "You scared the hell out of me."

Martin took a step back. "Sorry about that, what is going on with these newfound curiosities?"

"I don't know but they appear to change colors due to body heat." Alysia continued moving from vessel to vessel, enchanted by their singular beauty, the colors vibrant in the dark cave. Next to her, Martin placed his hands next to a container expecting the same reaction, but the liquid did not change color for him. Thinking only one vessel could be affected at a time, Alysia stepped away and let Martin try again. The colors refused to surface for Martin.

"Huh, maybe I just don't generate enough heat. My mom always said I had cold hands."

"They say cold hands mean a warm heart," Alysia said as

she continued to move from vessel to vessel enraptured by the intensity of their glow.

"If you are a lizard, I guess that might be true," Martin joked as he tried to heat his hands by rubbing them on his destroyed pants. He tried again and was becoming frustrated that he could not make the vessels react. First the stone and books, now this. He was beginning to feel like the Hawkeye of the Sovereign Guard.

He could not understand why certain things did or did not affect Alysia. The journals were one, but what about the Demon's Ink or these vessels? He admitted he did not trust people as a glass-half-empty kind of guy. She seemed like a hell of a great person, determined, and frankly fearless, but Martin sensed something darker about this young lady. He did not feel she was manipulating things, nor did he believe she was hiding information from them. She seemed as surprised as they all were with what was happening. Martin still sensed a darker presence, just underneath the surface of Alysia, a beast being contained. He had spoken quietly to Raegan about his concerns, but she told him it was his heightened sense of paranoia. She might be right.

Martin and Alysia continued to experiment with distance and length of time to bring the vessels to full brightness. Well, Martin watched and mentally noted time, his hands still unable to create the reaction. In contrast, over next to the wall with the six holes aligned to the vessels Alysia was testing Mary sat cleaning her weapon preparing for the next unholy nightmare they might encounter. Her cleaning was being distracted by what appeared to be different colored lights shining through the holes above her. Her gaze turned toward the ceiling when a solid rod radiating purple shot out from the hole above her, barely missing the backside of her head.

"What the hell," she exclaimed as she jumped from a sitting

position to standing in one swift motion. The purple rod disappeared back into the stone wall.

"What's going on over there, Mary?" Raegan turned to see what Mary was reacting to.

"Nobody else saw that. It could have killed me!" Mary's hands swept across the holes to see if rods were motion controlled.

Raegan walked over, "Mary, what are you talking about?"

"I was sitting here cleaning my useless weapon when a purple rod shot out of that hole. If I had been standing in front of it, the damn thing would have impaled me."

Raegan grabbed a light from her belt and shined it at the hole. She could see nothing out of the ordinary. Just as she was about to give Mary a whole ration of shit, a rod of vibrant green burst out another hole."

"Whoa," the two said in tandem. Watching the green rod grow more brilliant in color the longer it protruded from the hole. Neither were brave enough to touch the glowing material, too concerned it could start another sandstorm or release unknown creatures.

Their gaze turned to Martin and Alysia. Alysia's hands were hovering next to a vessel glowing a brilliant red, while the rod next to them continued to shine a bright green.

"Keep your hand next to that vessel, Alysia," Mary called out. "Martin, you're the mineral and gem guy, can you come over here for a moment?"

Martin left Alysia and navigated around the two stones separating them.

He recognized the rod was made from Beryl, or in this case, emerald. "I'll be damned," he exclaimed, "Alysia, move your hand over another vessel."

Alysia moved her hands over the vessel containing the fluid that glowed orange when heated, and as it burned bright, a blue rod protruded from the wall as the green rod slid back. "Corundum, or as you might know it, sapphires," Martin said as he examined the new material. "I have never seen minerals used this way. Their facets are too fragile. This is absolutely amazing. Some form of a chemical reaction is occurring, one mineral is affecting the other. It could be the vessels are a liquid variant of minerals which might be reacting to the minerals within the rods."

Martin watched the blue mineral glow and shimmer while a wild thought ran through his head. Red to green, orange to blue. Could he have the answer to one of these damn riddles? Maybe he could show the team some of his brains instead of just the brawn.

"Father Tealander, can I borrow your notepad?" he asked as he walked back to the middle of the room. "I think the first part of the phrase is referring to a color wheel."

"What makes you think it's a color wheel?" Tealander asked, sitting up.

"I dated a painter a few years back. She was fascinated with color theory. She spent hours fretting over the right colors for everything. We stood in a paint store for three hours once, just reviewing three tones of orange." Martin took pen to paper and began to draw as he spoke. "Anyway, I ended up learning a little along the way," on the paper he drew a circle and divided it into twelve pie wedges, "the wheel consists of twelve pie slices. Each slice represents either a primary, secondary, or tertiary color. Primary colors are located on the wheel at what I call the threes, between each sit one secondary and two tertiaries. The secondary is always directly across from a primary on the wheel. Between the primary and secondary lies a tertiary until the wheel is filled. Colors directly across from each other are complementary of each other so, yellow|purple, amber|violet, orange|blue, vermillion|teal, red|green, magenta|chartreuse. These colors comprise the twelve colors of the wheel" He turned the diagram around for everyone to see, "*wheel cannot exchange,* because they are compliments."

"I thought the color wheel did not come about until Isaac Newton discovered the spectrum?" Alysia said.

Martin turned to Alysia, his eyebrows raised. "That is some impressive recall. Physics class?"

"Netflix special on the controversy of color theory," Alysia quipped.

"Everything has to be a controversy today," Martin exclaimed as he continued to point at the wheel he had drawn. "That does not mean artists did not understand the power of color well before Newton. One only needs to look at ancient cave drawings or the Egyptians to realize color was a powerful medium before we understood the science behind them. Ancient civilizations understood how color affected people."

Alysia was interested but more interested as to how the two were affecting each other. "How are the vessels affecting the rods?" she asked Martin.

"I have no idea, but the vessels are activating their compliment." Martin stood up and moved towards the stones. "These two stones have six sides, twelve in total, completing the color wheel. My guess, the liquids mixed with the minerals will create some form of reaction. The question is, where do we start on the wheel?"

"I'm sorry, what do you mean where do we start? Don't we just start at the top and then move around the wheel clockwise?" Alysia said as she stood facing the two giant stones.

Martin put the color wheel drawing down, stood, and returned his entire focus to the stones that Alysia was standing in front of. "I don't think it is going to be that easy. There are two theories on the placement of colors within the color wheel. One believes yellow tones are followed by green tones. The other theory believes yellow tones are followed by orange tones. Which theory are these stones based upon? We also need to remember there are also two more parts to what Father Tealander told us, *start from beginning, mornings change.*"

"We have learned from past riddles that mistakes can be costly. One wrong answer and we are left scrambling to survive," Raegan said as she clapped her hands together twice. "I know time is growing short so any ideas or thoughts would be appreciated. To be honest, my brain is kind of mush right now. The side effects from the spider bites are not helping."

After a few moments of rumination, Alysia spoke. "Martin, you believe this riddle is based on color theory and color compliments. What if the meaning of the second part of the riddle *start from beginning* is a literal translation, start back at the beginning of the cave. Have we seen complementary colors within the cavern?"

"Red, there's a lot of red," Char's gravelly voice echoed in the chamber.

Alysia nodded in agreement. "Yes, but there was no green anywhere, which is reds compliment."

Mary blurted out excitedly, "How about those blood-sucking flowers, those carnivorous aholes!" Her arm shot out, showing the missing part of her finger. "The flowers were orange and the weird stuff glowing around them was blue. Martin's color wheel identifies them as complimentary." Mary bobbed her head in excitement. "By the way, this still hurts, should anyone care." Holding her hand up for everyone to see.

"Cry me a river. We can compare wounds later," Martin replied. "I think Mary's idea is worth a try. Now, if these two stones represent the color wheel, where do we start? And what is the penalty if we are wrong?"

Each task or riddle seemed escalated, becoming more complex, more deadly. It was only fair to reason a wrong move here would have serious consequences. Alysia looked around at the team members realizing they had never felt closer, even the new members from the Sovereign Guard. For the first time, she understood how combat must bring brothers and sisters together in a hard-to-break bond. Together they had come this far. She hoped by the end of this, they would all still be standing. And what were their destinies after they acquired the Kalama Dagger, well, if they found the dagger. Could she just hand over an artifact so well protected to Crimson to save the life of a child or the lives of a few children? There was a reason for the perils they survived. The children of Ka and Akh would not have taken such care if the dagger had only a little value. Yet, Crimson was one of those children and worked with Kalama to spread Ka and Akh's powers to disrupt their conquest. Was Crimson evil or working for balance?

She had huge doubts Crimson stood for anything good. Its actions and threats were proof enough, but what if the creature knew no other way? And what about the other five artifacts? Was the Sect of Light going to ignore five other objects of power?

No, this was just the beginning, if they survived, she was sure she would be involved with discovering the locations of the others. Somehow, she was bound to this, an integral part, something she could not understand. It indeed appeared her parents were aware or drawn into this madness by discovering Crimson's Book. Her life revolved around her parent's discovery. Of this, she was sure. Whatever the outcome, she was happy she was connected to those in this cavern.

Alysia spoke quietly, her voice barely a whisper in the cavern. "Team, I know time is not on our side, but I cannot afford to lose any of you, so, lets be certain we make the right decisions with this puzzle. I must admit, I am as baffled as Raegan at this point. I'm pretty well drained of inspiration. But sometimes I find if you concentrate on something other than the challenge at hand, the answers will come to you, right Mary?" Alysia looked over and saw Mary return her smile. "Let's take a moment to write down which vessels affect which rod, so we can move quickly when the time comes."

The team agreed and separated to begin documenting the vessels affects. Alysia moved her hands over the vessels, Mary and Martin recorded the colors, placing them in order on the drawing of the wheel, numbering the vessels and the holes on the paper. While Alysia worked the vessels, she watched Redstone and Father Tealander talking together away from the group. Tealander kept touching Redstone's arm as he talked. At one point, the conversation became tense, but it seemed to calm down quickly. The meeting ended with Redstone patting Father Tealander's shoulder and glancing over at Alysia. *Wonder what that is about?* she thought.

Once the colors were documented, Father Tealander called for everyone to regroup. Alysia could not remember when he seemed frailer. His body was hunched over, barely holding himself up. His palsy made his hands tremble uncontrollably, even as he rubbed them together. "I think I understand the meaning of the last phrase. I believe it refers to the parchment. I cannot be one hundred percent certain, but I believe *mornings change* refers to the rising of the sun. If we look at the two stones, my guess would be the vessel is poured in the east while the rod is placed in the west. The liquid flows through the groove, into the funnel and somehow interacts with the rod placed within the groove of the other stone."

Excited chatter filled the air as the team celebrated what they hoped was the last key to the puzzle. Char tried to share in their excitement, but it was an emotion the demon could no longer understand. Standing to the side and wanting to be a part of their discovered joy, it realized it would never again be able to feel that way. Nor would it ever truly be an accepted part of this group. The demon understood disappointment, its foundation was built upon it, along with fear, pain, terror, and rejection. It knew they appreciated its sacrifices, but no amount of sacrifice could cover the scars of its past or its present. Redemption was nothing but a selfish dream, unobtainable.

Char was pulled from its despair by a distant sound coming from the passage they had exited. A demon's hearing was exceptional, made that way to absorb the cries of pain from their brethren, the anguish of others added to their own. It rushed back towards the entrance, no longer focusing on the excitement behind it but the increasing rustling ahead of it. Arriving at the opening to the passage, it concentrated and recognized the sound. It was the same sound that had filled the spiders' cave. The arachnids were on the move, and they were coming in full force.

Char turned towards the group and growled, "The spiders are coming. And when I say they are coming, I mean all of them are coming, it sounds like the entire colony is on the move."

CHAPTER 39

C rimson looked over his impatient army, their desire to destroy so strong that they attacked each other, defiling their own to release their pent-up aggression. Crimson smiled at the creatures' blood lust, which only increased after sharing Alysia's progress. The informant amongst Alysia's group was reluctantly loyal, a favor for a favor granted. Humanity's souls were sold cheaply. It was no wonder Crimson's army was twice the size of his opponent. The balance of power between good and evil shifted so greatly that the demon was surprised it had taken this long for the Council of 120 to recognize it. Once the demon controlled the Kalama Dagger, it was confident it could strike at the heart of all good and wipe it out, turning creation on its head, splintering further the good and evil divide. It regained its throne and watched as its thralls tore each other from limb to limb, only to be pulled back together and torn apart once more.

The demon's laughter rolled through Jarapenth in great waves, further inspiring the demon's brethren to imagine new ways to torture the forgotten. Their pain joined its laughter in a cacophony of sound reaching the center of Jarapenth, where the forgotten and disparate celebrated, feeding and growing, preparing for their time.

CHAPTER 40

M ary was first to react when Char warned of the coming horde, the last thing she wanted was to face off against those nightmares again. The thought of them crawling over her, biting her, wanting to feast on her, caused her heart rate to increase and sweat to instantly bead up on her brow. She looked down at her arms recalling the amount of time she had spent in a tattoo artist's chair getting these important stories drawn. Now they were puffed and swollen. Her well scripted stories ruined by the spider bites which would create scars further destroying the countless hours of work. Her anger and fear moved her into swift action. She grabbed one of the last ammo clips from her belt and slapped it into her weapon. The sound echoed through the chamber drawing everyone's attention to her.

"We have to make a decision. We are not surviving another onslaught from those bastards. I sure as fuck will not be made into a spider Slurpee," Mary said as she turned to her teammates.

"You're damn right about that," Martin called out. "Time to

shit or get off the pot, people. Char, how long can you hold those fuckers off."

"They are not here yet," Char cried out. "I will hold them back as long as I can, but I cannot guarantee for how long. I am worn down."

"Can you use that voice thing again to pop those bastards into oblivion?" Martin asked, a tinge of hope in his voice. Earlier in this journey, he had hoped for more action. Now, he only hoped he and those with him would survive, all thoughts of gun battles and confrontations a distant dream.

"I don't think so. I have little energy left, Martin. I doubt I can hold them off for long. I am fragile at this point. A demon can only expel so much energy before it needs to regenerate."

Alysia heard Char and agreed with Martin, they either died trying to solve this puzzle or by a million spider bites. She would take her chances with the mystery. "We have to move with what we've got. I appear to be the only one who affects the liquids in the vessels so I will work on those. Martin, you take the mineral rods. Let's keep it to just us two to start, the rest of the team get up against the back wall. Raegan and Mary do what you can to protect us if those carnivorous soccer balls reach the entrance before we find a way out."

Martin moved into position as the rest of the team followed Alysia's lead. Raegan and Mary took a defensive stance in front of the two stones, covering Char, who stood at the entrance to the room.

Martin breathed deep, pulling a massive amount of air into his lungs, expanding his chest. He cleared his mind preparing to focus on completing the puzzle. He let the air out slowly and rallied the team. "Once we start, we are not going to be able to stop. We must keep going. Alysia, as you pour the liquid into the groove on your stone, I will place the rod into the groove on the opposite side of the second stone. Are you ready?" Martin said as he prepared to pull the first rod from the wall. Alysia shouted yes.

Martin turned to Char, praying the spiders had found something else to eat or distract them, such as heading to the Cineplex to catch a double feature of *Arachnophobia* and *Eight Legged Freaks*. A miracle would be appreciated right about now. "Char, give me a sign. I know good news is not a demon forte but give me something."

"I cannot see them yet, but they are getting closer, and there is a shit load of them from the sounds coming out of this passage," Char replied, its voice intense, hammer hitting nails sharp.

"Char, we need to work on what good news means," Martin yelled. He turned to Alysia and the vessels. "Alysia, starting with the vessel holding the orange liquid, pull it from the shelf, we will then see if the rod loosens within the stone."

Alysia reached up to lift the vessel from the shelf, but the jar would not move. "It won't come out," her voice tinged with panic. She tugged again. It was cemented in place. Letting go, she looked to see if it was stuck due to age, but it did not appear to be attached in any way. She tried to lift and pull it forward. The damn thing would not budge. The liquid within burned a bright orange.

On the other side, the Sapphire rod was glowing brightly in response to the orange liquid.

"Is the rod coming loose?" Alysia called out as she continued trying to maneuver the vessel.

"No, it's wedged in the rock," Martin replied.

Char released a growl from deep within his throat, "The spiders are here, and they are pissed off!"

CHAPTER 41

Char watched as the spiders rolled across each other, filling the passage full of their bloated bodies. They were pressed closely together, their gelatinous forms breaking from the pressure. The thrashing of legs was joined by the awful sound of crumpling gut-filled bags as the spiders forced their way to be first to a juicy meal. As one exploded even more took its place, falling over each other, climbing, crawling, hurtling ever forward, a hairless mass of eight-legged death. Char reached deep within itself and called forth the Shield of Gargolot for the second time in as many days and pushed the shield into the cave. Without time to regenerate, Char's ability to hold any power for long would be limited. The spiders splat against the invisible wall, even to Char the sound was nauseating. Fighting to gain purchase but finding none, the bodies piled up as the spiders pressed against the invisible shield, desperate for sustenance. Char fought to hold the shield in place, but the mass increased as more spiders pushed from behind. The sheer weight of all those bodies forced the protection back. Char concentrated, trying to hold its position and save its teammates.

"There are too many of them! I cannot hold the shield for long," Char's voice reaching a fevered pitch as it fought for control.

"Alysia," Raegan called out over the vile sound of popping spiders. "In the sand room, you were the only one who could lift the books. Maybe it is the other way around in here, let Redstone try."

Redstone rushed toward Alysia from his position against the back wall. His ears were filled with the sound of the spiders exploding as they hit the shield, and his nose was assaulted with the acrid smell of their burst bodies and the sweat, grime, and stress of his team. The arachnids popping was unnerving. One thing was for sure, if Redstone escaped this nightmare, he would never be able to listen to his daughter pop bubble wrap ever again.

Alysia stepped aside, and Redstone grabbed the vessel. It released with ease. Redstone removed the wax seal from the top of the jar, the chemical odor filling his nose as pungent as smelling salts, his head turned reflexively away. He poured the liquid into the groove, watching it flow towards the funnel in the center of the stone and swirl down. The liquid appeared in the center of the second stone and began to fill the groove opposite it. Martin yelled yes as the rod released from the rock. He placed it in the track with the orange liquid, the sapphire melted, glowing hot, and the two stones turned clockwise.

"Holy shit, yes," Martin called out as Redstone returned to the vessel shelf, reaching up for the next liquid. Redstone's enthusiasm was rewarded with a sharp release of pressure pushing through his body, throwing him back against the stone wheel. His head made a resounding crack, his vision darkened and sounds dampened.

Raegan could not see what was taking place behind her. Her whole attention was on Char and the swarm it was holding back. As Redstone hit the stone with his head, thin blue rods shot from the holes in the floor under where Char stood. Its body impaled, shoving the demon towards the ceiling. For a moment, Char lost concentration and the spiders almost broke through into the chamber. Raegan prepared for the horde, tightening her grip on the weapon she held, but Char was able to regain the rite and push them back.

"Get us the hell out of here," Char's voice rang through the cavern.

Raegan watched as another row of bars shot from the floor behind Char, their tips razor sharp. Raegan understood the challenge. The group must get all the colors into their proper places before the rods reached their location. Another row of rods shot from the floor. She counted rows and estimated the time between bursts. If her calculations were correct, they had roughly three minutes to complete the task.

"Guys, you have three minutes at best, hurry the hell up back there. Char is falling apart," Raegan shouted. She glanced over at Mary and could see beads of sweat falling from her forehead, her eyes large, frantic. Raegan wanted to survive just to give Madame hell for putting her and her team in this situation.

Behind Raegan, Alysia kneeled beside Redstone. "Hey, hey, can you hear me? Redstone!" Alysia slapped him in the face, hard. Redstone's vision cleared. He could feel blood running down the back of his neck. He had never suffered a concussion, but if blurry vision, wanting to vomit, and a raging headache were symptoms, he had one now.

"You need to warm the liquid in the vessels first before I remove them," Redstone said as he took Alysia's hand and stood, swaying as he regained his balance.

Alysia placed both hands in front of the next vessel, the liquid began to glow, this one vermillion in color. Reaching its brightest point, Redstone removed the vessel and poured it into the groove. Alysia, trying to be proactive, moved her hands to the next, only to be pressed back. The punch was less than the one which hit Redstone.

"The chemical reaction looks like it needs to complete before I can warm the next one," Alysia said, turning to Martin and Redstone. As the mineral liquified, the stone wheels turned.

THE RODS that pierced Char's body, physically lifting the demon off the floor, retracted, hammering Char into the hard rock floor. Spiders were on the demon before it could lift itself back up and hold the already weakening shield. The spiders which bit into its malformed body ignited, turning Char into a walking torch. The demon stumbled, placing its back against the hard rods released from the floor behind it. As those bars retracted, Char stepped back once again to the next row. The spiders fought to reach it, only to ignite and flee into the spiders behind.

Raegan and Mary had their weapons ready, should any of the spiders get through the shield. Raegan watched as flaming eight-legged torches scurried back into the mass, only to ignite others. Now they were facing flaming arachnids, this just kept getting better. Raegan turned to see progress on the wheels.

ALYSIA FINISHED HEATING up the fifth vessel, and Redstone poured the content into the stone groove. The red liquid interacted with the emerald rod. The wheel ground into the sixth and final place while the metal rods detonated out of the floor ten feet from Raegan and Mary. The two could feel the heat from Char and the wildfire of spiders in front of them.

"We are seriously running out of room here," Raegan yelled to the team behind her, "shit is going to get real, real soon."

The race was on as they worked to heat the liquid and pour the last vessel into the color wheel before either the rods impaled them or the spiders dined. Alysia's hands warmed the final vessel to a fiery bright magenta. Martin yanked the last rod from the wall and placed it into the groove. The wheels spun, completing their 360-degree journey.

The test complete, the team awaited escape. The groups' reward was rods of blue firing from the floor two feet from Raegan and Mary. Both scrambled behind the stone wheels, taking a firing stance against the wall.

Char continued moving towards the team as the rows of rods retreated into the floor. The spiders struck against the weakened shield and Chars body like waves against a jetty. Char slid down the last row of rods as the spiders overwhelmed it, unafraid of the demon or what its heated form could do to them. Their hunger was a driving force, the pain within their guts tightening with the smell of fresh blood.

Under the teams' feet, the last row of holes teased them. In Raegan's head, she had been counting down to their impalement. How quickly would it be over, would it be instantaneous, or would they be eaten alive, spider-shish kabob? She counted down from ten. If it happened sooner, at least the tension would end. She would be damned if she died defeated. Raegan stood ramrod straight, grabbing Mary's hand to her left and Alysia's hand to the right, and yelled, "Sovereign Guard, *stand.*"

Mary and Martin yelled in unison, "*stand proud!*"

The color wheels sank into the floor, and a panel opened behind the team. Stale air blew across Raegan's back from the opening, the sigh of a held breath.

"Alysia, Char is still behind the last rods," Raegan cried out as she moved forward to assist the demon.

Alysia dropped beside Raegan, the heat of the inferno in front of them, forcing their heads back as their arms worked to reach Char's fallen form. The sweat on their bodies steaming, the hairs on their arms melting. Raegan reached over to Alysia to push her away, afraid their clothing would ignite.

"We are not going to leave Char here. No!" Alysia shook Raegan off while continuing to help the demon.

"Damn it, Char, come on, hold on, go through these fucking bars. I know you can."

Char turned its burning face to Alysia. Its blue eyes filled with regret. She realized she was crying for this demon, which made her shout at the creature in further fury, unable to comprehend why she felt this way.

Char began to fade, its form phasing, she was confident the creature passed, returning to Jarapenth, but the demon's upper half slid through the bars. Raegan and Alysia pulled the beast the rest of the way through.

Redstone assisted Alysia and Raegan, helping to move the demon as far as they could before the heat from its body became too much, their hands turning bright red.

The spiders crammed themselves against the last row of rods, trying to press their bloated bodies through the small gaps. Spiders continued to flow into the room, hundreds of thousands of bodies squirming, fighting to approach the front. Within moments the bars were filled floor to ceiling with burning spiders. As the pressure from behind increased, it became a cider press, spiders turned to a pulp, squeezed through the gaps, their insides flowing, a waterfall of slime. As the team maneuvered farther into the passage, the panel closed behind them. The sound of raining spider heads detached from their abdomens vanished, and quiet enfolded them.

CHAPTER 42

Martin attended to Alysia, Redstone, and Raegan's hands as best he could, using what was left from his water bottle to clean them.

After being tended to, Redstone lowered onto his haunches next to Char, looking over the creature. Twice since he met this demon, it had sacrificed for this team. Redstone wondered why. He recalled seeing it in Vegas causing him to turn away from helping this group. Peering down at the creature, Char's eyes opened and returned his gaze, crystal blue orbs. Redstone could see some form of intelligence in them, along with a world of pain.

"You wonder why I help you," Char's voice came out low, barely a whisper.

"It has definitely crossed my mind," Redstone responded as he continued to watch the demon's body glow and pulse through the multiple holes and incisions in its tattered form.

"There is no redemption, no hope, but when I forced myself onto this plane, I started to see there might be a chance, a slim one, but a chance. In Jarapenth, we are all forced to relive our sins, and you would be amazed how even the smallest of sins becomes such a burden when you are down there. A culmination of small steps leading to a massive boulder that falls upon your shoulders and forces you to feel the ache of regret and shame, over and over. Here, I thought forgiveness might be found, but I am not sure anymore. I think we are all doomed to stew within our regrets and failures, to spend our time in anxiety over what we should have or could have done. I need to rest awhile."

Char's eyes closed, and Redstone stood. What Char said resonated. His failures flowed through him as his blood flowed through his veins. We are imperfect creatures, creatures filled with fear and anxieties, all of us longing for acceptance and a desire to fit with our fellow humankind. He did not want to imagine an eternity of suffering, but this demon was proof it existed. How could it be avoided? What worried Redstone most of all was the realization that maybe no one could avoid what awaited once this life passed, as there was no sign of the good. They were left to fight alone. He returned to the rest of the group, who were planning the next moves.

"I think we need to send a couple of people down the passage and do a recon before we move on. We cannot afford any more surprises. Char needs some downtime, not to mention Father Tealander," Raegan was saying as Redstone approached.

"I would like to be part of the forward group," Redstone said as he stepped into the circle. "I am well enough to assist."

Raegan turned to Alysia, "Your thoughts moving forward?"

"I like your plan. I don't know about anyone else, but I don't know if I can go further right now."

"Okay, Redstone, you are up, but I am sending Martin and Mary with you," Raegan said as she reached down to help Mary up from her sitting position.

"You know my finger was eaten, right? Don't I get to rest?" Mary said as she took Raegan's hand.

"A piece of your finger is gone, not your whole damn finger. Quit your bitching," Martin said.

"But it is the most important part of my finger if you get my drift."

"Seriously, even beat to shit, you are one disgusting human being, you know that?" Martin gently pushed Mary away.

"What? I am talking about my nose-picking finger. What are you thinking about, sicko."

Alysia found herself chuckling at the banter between the two. When Martin gave Mary an OMG face, mouth hanging wide, forehead wrinkling, Alysia's chuckles turned to laughter. Others joined, not because they found the banter funny, but because they realized they were still alive, and it felt good, even with the aches and pains.

Alysia watched as the three scouts rounded a bend in the tunnel, disappearing from her view.

THEY TRAVELED for some time before coming to a set of stairs carved from the sandstone. Redstone recognized this from the petroglyph, the ladder climbing up. A soft glow shone from far up the narrow, steep stairs. This was going to be a dangerous climb for the weakened team.

"Well, do we journey up, or do we send someone back to collect the rest of the team, and we face this together?" Martin asked.

"I think we need the group," Redstone answered, "so far, we have needed all of us to complete these tasks, I worry if we go up those stairs, we might not come back down."

"I concur. I will head back down the passage and collect the team while you two get some rest. I think we will need to assist some of the group so rebuild what energy you can. Mary, rest that nose-picking finger, there must be a mine of dirt and grime up there just waiting to be freed," Martin said as he turned to go back.

"Sick," Mary replied as her body slid down the cave wall.

BY THE TIME the rest of the team stumbled into view, Redstone and Mary felt a little better. Raegan approached the stairs making the same assessment her forward team had made. The damn things were steep, narrow, and abnormally tall. The team would be forced to lift already tired legs high to climb. If someone slipped and fell, she was not sure how they could arrest a fall. Most of the gear was lost or beyond repair. Only two packs remained, Alysia's, holding the critical journals and Martin's, which he barely salvaged from the color wheel test. They had no choice but to climb, rest was not an option as she feared their time was almost gone.

Alysia came up beside Raegan, concern on her face. "How is Matthew going to make this ascent? I don't think he can go much further."

"I don't think most of us can continue," Raegan said, turning to look at Alysia. Alysia had spunk, she was growing to like her, even with their confrontations and disagreements. She had a lot to learn about leading. Still, under the circumstances, she had held the team together under intense strain, an impressive feat. Hell, even her two mates liked her, more importantly, they trusted her, even Martin, who still questioned why Alysia was or was not affected by objects. Raegan observed the scar on Alysia's face, cutting across her left eye. The damage was severe enough to turn the eye a milky blue, but her other eye was still a brilliant topaz blue. It held Raegan's own, bright, and aware.

"I agree," Alysia said through a deep breath, "unfortunately, the only way out is up, we will do the best we can. I will work with Matthew to help him."

The team began their ascent. The stairs so narrow they used the pads on the front of their feet to hold themselves in place. Their hands were used as braces against the narrow stairwell walls. Soon the team's legs were on fire, the pain excruciating. Father Tealander was boxed in by Alysia and Redstone, so they could arrest his fall should he stumble.

Mary led the team, and Martin could hear her count every step as her foot came down. It was driving him mad, but he knew she was just dealing with the stress, and he was so tired the sound of a cockroach scuttling across the floor would have set him off.

Mary called the group to a halt as the light grew brighter ahead. Alysia volunteered to travel up the rest of the way with Mary to see what was causing the glow.

The two began trekking upward. As they approached the top, the radiance grew stronger, forcing their eyes downward. "Who would have thought I would need my shades in here?" Alysia mused as they approached the final stair and entered a new room.

"Three hundred and thirty-three stairs," Mary called out as she bent over to relieve a cramp.

Alysia shielded her eyes with her hand, trying to see what was behind the glow, but it was as if she was investigating a star, its brightness fierce. She dared not look directly at it.

"What the hell is it?" Mary asked as she caught her breath.

"I can't tell, it's too damn bright, and I am not moving any closer, not without everyone here. The stairs could disappear for all I know," Alysia said as she circled the object.

"Do we have to climb back down those stairs?" Mary pointed behind them.

Alysia sighed, "I hope not." Instead, she turned and yelled down the stairs, "Can anyone hear me?"

A few seconds later, Raegan's voice, "Yes, barely."

Alysia yelled even louder, "Come up, all clear."

"On our way."

If this were the last test, Alysia was uncertain they would pass it. They could barely walk, let alone face another challenge. In the middle of the room, the object continued to pulse and glow.

CHAPTER 43

Madame was tired of waiting around for her team to be slaughtered. She was not going to stand back like the shadow figure required her to do. Alysia's life and the rest of her crew were not throwaway pieces.

She contacted her assistant Christopher and asked him to come to her office.

"I want a security team dispatched to Bethany's location." She handed him a USB drive. "This is the GPS tracking device we had implanted into each of the Sovereign Guard. We will be able to locate Christine through her device and, in turn, Bethany's location. Tell the security team they are to do all they can to protect the child. That is their priority."

She waited for Christopher to finish writing her first instructions down.

"Second, have a helicopter at the ready in Vegas. This USB stick has Raegan's tracking information. When Raegan comes out of the cave, the pilot will get a read on her location. He is to immediately extract the dagger team."

"Anything else, Madame?" Christopher asked as he finished taking notes.

"Have our connections in Vegas ready a team at the best hospital in the area. If we have injured, I want them cared for quietly. If we have dead, I want them cared for respectfully. Offer them a large donation for their silence, if necessary. At the end of this fiasco, we do not want the press hunting us down."

Christopher stood and left the office. Madame sat in her chair and awaited the wraith of the shadow for her disobedience.

It was time. Crimson stood before its army of six hundred and sixty-six warriors and riled them up, increasing their blood lust. "Our time has come. I release you upon the world. Bring me back the dagger and the woman Alysia, the rest you may do with as you wish. And as for Char," the demons howled in fury, "tear the creature apart and bring me the pieces so I may toy with its pain."

Crimson waved its hand, and the soldiers disappeared. The demon then turned and faced the larger army of six hundred and sixty-six thousand demons. "Pick up the cages you have made, go and embed yourself. Let us draw real fear, let us feed on sadness, let us feast on despair. Prepare yourself to become what you have desired to be, retribution for our eternal punishment."

Its second army vanished, Crimson looked over Jarapenth and counted the hours to its freedom from this place. Its glorious reign upon the Earth that its creator denied it almost within its grasp.

CHAPTER 44

"Thought you said all clear," Raegan said as she came out of the stairway.

"Well, I couldn't scream, there is a glowing mass in the middle of the room, and we have no idea what the hell it is," Alysia responded.

"Point taken."

The team crowded together but avoided approaching the glowing object in the middle.

"That has to be the Kalama Dagger," Alysia said as she circled. "What else could it be?" But was it? She felt no connection, no pull. It could just be another damn test, another opportunity to kill them all.

"Oh, I could think of several hundred horrible things it could be," Mary commented, "after everything else we have seen, who knows what it could be."

"I agree with Alysia, I think we are in the final room. This has to be the dagger," Father Tealander said as he withdrew the battered notes. "*Blessed be thee who touches light, placed within a demon's plight, handed down the world ignite,*" he read.

Tealander was sure it was the dagger. For him, the pull was enormous, the weight dragging him down. His frail body barely able to stand in its presence.

Alysia stepped towards the object and reached out a hand, but the light intensified, and she withdrew. "Damn it, we are so close."

Father Tealander watched Alysia's frustration grow. He worried for her more than she would ever know. He loved her as his own, which made what was going to happen much harder. Tealander understood the phrase, it was why he was here, and, glancing over at Char, he understood why the demon was here as well. He did not want to become what Char was, but his deeds would not warrant forgiveness. This was to be his destiny.

Tealander glanced over to Char and saw the creature intently looking at him, it gave him an almost imperceptible nod. It knew. This demon knew. How long had it known? His knees grew weak, *Lord*, he thought, *please guide my hand, allow me the ability to do what is right. Please forgive me for what I have done. I accept my fate. I have no hate in my heart.*

Tealander approached the fiery object and reached out his hand. Light exploded within the space, temporarily blinding the members of the group, including Tealander. As people's eyesight returned, a creature nine feet tall stood before them. Its lower half was human, but its upper half was that of a ram. Its massive horns curled upon themselves.

Tealander retreated. It was Satan himself, come to drag him to hell. He had been wrong. He had doomed them all.

Martin and Mary raised their weapons, ready to engage when Redstone stepped in front of them and shouted, "Lower your weapons. This is no enemy."

Redstone addressed the creature, "Qui-am-I Wintook Poot-see, great North Star, we come seeking your wisdom."

"You come seeking the dagger," the creature replied, its voice a mix of human and goat, deep and guttural.

"It is true, we seek the Kalama Dagger, but not for ourselves. We seek it to protect the world," Redstone said, raising his hands before the North Star.

"A noble quest, Redstone, yet I fear you do not understand the true power the object wields, nor do I believe you understand the journey still in front of you. You turned your back on this quest, and only through fear for yourself and your family did you return. That is not noble. Ask yourself, do you seek for others or for yourself?"

Redstone was taken aback. The North Star was right. It was for selfish reasons Redstone had agreed to come on this quest. Throughout this journey, his mind had been on those he loved, the rest of humanity but an afterthought. He was not worthy to carry this burden.

The creature read his thoughts and responded. "You are not Redstone, but you are worthy to continue. You must accept your fate, for it is predestined. You will need to stand strong as others grow weak. You must place your own needs and fears behind you and turn your focus inward. Your challenges will only increase."

The creature then turned to address Alysia. "Why have you come to seek this dagger?"

Alysia felt all the terror and fear, stress, and anger flow out from her body. She took one step towards the creature and lifted her head, staring into the eyes of the one calling her out. She had led them to this moment, she would lead them out, alive. "To save a child. To save many children."

"Yes, but you must understand by now there will be no saving the child, for an object of this power can never be handed to either good or evil, it must remain in balance. Are you the one to provide that balance?"

The creature bent closer to Alysia, its eyes peering into her soul, relentless, searching her thoughts, an intruder in her mind. "I don't know. All I can promise you is I will try. I will sacrifice myself if necessary. I do not know why I am here. I do not know what my parents started. I stand before you with fear in my heart, great doubt, and uncertainty. I am unsure if I am worthy of such a task, but I will try and do what is right, I will try and undo what has been done."

The creature continued looking at Alysia, its eyes narrowed then widened with surprise as it read her thoughts. "You are more than you know, child. You are tied to this just as all who stand before me are. You will discover truths that will make you doubt yourself and those you love, but the truth is a key."

The North Star stood up straight, turning its gaze to all of them. "Once this object is handed to you, you all are beholden to it. You are tied to its destiny." Behind the creature, a new set of stairs appeared. "These stairs will lead you to the beginning. You are free to leave now without the dagger, and I will continue to guard over it as I have for centuries, but I can no longer assure its protection should you go. Feel no shame, for what is being asked of you is no easy task. Some of you will sacrifice your very lives."

Father Tealander felt the North Star's gaze fall on him as it spoke this last sentence.

"We cannot leave without it," Alysia said standing straight, "we have all suffered to get here, to leave now would be to abandon all that we have overcome."

"You have not yet suffered, child. What lies ahead of you will begin your true suffering."

Redstone turned to the team, "The North Star speaks true. If we do this, there will be no turning back for any of us if we take the dagger. We will be hunted, the power of the artifact too great for either side to ignore. Our future will be wrought with peril. But if we decide to do this," he paused thinking on what he was about to commit to. He had a family to care for but to deny his future would only bring greater pain to his tribe and his family. "I will stand with you."

Alysia approached the North Star, "I am ready to receive the dagger." She lifted both hands to accept the gift. She could already feel the burden weighing on her soul.

"You may not accept it," the creature rumbled, "only the blessed hand may take the dagger."

Alysia did not expect this. She was chosen to carry this burden, no other. She did not wish it to fall on anyone else. Alysia felt her heart break when Matthew stepped before the creature and fell to his tired knees. His old frame was beaten and worn. She wanted to call out to him, to tell him, no, but the voice of the creature rang in her head, telling her to stand silent.

"I am willing to take the burden of the Kalama Dagger," Tealander said, raising his hands and head to the North Star.

The North Star raised its hands to the sky, "Heavens, one of worth has appeared before me to take the legacy of this object and protect it. He accepts its burden without objections, he accepts its fate. Allow me to hand this burden to him and let me return to you so I may rest at your feet."

From above the creature, a light shone. An object appeared. The Kalama Dagger burned bright, a flaming torch. The handle jeweled in precious stones and its blade about a foot in length with etched carvings that glowed within the metal. As the North Star brought the dagger down to Tealander, it spoke to him and him alone, mind to mind. "You know what comes next, you understand the meaning of the words. Are you prepared to do what is necessary, no matter the cost?"

"Yes, I understand," Tealander said as he looked upon the North Star. The dagger fell into his hands, the weight forcing

Tealander to rebalance himself. "Please give me the strength to do what must be done," he whispered under his breath.

"You have always been strong Father, you have only doubted yourself. Others have not. Your debt is heavy, but fear not your future, for you have set in motion a turning. By your hand, you have led a child. She will determine our fates."

The North Star grew brighter for a moment then faded away. Leaving only the light of the dagger within the room. The burning blade was cold in Tealander's hands as he continued kneeling. He saw Char approach him from the left before the others could come to him.

"I am sorry, Father," Char whispered, touching the Father's shoulder gently before pulling its hand back.

"How long have you known?" Tealander looked up into its crystal blue eyes and saw his fate better than he had ever seen it.

"A guilty soul connects with others. I knew from the moment we met."

"When the time comes, will I suffer?" Tealander pleaded to the demon, wanting some form of reassurance, but it was not the reassurance he desired, his head fell to his chest as the demon answered.

Char wanted to lie to Tealander. It wanted to tell the Father that everything would be okay, that he had suffered enough. But Char would not lie to his friend even when it new the truth was more horrible than Tealander would be able to bare. Char moved closer to Tealander and with fetid breath whispered, "More than your human mind can even imagine." Char walked away as the others gathered to help him back onto his feet.

"MORE FUCKING STAIRS," Mary muttered as she lifted her weary legs to the next and then the next. The group trudged upward, bruised and battered. Road weary travelers simply wanting to be home. They climbed in silence, only speaking to give encouragement to one another.

Alysia trudged along behind the rest. She could feel infection seeping in. There were too many wounds received not to have her body burning from within. Alysia was unsure how she could face Crimson in her state but knew she would be forced to do so. The words of the North Star was like a skipping record, *there will be no saving the child.* She would try anyway, damn the costs. Alysia shook her head, trying not to focus on the what if, instead she focused on the must-do, and the first thing was to get the dagger from Matthew. Without the blade, she could not negotiate.

From the front, Alysia heard Raegan call out excitedly, "I feel fresh air."

The prospect of being in the open once more motivated the team to pick up their pace. At the top of the stairs, a crack appeared. Raegan felt cool air coming through, the sweet smell of dry air filling her lungs. She squeezed through the tight rift, resisting the urge to rush, she did not expect further traps, but caution was still warranted. Her body slid out of the split and into the open air. Air never felt or tasted this good.

Mary exited behind her. "Three hundred and thirty-three more stairs. Should have known, a total of six hundred-sixty-six stairs." She bent down, gasping in a big gulp of dry Nevada desert air, and was grateful she was alive.

Alysia was the last to clear the crevice. She shivered as the cool night wind blew across her tattered clothing. Not much was holding her garments together, the wind could blow the damn things off. She was a mess, her body crusted in guts and mud. She watched Redstone climb up a small hill as the others did their best to stand, finding rocks to lean on or falling to the ground in exhaustion.

REDSTONE WALKED over to the edge of the plateau they had exited and found the opening of the Firecave directly below them. They had come full circle, which seemed strange as it always felt like they were moving straight. He looked down at his watch, which was once again working. The date and time displayed Friday eleven-twenty-six at night. He turned from the edge of the cliff, looked out over the plateau, and felt his heart stop. The others could not see what he could see as they were too low. In the distance, barely visible in the moonlight, stood an army of demons, the red of their veins contrasting against the blackness of night. There had to be several hundred of them just waiting and watching. The North Star told him what was to come, but even with the knowledge, the sight was terrifying.

Below, Father Tealander strolled up the hill to where Redstone stood. When he arrived and looked back at the army of demons, he did not act surprised.

"You knew?" Redstone said with a questioning tone.

"As I told you in the caverns, I have done things I regret, Redstone," he said as the wind whipped what little grey hair the father had left on his head. "I now must make amends. In doing so, I leave Alysia in Roland's care. I fear it will be too much for her to bear. She will hear things, learn of things, they will shatter her. I know you have a family of your own, but I must ask you to help her understand. Roland is not here, it will need to be you."

Redstone looked at the old man, his years clearly present,

defined by the lines of stress deeply etched on his face. "I don't know if I can."

Father Tealander reached out his hand and took Redstone's, "You are strong. I know you will find a way. When I leave here, you will call Alysia and Raegan up, and you must promise to allow neither to interfere, no matter what it takes." Tealander turned to walk away, then stopped and looked back. "Tell her I am sorry, tell her, I love her as my own daughter. I hope someday she can forgive me what I have done."

Father Tealander reached the bottom of the hill where Char had been patiently waiting for him. Redstone watched as Tealander and Char walked towards the demon army, the dagger held at Tealander's side. Redstone waited for them to advance too far for Alysia to interfere.

"Raegan, Alysia, could you come up here for a moment?" He called down. The two began climbing up the slight incline. "Come on, seriously, you are making us climb again," Alysia said, half-joking.

As they approached, he placed a finger to his lips and motioned with his head to look behind them.

"You have got to be fucking kidding me," Raegan said as she turned.

Alysia collapsed to the ground, her body sagging from the ordeals of the last few days. They had been close, so damn close. "We can't defeat them, can we."

"No, there is no way. We will run out of what little ammunition we have left in a matter of minutes. Then it will turn into a blood bath, our blood." Raegan said as she watched the army.

"Wait, Redstone, where are Matthew and Char. I saw Matthew up here with you." Alysia asked, afraid they both would be overtaken and not even know the army was out there.

CHAPTER 45

In Seattle, the security team assembled and headed towards the Oregon Coast thirty minutes after receiving orders from the Madam. The ride was bumpy as a storm had settled over the Pacific Ocean, and it was one hell of a storm. With heavy rain and wind gusts of sixty miles per hour on land, they were experiencing eighty-mile gusts at their altitude, which caused the helicopter to sway and jump.

Turbulence could have been avoided if they flew over land and come over the coastal mountains of Oregon, but Madame informed them time was critical, so they took a more direct route, right along the coastline. As the team approached the GPS location, they could see at least thirty threats standing along the ack of the property with their backs to the ocean. The team was informed the enemy would be something different, but looking down on creatures the size of cattle, with mouths of whirling teeth, was otherworldly. Being security for the Sect of Light, the team experienced the weird and bizarre every day. Creatures built like tanks were a new item to add to the catalog.

The team came around a second time. As the chopper flew

over the top of the home below, the creatures released a nerve-shattering roar and charged the house.

"Shoot 'em down, shoot 'em down!" Greg Taylor, head of security, yelled at the team.

Blessed bullets tore up the yard and dunes as the crew opened fire.

Inside the house, Christine and Roland heard the helicopter fly overhead. The blades were barely audible over the surging storm. Upon the second pass, the creatures released a scream and careened towards them.

"We are dead," Roland whispered as the demons hurtled towards them.

"The hell we are, Roland! Get your ass ready to fight, damn it. Weapon at the ready," Christine turned from Roland and yelled to Martha to return to Bethany's room. The frail door would not hold these creatures back, but she needed Martha out of the current equation.

Martha ran from the living room, her ruined brown hair flying, at least what was left after the Moclips incident, behind her as she rushed into the bedroom, slamming the door.

"Roland, I hope you are what I think you are. No pulling back, we defend the child at all costs. Back me up."

Roland nodded, and the two of them brought their weapons up, training them on the War Hounds.

Gunfire erupted outside. The two watched as a hailstorm of bullets ripped into grass and sand, hundreds of rounds firing simultaneously into the oncoming hounds. War Hounds flipped head over back as they were ripped apart by hailstorm of bullets above. One War Hounds' head was shot clean off, its body continuing to pitch forward, dancing to the bullets raining down on its torso. One threw itself at the window but exploded in midair as bullets sliced into its charred flesh. The momentum of the War Hound sent its carcass through the plate glass window. Glass exploded inward as Roland and Christine fled towards the kitchen to avoid the cutting shards. The storm entered, the wind driving rain into the room. Whoever owned this home was going to be pissed, Christine thought as War Hounds were torn apart by gunfire.

"I think our guardian angels are wiping them out," Roland exclaimed. But his enthusiasm was blown apart as one of the War Hounds bounded through the window, landing in the middle of the room, and barreled towards the two of them. Christine and Roland opened fire, but they could not hit the body, just the open maw. The teeth whirled in its lamprey mouth, shredding the bullets on impact.

The creature was massive in the room, more prominent than it appeared outside. The smell of it made it difficult to take a breath without gagging on the cloying scent of dead fish left in the sun. Its human arm legs, human hands feet were more agile than Christine could imagine. It moved with the grace of a dancer, side to side, watching for an opportunity to get to them. Roland tried to flank the creature, but it swiftly corrected its movements, considering each of their attempts.

The War Hound bellowed, black fluid splattering from its mouth, and stampeded towards Roland, knocking him underfoot, or in this case, hand. Roland tumbled under the creature, the hands striking his chest and head. His body hit the kitchen island. He tried to hold the beast back, but its weight was too great, a little more pressure, and his chest would collapse.

Christine fired into the War Hounds back as it trampled Roland. The creature roared at her, embers erupting from its maw. It turned from Roland and advanced on Christine. She led the creature from the kitchen into the open living space. It charged like a pissed off bull released from its holding pen. She jumped over the couch, working to keep something between her and the hound. The creature stood on its back arms and lifted the couch with its front arms. The couch flew over her head, crashing through another window, rain and wind pelted her from the back, immediately drenching her.

"Holy Shit, you are one big fucker!" she yelled at the creature as it stood to its full twelve-foot height. She shot into its underbelly. It fell to all fours and charged like an enraged bear. She rolled left, lifting her weapon and firing into its side. The creature began circling, not allowing her to get another shot. Each circle brought it closer. Christine was running out of room to maneuver. The War Hound's arm reached out and grabbed her before she could find a way to escape it. She beat the appendage with her weapon, trying to break its grip. The creature was incredibly strong, her attempts to free herself no more effective than a fly trying to escape a web. Its mouth opened wider, the hot, fetid breath washing across her as hot ash and embers burned her face.

Christine lifted her weapon and fired directly into the hound's mouth. It pushed its face forward, the gun entering the whirling teeth, her weapon chipped to sawdust in seconds. Before she could react, her hand went into the teeth, and as went the gun, so did her hand.

Her scream echoed through the house as the creature threw her across the room and into the television hanging on the wall. Her last image was Roland stabbing the beast with a carving knife.

Roland awoke from the nightmare only to be faced with a new one. He watched as Christine's hand was obliterated into blood, bone, and gristle. Standing, he located the blade on the island and jumped on the creature from behind, driving the edge deep into its back.

The creature threw Christine and turned on Roland, grabbing him as it had grabbed Christine. It once more stood to its full height and pushed him against the kitchen island, his back bending.

Roland, in tremendous pain, was shocked when the creature spoke. "Just a little more pressure and your back is going to shatter," its voice a symphony of razors cutting into flesh. Roland felt and heard his back crack as the War Hound continued to press him into the lip of the island. His cry of pain made the War Hound howl. One more push would snap his spine.

The hound's mouth pressed forward. Roland watched as his face approached the circular saw of death. he lifted the blade, but the other hand of the hound swatted it away.

Roland was inches away from death when he yelled, "Wait!"

"What, you worthless piece of meat," the War Hound shrieked.

"You need a breath mint, you fucking bastard."

The War Hound screeched, dropping Roland to the ground. Behind it stood a woman dressed in black, a large sword in her left hand. It dripped a black ooze onto the floor. The War Hounds back was torn open from neck to ass.

She reached down, taking Roland's hand, helping him from the floor. "Where is the child?"

"She is in the back bedroom, but Christine needs medical help immediately, that thing destroyed her hand."

"We have a medic onboard. Can I leave you to attend to her?" She asked, making sure he was not going to pass out.

"Yes, help her, please." Roland watched as the woman took

off her belt and placed it around Christine's wrist. She spoke into a headpiece, letting the medic know immediate assistance was necessary.

Within moments Christine was being removed from the home and flown to the nearest hospital. The young lady who had saved his life stayed behind with others to protect in case of a further incursion.

"How the hell did you know where we were?" Roland asked as the medic cared for his wounds.

"The Sect always knows where their people are," she responded, returning to the room where Bethany slept. The child not knowing how many times she had come close to death.

CHAPTER 46

s Alysia climbed to meet with Redstone, Matthew and Char began the slow walk out to the waiting army. "I suppose we are two peas in a pod at this point," Matthew said to Char, "A man of the cloth and a demon, the irony."

"Not so ironic. Are we much different you and I, both sinners, both knowing what awaits us when this is over? Well, I know what awaits," Char said.

"This is it?" Tealander said.

"This is it," Char repeated. "You know what must be done?"

"I do," Father Tealander reached his hand out to Char. "I am sorry for all your suffering, and I am sorry it will continue but thank you for doing what you have done for Alysia, I wish I had trusted you sooner."

Char took the Father's hand, and although it burned, the Father did not flinch, he squeezed Char's hand harder. In this moment, Char found a small piece of redemption. Its blue eyes watered. A demon could cry, but its tears evaporated before they could form. The two turned and continued moving towards the army.

"WHAT THE HELL ARE THEY DOING!" Alysia exclaimed as she watched Char and Tealander advance towards the demon horde, hand in hand. The rest of the group heard her cry out and hurried up the side of the hill. Watching as the two stumbled tiredly towards the waiting force, unable to comprehend what was happening.

"No, no. NO!" Alysia shouted as she moved to go to them. Redstone grabbed and held her from behind. "Let me go, you son of a bitch. You have no goddamn right, Redstone. Let me go right now!" She fought and struggled, kicking Redstone's legs, each strike painful against his already bruised and bitten calves. Redstone held her tightly in a grip she could not break. Father Tealander had been clear, no one was to interfere.

The Sovereign Guard watched as their friends walked into what they all knew would be their deaths, and their hearts shattered as they watched Alysia struggle in Redstone's grip. A part of Raegan wanted to pry her from Redstone, but she knew what he was doing was for Alysia's safety, even as she saw the look of suffering wash across his filth caked face.

Alysia's struggles intensified. She was not going to let Matthew sacrifice himself for her. She had dragged him out here, this was not the way it was meant to be. She screamed into the night, her throat tearing from the velocity of her voice.

"It's too late," Redstone spoke in her ear as she screamed and clawed, it was taking the last of his strength to hold her. Even as Redstone felt his very soul being torn apart, he would do as he was asked. He held Alysia, trying to absorb some of her pain.

Tealander and Char stopped when they were one hundred feet from the demon army.

One of the demons stepped forward, larger than the rest. "Infantmeal, you worthless shit. We are going to have such fun tearing you apart." The demons screamed in unison, filling the night with the sounds of their deafening roar.

As the demons' roars died down, Tealander could hear Alysia's screams in the distance, and it took everything not to turn to her.

"I hear your bitch screaming back there, Teabagger. Crimson has big plans for her, yes it does. As for the rest of your so-called friends, we are instructed to have a little fun with them this night," it laughed as the army cheered behind it.

"Unfortunately for all of you, this is about as far as you will get tonight," Father Tealander said as he took one courageous step towards the army.

"Father, you delusional man," the demon growled. "No, you are the unfortunate one. Tonight, you will know true fear and pain, tonight you will fall upon your knees and beg Crimson for mercy, which you will not receive."

"What do you think, Char? You think this demon speaks the truth?" Tealander turned to Char, raising one tired eyebrow.

The demon laughed, "Infantmeal is a coward and a traitor. What it says means nothing."

Char stared the other demon down, its eyes burning bright as flames within its skull. All its rage, pain, and terror flowing through, intensifying its glare. Its eyes turned to blue fire, engulfing the demon's entire head, it took one step forward and spoke. "My name is not Infantmeal, it is Char. And I bring a message from the North Star."

Char's entire body glowed blue, hot as a welder's torch. Tealander stepped behind the demon, his skin scorching from the heat coming off Char in waves. His hair and clothing caught fire, and he cried out in agony as he plunged the Kalama Dagger deep into Char's back, right where its heart would be. "Back to hell motherfuckers!" the Father yelled as he turned his burning face to the heavens.

The demon army cowered back, a touch too late to save them, to save anything. Char detonated in a brilliant flash of light, evaporating all living things instantly in an all-consuming arch of fire.

Alysia's scream echoed in the Valley of Fire along with the blast as she slipped into unconsciousness.

CHAPTER 47

"Rose, you are awake, I see."

Alysia did not want to awaken, she just wanted to be left alone, to mourn her loss, and to sleep for years if she would be allowed.

"Rose, we had a deal, awake."

Alysia opened her eyes. Standing above her was one of the most striking men she had ever met. If a Greek God were to become human, this is what he would look like. The man offered her his hand, and he lifted her into a standing position. Adonis could not hold a flame to this creation, eyes the blue of the demons, his hair a dark blonde, flowing over his shoulders in hypnotic waves. The face angelic, one look would mesmerize both men and women. He was muscular but not as large as Martin. Most thought of this as an ideal man, which made it all wrong, a deception, a dream. If this thing were a temptation, it had picked the wrong gender. Aphrodite would have been a better choice.

"You are Crimson?" Alysia questioned but already knew the answer.

The gentleman bowed deeply, "I am, lovely Rose," he said, taking her hand and kissing the top of it.

"Where are we?" she said as she pulled her hand away.

Crimson ignored the slight and turned to look over the colorless landscape. "You are in Jarapenth, my kingdom." His hand flowed left to right. "Of course, this is just one small part of it. It is truly infinite. I am sure Char has told you of it?"

Alysia stared out into a wasteland. It was unlike anything she had ever seen or could describe. The landscape was alien. Weird formations thrust themselves from the ground, some of them filled with mouths, some with eyes. Steam erupted from fumaroles as tall as the tallest mountains. As she watched, they shattered, disappearing into the ground to be replaced with some new horrors. The landscape became more terrifying the longer she stared into it.

"To each, this place has a different appearance, its shapes, its smells, all changing based on the person glancing upon it. I cannot even see what you see, for Jarapenth means something different to me." Crimson said as he placed a hand upon her shoulder.

"Where are all the demons?" she asked.

"Oh, I figured it would be better if you and I had the opportunity to speak alone. I can always muster a few if you wish. Add some torture into the background, help to create that hell feeling your mind is trying to conjure."

"No, I have had enough of your kind for a while," Alysia said, pulling away from Crimson's hand on her shoulder.

"My kind? That is a harsh statement, Rose. You do not even know me. Do I look like one of those who attacked you? So quick to judge, your kind."

"No, but Char told me about you and the horrible things that happen down here and what you did to it," Alysia said as she took one step away.

"The horrible things here? What happens here is simply a reflection of your own humanity. These demons are simply shadows of their former selves. You judge our judgment, yet your kind call for the death penalty, genocide, war, terrorism, bioterrorism, road rage, child abuse, beating women, gang shootings, drug overdoses, slum lords, homelessness, should I continue? No, those down here bring their own torture. As Char discovered, they are free to leave at any time, but first, they must allow themselves to leave. How is that my wrongdoing?"

Alysia could not provide an answer, so she turned the question. "Are Char and Matthew here?"

"Well, of course they are. One good deed does not erase many," Crimson said with a warm smile. "You don't believe all that, ask forgiveness at the end, and all is forgiven nonsense, do you? Imagine if a serial killer could simply wash away all their wrongdoings with a simple, I am sorry at the end. I mean, even if they meant it with all their hearts, do you think that would be fair, as you humans call it? A Mother Theresa with a Ted Bundy?" Crimson laughed.

Alysia let her eyes meet Crimsons. "How can I get them out?"

Crimson stepped back over to her and patted her on the back like an insufferable child. "You can't. Did you not hear what I told you? Only they can free themselves. I could not even show you where they are as each is still constructing their own hells, but I can imagine they will be wonderful hells to see when they are complete, especially Tealander's. His guilt is righteous."

Crimson stepped away and stared into Jarapenth for a moment, "But, should you give me the dagger, maybe I can find a way to free the Father, and maybe even the traitorous Char. The other demons would not be happy, of course, they have been looking forward to torturing that demon since Tuesday, or as you know, several hundred years."

"Even if I wanted to trade the dagger for their souls, I could not. It was destroyed when Matthew and Char used it to defeat your army," Alysia answered angrily.

Alysia took a step back when Crimson turned and looked at her, his face appearing to blur. Underneath the handsome features, something darker slithered. But as quickly as it appeared, it was gone. The frown on Crimson's face remained.

"I would not call what they faced an army, Alysia. Truly just a drop of my servants. Also, I am terribly disappointed in you. I was under the impression you were smarter than you appear to be. I expected much more from someone my council fears. Do you even know what your name means?"

Alysia was becoming flustered, this conversation was going in many directions, "Of course, it means flower. It is a family name."

Crimson's response was one of annoyance, "No, Alysia Rose, your name means of noble type, famous type. Both your first and last name are of Germanic heritage. Both signify a person of importance. I find it interesting you are so naïve. You were born of greatness, but you show little of it. One would almost be disappointed with you if they did not know of your past."

"Why am I here? What do you want from me! "Alysia said, throwing up her hands angrily. Crimson's face became one of intense rage, its aggression barely contained. "I want the dagger!" The demon's voice echoed throughout Jarapenth. From a distance, Alysia could hear cries of fear as Crimson continued to rage. "I want what is rightfully mine, what I deserve. But it must be given to me, I cannot simply take it. Did you learn nothing from the tasks within the cavern? Even your precious Father understood, yet you stand before me, your innocence defiling my home. Your charade does not fool me. Give. Me. The. Dagger."

"I don't have it," Alysia cried out, standing her ground.

Crimson took two steps towards her. Alysia cowered before him. She did not want to, but she could not contain the fear in her heart. She took two involuntary steps backwards and found a wall against her back that had not been there before. Crimson stood over her. Under his beauty swam such ugliness, it made Alysia's stomach turn. A cloying smell seeped from its pores, sickening sweat. "Your insolence was cute at first. Now I grow tired of it. Let me refresh your small brain, *blessed be thee who touches light, placed within a demon's plight, handed down the world ignite.* Father Tealander understood the meaning of this the minute he read it, do you know why? Because I told him the meaning. Tealander sold his soul to me to protect you. And to protect you, he informed me of everything. Every move, every attack has been instrumented by me because of the Father's information. I played you like a pawn, forcing you to move in the direction I wanted. None of this was by chance."

It secretly gloated as it watched Alysia's face change from one of fear to one of being betrayed.

Crimson continued its rant. "First, only one who is blessed can take the dagger. It was part of our game when we hid the blade. Second, it must be used against a demon who sought redemption. Third, upon completing both, the Kalama Dagger is handed down to the heir of the one who took the blade, and that heir is you. You are to ignite the world. Now hand me the dagger."

Terrified, confused, and saddened, Alysia tried to comprehend everything at once. Matthew had been spying on her and the team to protect her. Protect her from what? From this? Did he not know in the end, none of what he did would matter? She felt her anger rising, her hands balling into fists. How could he have betrayed her? How could he not have told her? She loved him like a father, maybe more than her actual father. She felt tears fall from her eyes. Her hatred for him and Crimson burned deep within her, and suddenly, she felt a weight within her hands. When she looked down, the Kalama Dagger burned. Its cold heat flowing up her arms and into her body. She lifted it in front of her. It fed on her anger and fear, burning brighter. Crimson flinched.

"Ah, there is the Rose I know. So much anger. Your father would be proud."

Alysia took a step towards Crimson holding the dagger in front of her like a shield, "Give me a reason to not kill you, give me one."

"What if I could share with you why you fear Santa Cruz and your past, what if I did that?"

Alysia felt the sword slip in her hands, grasping to hold on. "You can tell me what happened?"

Crimson reached over and brushed a strand of auburn hair from Alysia's face. "Yes, child. I can tell you what happened and what it meant. Ah, I see. Your father blocked your memory while enhancing your other gift. Hmmm, interesting. I can see the wall he built beginning to collapse. Your memory monster is barely contained. If the monster breaks free, the damage to your mind could be catastrophic. Come, Alysia, you need not wait to understand, I can help you. Together we can tear down those protections, and you can be free."

"Why would my father block my memories?"

"Alysia," Crimson spoke to her as if she were a petulant child, "why do parents do the things they do to their children. Trying to protect them when most times they only cause greater harm. Come, hand me the dagger."

Alysia could feel her hand begin to reach out to Crimson, but she pulled back.

"No. I want to know, but not at the cost of mass destruction. There must be a better reason."

"What if I offered you six hundred and sixty-six thousand more reasons," Crimson said as he waved his hand, beckoning her to look behind her. Alysia glanced behind her where the wall had been. It was now gone, and in its place, for as far as she could see, was row after row of silver cages, each one holding a child. In the front was Bethany, her pleading eyes boring into Alysia.

"You promised me you would come back," Bethany wailed from behind bars, "you promised you would save me!"

Alysia fell to her knees, powerless. The dagger flickered and died, now only a relic one would find in a museum.

She felt Crimson approach her from behind and the weight of his hand fall upon her shoulder. "Rose, give me the dagger, and I will spare these children. I will also free your friends from here, allowing their souls to move on. I will share with you the secrets that haunt you, isn't that value enough, child."

Alysia felt the weight of the dagger in her hand. To give it to Crimson would be handing a weapon of great destruction to a spoiled child. If she did not hand it over, she only enraged the bad child to use its magnifying glass on the anthill. She lost either way. The weight of the dagger was the measure of human life, would she save 666,000 to sacrifice billions or sacrifice millions for hundreds of thousands? And what if she saved their souls now? Crimson would just take them later.

"I feel your pain Rose, I do. You wonder if the sacrifice is worth it, you wonder if, in the end, it would matter. Consider this, there are still five artifacts left, each as powerful as the dagger you hold. Maybe you could find them and defeat me now that my spy is gone. Perhaps you could do so without my knowledge. Even with the dagger, it will take me time to prepare to invade your precious plane. Imagine what you could do with that time. Imagine the joy the parents of each of these children will feel with one more day to hold them, love, and cherish them. You would give them the greatest opportunity."

Her willpower shattered around her. Alysia's head bent forward, almost an act of supplication. The cries and whimpers of children filled the void, each one an individual pinprick in her ear. She felt her hand holding the dagger begin to rise, but it stopped midway when she heard the voice of the North Star, "You agreed to this burden. It is yours to bear, from this point forward, a great sacrifice is required. There will be no easy solutions. You promised to take this burden when you stood before me. Now carry it."

Alysia raised her head, forcing herself to look the children in the eye, "I cannot give you the dagger, Crimson."

Alysia felt the hand on her shoulder tighten, making her wince. She could feel everything around her grow hotter as Crimson's other hand appeared before her, palm up. It was three times the size of any human hand, crimson red, worn like old leather, filth caked within the creases of its palm and under its long, thick, cracked, yellow nails. She could smell ages of blood and much worse wafting from it.

This time, when Crimson spoke, its voice was not smooth and soft as butter, but rough as an ax on a grinding wheel, deep and hollow, filled with the reverberations of millions of tormented souls. "If I close this hand into a fist, you will watch as the children before you are crushed within their cages, their lives ended. I have created a whole new level of pain for them in Jarapenth. When they pass to me, oh Alysia, they will suffer in ways your little mind cannot even fathom. Hand me the Kalama Dagger or carry the weight of what will come."

Alysia's tears fell like rain on the stone underneath her. She could not give Crimson the blade. Slowly Crimson began to curl his hand into a fist. Alysia was forced to watch as the children struggled to make themselves smaller. Forced to listen to their screams of anguish. Crimson's hand stopped midway to closed, the cages mangled before her. "You can stop this, Alysia. You can save them. Simply put the dagger in my hand and it will all be over. I can free your friends and spare you the pain of learning the past."

Alysia looked up at Crimson, tears running down her face, sobs hitching her every word, "Please, please don't do this, you don't have to do this."

Crimson's hand on her shoulder softened, its words merely a whisper, "I'm not doing this, Alysia. You are. This is your choice. The blood of each of these children falls on you." His hand continued to slowly close, the wails of the children now mixed with her own primal scream as she raised the Kalama Dagger and cut off the demon's hand at the wrist. She watched as the hand tumbled across the floor. Alysia slipped into darkness surrounded by the sounds of Crimson's primal rage and the shrill screams of the children she had sacrificed.

CHAPTER 48

"Was she successful?" the shadow asked from its customary corner.

"Yes, she retrieved the dagger," Madame answered, watching the entity as it watched her. Sometimes the light would catch its eyes, and she could see them glow like a feral cat.

"Did she fulfill the promise?"

"No, she did not give Crimson the dagger. Have you not seen the news? She is much stronger than I ever imagined," Madame said as she turned in her chair to stare out into the darkness.

"Did she learn of her past, does she know? Did the demon Crimson share with her?" The entities voice sounding of worry.

Madame certainly hoped she had not discovered her past. She did not want to be on the other side of Alysia's wrath. "I don't know. She has been in a coma since we pulled them out of the desert. Besides, I have been spending every waking hour doing clean-up. The whole thing is a damn mess. If she did find out, and she possesses the dagger, she is a serious threat."

"I am aware. Let us hope the past remains a secret for a while longer. With the dagger in her possession, she will need to seek an artifact of darkness to balance her. If not, well, it could be catastrophic. Send her after the dagger's compliment when she awakens."

"If she awakens," Madame replied. "She lost a lot. We might have lost her."

"No," the entity said as it retreated into its ethereal plane. "She will soon recover. Be ready. Time is of the essence."

The shadow melted into the others within the corner. Madame continued to stare out into the darkness.

CHAPTER 49

A lysia awoke alone in a hospital bed. Her head hurt. It felt
soft, lofty as a balloon. Through the speakers in the ceiling, she could softly hear Debussy's Claire de Lune playing, a
cruel joke. Gazing at her arms, they were bandaged along with
her hands, except for the tips of her fingers. Her eyes wandered
to the windows, where darkness pressed against the glass. Its
eyeless face looking into her wounded and damaged body. Her
eyelids began to close when the glow of the television drew her
attention forward. The headline scrolling across the bottom of
the news report made her grasp for the remote. The first button
she pressed lifted her head, the next the volume.

*"We continue our breaking news as a special United
Nations meeting has been called to discuss the current
pandemic circling the globe. Four days ago, hospitals worldwide
began to receive patients into emergency rooms suffering from
what doctors are calling a coma-like state. So far, it appears to
affect only children between two to sixteen years of age. At first,
governments thought they were witnessing an act of terrorism,
but no country has been spared as the cases mount. Children*

from around the world continue to be admitted with unusual symptoms. On the line, we have Dr. Diana Lamb from the World Health Organization. Dr. Lamb, thank you for joining us. What new information can you share with us this evening?"

"Thank you, Trina, for having me on. We are still in the early stages of discovery in this quickly evolving pandemic. As you mentioned earlier, our first thoughts were focused on some form of bioterrorism. Still, as cases grow, we are quickly dismissing this notion. We are receiving cases from every country. Doctors from around the world are working hand in hand to diagnose and treat these children. Trina, this is truly a worldwide effort, and we see support from countries that are usually less willing to participate. This is a crisis not seen before, as cases continue to rise."

"Dr. Lamb, are we seeing a decrease in cases?"

"Unfortunately, we are not. Current count is well above four hundred thousand, but cases continue to flood in."

"Have you been able to identify anything that could pull these cases together?"

"We have conducted tests on water and food supplies, but since all nations are affected, it has been an overwhelming task. Some scientists are indicating potential global warming and new bacteria or other living organisms. First thoughts pointed to Naegleria fowleri, or commonly known as the "brain-eating amoeba', but in the past, we have only seen eight to twelve of these cases worldwide per year, and between July and September. Although some of the traits are the same, a coma state is the last symptom. What we are seeing is instant coma with no prior symptoms."

"Do you believe your organization is capturing all cases?"

No, Trina, absolutely not. Due to the immediate effects of the coma, we fear that many cases are still unreported. Researchers are looking for accidental deaths from drowning, falls, and other

incidents as innocuous as falling from a park swing. As I said,
we are at the beginning working with officials to figure out
commonalities among cases."

"Thank you, Dr. Lamb, we will continue to touch base with
you over the coming hours. I know the world is with me when I
wish you speed in finding the cause."

"Thank you, Trina, we can use all the prayers we can gather
right now."

Alysia raised herself further in the bed. Her attack on
Crimson appearing to have stopped the demon from killing the
children, but not enough to avoid injury. Had all been for
naught?

"We continue to follow other breaking news this evening.
Federal agents and park rangers are asking for any information
the public might be able to provide regarding a massive explo-
sion within the Valley of Fire State Park about forty miles
outside Las Vegas, Nevada. We have Ranger Steve Tobin joining
us this evening. Steve, thank you for joining us."

"Thank you, Trina."

"Steve, what can you share with us this evening?"

"Trina, we continue to be baffled by the events that continue
to unfold here. Locals reported a brief but bright light and a sonic
boom that shattered windows ten miles away from the blast area.
Reports from the Las Vegas strip of hearing a loud explosion and
mild shaking continue to pour in. First thoughts from investiga-
tors on the scene believed it was a meteor strike, but the unique-
ness of the blast zone has taken that theory off the table."

"What uniqueness are you referring to."

"I think it would be easier to see from pictures, Trina, can
you pull those up, please?"

"Steve, we have them on screen so our viewers can see. Wow,
those are amazing shots."

"Yes, they are incredible. As you can see, the blast is not

circular, it arches in one direction. The blast decimated an area roughly a half-mile wide, killing every living thing, basically incinerating all life. What is even more baffling is that an area roughly the size of a football field was turned completely into glass."

"Wait, Steve, you are saying turned into glass? What was turned into glass? And how hot would a blast need to be to turn the area into glass?"

"Temperatures would have needed to exceed three thousand degrees Fahrenheit, roughly the same temperature reached as the space shuttle reenters the earth's atmosphere. Also, nothing behind the blast is affected, the temperature was directional. We have specialists coming from around the world to assist in our investigation. But for now, we remain baffled."

"The blast occurred roughly around the same time as the current pandemic began. Do you or others believe they have connections in any way?"

"I am the wrong person to ask that question, but we have had specialists in to take samples from the area. So far, no evidence pointing towards a connection can be found. Again, it is early."

"Steve, thank you for your time this evening."

"You're welcome."

Alysia turned the volume down and once again looked out the window, lost in thought as Redstone and Raegan knocked on her half-open door.

"May we come in," Redstone asked.

"Of course," Alysia said with a weak smile as she raised her head further. "How are you, and what about the rest of our team?"

Redstone answered as Raegan took the chair next to the bed, reaching out to take Alysia's hand. "I am okay. I have had enough shots to last a lifetime," he chuckled. "The rest of the team is also well, except for Christine. She is still in the ICU. She lost a hand to a creature Roland said was like a riding lawnmower on human hands. Roland and Martha are okay. Roland has several cracked ribs. Martha is afraid to leave her home, the Sect of Light has assigned security personnel to watch over her. I believe Martha is the most mentally scarred through all this. Bethany is another story. Her parents retrieved her and returned her to their home. Madame is working to smooth those relations."

Alysia turned to Raegan. "How did we get out of the area before authorities arrived?"

"Madame arranged air support," Raegan patted her upper arm. "Each of the Sovereign Guard is tagged with a GPS locator for situations such as this one." She gently squeezed Alysia's hand. "We have all been anxious about you. You have been out for four days." Raegan looked up to the television, "You have heard?"

"Yes," Alysia said. She heard the sadness in her voice, the hurt and the pain. She did not want to cause her friends further suffering, but she could not bear it alone.

"Will there be more Alysia? Are there more children?"

"Yes. Although I thought the children would have been found dead," Alysia said, closing her eyes, seeing the children in their silver cages, hearing their screams, knowing she could not help them.

"Excuse me?" Redstone said, shocked she would think them dead.

Alysia told them what occurred after the blast, that killed their friends, leaving out Tealander being a spy. Still, her eyes welled up as she explained that both Char and Tealander were trapped in Jarapenth.

"666,000, as if I should be surprised after everything else that's occurred," Redstone commented as he shook his head.

"By cutting off Crimson's wrist, you probably saved these children's lives."

She did not want to think about it right now. The thought children around the world were in the state they were in due to her choice was too difficult to bare. She raised her arm. "How did the Sect explain all these puncture wounds to the medical teams?"

Raegan provided a weak smile. "The Sect is enormously powerful. A large donation arrived for a new cancer ward the hospital is raising funds for. No further questions were asked. I did have to explain to the doctors the punctures were from spider bites, but they all looked at me as if I had lost my mind. They pumped us full of antibiotics, and we have been reporting in daily to let them know if we have any symptoms." Raegan shifted in her chair, her body still sore from the damage it had taken. "Alysia, if you did not hand Crimson the dagger, where is it? We could not locate it after the blast, yet you say you had it in Jarapenth."

Alysia closed her eyes, concentrating on the dagger. She heard the two of them gasp, and Redstone say ,"holy shit," under his breath.

"Holy something," Alysia said weakly as the dagger became whole and sat within her hand. "I figure the Kalama Dagger is not a physical object, but a metaphysical one. I think it represents a part of the powers dispersed to each of the artifacts. That power now resides in me, well, until I gift it to someone else. I believe as the artifacts are collected, the powers are consumed by the collector or one worthy of it being collected, I don't know for sure."

Redstone stared at the dagger, heart racing. Everything Father Tealander told him while in the cave was true. Matthew sacrificed himself to pass the blade to Alysia. Redstone hoped Tealander's sacrifice was worth the damage done.

Redstone looked at Alysia, "You know that Matthew loved you very much. He spoke admiringly of you. He knew the sacrifice for taking the dagger. He accepted it with an open heart." Redstone looked at Alysia from the bottom of the bed, desperate to impart the love Matthew had held for her.

"That is why we are going after them," Alysia said quietly.

"Alysia, you are tired and weak. We cannot get them. They are gone, stuck in hell or this Jarapenth," Redstone replied, his tone a mixture of worry and admonishment that she would be thinking anything this crazy.

"I saw a way in when I cut off his hand. I don't think he wanted to show me, but for a moment, I saw through his eyes, and I saw how to save them. I have to save them."

"Alysia, listen to me," Raegan drew Alysia's attention back to her face. "We have to go after the next artifact. Madame has seen it. It is the daggers compliment, Ehecatl's Breath. She told me without it, balance will be lost, and we will be in further danger. Without it, you could be consumed by the power of the dagger."

"Fine, then we must go after both. Redstone and I will travel into Jarapenth to save Matthew and Char you will take the other team and start searching for Ehecatl." Alysia said as a deep drowsiness began to envelope her. "If you are willing, I would like to have Mary with Redstone and me."

"Sorry, Alysia, if you are going to hell, I will not be sending Mary. It will need to be me. Besides, you still have much to learn my young Padawan." Raegan said lightly grasping Alysia's hand.

"I thought only Martin quoted movie lines?"

"He kind of rubs off on you, you know?" Raegan said with a sad smile.

Redstone paced in front of Alysia's hospital bed, his body tense. "You are out of your damn mind, Alysia. I am not going into Jarapenth. We are dealing with hell on earth already. Why would I want to go to the heart of it all." Frustrated, he went to the window, staring into the darkness, watching the cars travel along the freeway.

"You want to leave them there, Redstone? You heard what Char said. Their torment will be legendary. We cannot leave our friends to that, can we?"

"Damn it." Redstone turned back to Alysia. "What do we need to do?"

"We have to find the Phaistos Disc," Alysia replied as she closed her eyes and allowed herself to fall back asleep. Raegan's gentle hand holding hers, providing comfort, a moment to heal.

Coming 2022
Alysia Rose Volume 2 - Ehecatl's Breath

ACKNOWLEDGMENTS

I enjoy writing about real places but with a fictional take. You might recognize many of the places I reference but have modified to fit my tale. I love natural locations, national parks, monuments, state parks, and historical sites. I love when I realize the author is mentioning an actual place, it allows me as a reader to visualize what they are trying to capture. My mind builds the set immediately. I feel deeply connected to the story, my brain yelling, "Hey. I've been there."

Valley of Fire State Park is about forty-five minutes outside of Las Vegas, and I highly recommend visiting when you are in Las Vegas. You will not be disappointed. Its rich hues of burnt sienna, reds, purples, and greens will have you stopping every twenty feet for pictures. Atlatl Rock is located within the park. All of the puzzles and riddles the team had to solve are located on the drawings. The color chamber, spider chamber, and hourglass chambers represent symbols found on the rock formation.

There are many petroglyphs located throughout the park. Please be respectful of these beautiful designs. They are thousands of years old, and once destroyed they are gone forever.

How would you feel if someone came into your yard and destroyed your landscaping? Go look, feel the history, but let your eyes soak it in and keep your fingers off the stone. Our natural oils slowly erode the rock, oh, and keep to the trails. There is a location called Firecave in Valley of Fire State Park, but it does not lead to a remote cave system under the park. That is just my imagination running wild, please do not bring a demon with you in hopes of accessing the secrets of the dagger.

John Redstone is a character of my imagination, but his cultural references are based on facts. Redstone is a Southern Paiute from the Moapa band, and their reservation is in the Nevada desert area. Information on the Moapa band provided in the book is based on research, if I missed something or misquoted it, I apologize to the reader and the Moapa people. I tried to stay as factual as possible while tailoring a fictional piece. I fell in love with the story of the North Star as told by the Paiute. I loved it so much that I modified it to fit within my storyline. When I discovered the tale of the North Star, I had already written the ending to the Kalama Dagger. I went back into the story and reworked the narrative to reflect the journey of the North Star and Alysia Rose. I felt their journeys were one and the same.

Is there an actual carnivorous orchid? Yes, there is. Does it eat people? Maybe, if you are about an inch in height. *Aracamunia liesneri* was discovered in 1987 by R. Liesner and F. Delascia on Cerro Aracamuni in Venezuela. It is the first orchid species to be considered carnivorous. At this time, no one thinks it mimics human speech, but I was such a fan of *The Ruins* I had to pay a little homage.

How about soccer ball-sized spiders? No. Softball-sized spiders? Yes. Califorctenus cacachilensis was discovered in 2017 by Jimenez, Berrian, Polotow and Palacios-Cardiel. It is known as the Sierra Cacachilas wandering spider. It was discovered in an abandoned mine in Baja California Big Sur. My description within the book is reasonably accurate, other than its size and red fangs.

Most of the information I have written in this novel regarding color theory is also based on fact. Yes, there exists a heated battle about which color follows green, fascinating reads if you ever have an opportunity to investigate it.

I hope you found this story as enjoyable to read as I did to write. This is my first novel. I still have much to learn and process. If you would like to reach out to me, visit my website at https://www.ascottwest.com and contact me with your thoughts, I want to make you a fan and hungry for my next novel. If you are interested in staying in touch, please follow me on Twitter: @ascottwest1 or Facebook: kalamadagger.

I would also like to thank those who subscribed to my e-mail list before you even knew me or read my book. You are appreciated.

To my editor Tyrean Martinson, I know you had not edited horror before but thank you for diving in and allowing me to be your first. Your edits and suggestions made this book stronger. After Tyrean finished edits, I added 15,000 words to this novel to strengthen the characters and plots. Without her, you would have been reading a weaker piece of work.

To my wife Traci, who has believed in me for over 34 years, I love you more than you will know. This novel would have never been published without your support, and constant reassurance all would be well. She was also my secondary editor, working with me to catch the little things I missed as I edited and rewrote parts of the story.

To my daughter Raegan, who allowed me to use her as a character in the novel and encouraged me to continue writing. She gave me the idea for my third novel coming soon.

To my son and daughter-in-law, Jared, and Brianna, who

lifted me up even from Georgia. Two years ago, they brought our first grandchild, Oakley, into the world, and seeing that smiling face through FaceTime is such a treat.

To my parents, who have been my biggest cheerleaders for 53 years, Edwin and Cathy, you are my rock, and I love you.

My sisters, Tricia and Michelle, brother-in-law Dan, my nephew Frank and my nieces Emily and Mira, each a light on my path.

To my uncles, aunts, cousins, and friends who cheered me on as I sat at a keyboard and pounded out words to make a story, your support is greatly appreciated.

To Mary Mueller, who also allowed me to use her name within this piece of fiction and was one of my first beta readers.

To you, the reader. Thank you for choosing me when there are thousands of other choices. I cannot share my happiness and appreciation. This book sits in your hands!

ABOUT THE AUTHOR

 A. Scott West lives in Washington State and has been with his spouse for 34 years. They have a son and daughter, both adults. Scott loves reading horror and watching horror movies. His love of horror blossomed at thirteen after reading Christine by Stephen King. His passions include Coke Zero, Bad Dog Bourbon, Friday opening movie nights, horse races, music, and his smoker. When he is not writing, he works in the yard, cooks, or messes with technology. Although the author is skeptical about ghosts, he admits to living in a haunted house for ten years and still wakes with nightmares. His greatest fear is flying and dreads getting on planes.

Website:https://www.ascottwest.com

Twitter: https://twitter.com/AScottWest1

Facebook:https://www.facebook.com/kalamadagger

Made in the USA
Monee, IL
08 July 2021